Paul Gallico was born in New York City, of Italian and Austrian parentage, in 1897, and attended Columbia University. From 1922 to 1936 he worked on the *New York Daily News* as sports editor, columnist, and assistant managing editor. In 1936 he bought a house on top of a hill at Salcombe in South Devon and settled down with a Great Dane and twenty-three assorted cats. It was in 1941 that he made his name with *The Snow Goose*, a classic story of Dunkirk which became a world-wide bestseller. Having served as a gunner's mate in the U.S. Navy in 1918, he was again active as a war correspondent with the American Expeditionary Force in 1944. Paul Gallico, who later lived in Monaco, was a first-class fencer and a keen sea-fisherman. He wrote over 40 books which include *Jennie* (1950), *The Small Miracle* (1952), *Snowflake* (1952), *Love of Seven Dolls* (1954), *Ludmila* (1955), *Thomasina* (1957), *Mrs Harris Goes to New York* (1960), *Too Many Ghosts* (1961), *Love, Let Me Not Hunger* (1963), *Flowers for Mrs Harris* (1963), *The Hand of Mary Constable* (1964), *The Steadfast Man*, a scholarly study of St Patrick, *The Hurricane Story* (1959), a 'biography' of the famous fighter, *Mrs Harris, M.P.* (1965), *The Day Jean-Pierre Went Round the World* (1965), *The Man Who was Magic* (1966), *The Story of Silent Night* (1967), *Manxmouse* (1968), *The Poseidon Adventure* (1969), *The Matilda* (1970), *Zoo Gang* (1971), *Honourable Cat* (1972), *The Boy Who Invented the Bubble Gun* (1974), *Mrs Harris Goes to Moscow* (1974) and *Miracle in the Wilderness* (1975). A posthumous work, *Beyond the Poseidon Adventure*, was published in 1978. Paul Gallico, one of the most prolific and professional of American authors, died in July 1976. He was married four times and had several children.

PAUL GALLICO

THE ADVENTURES OF
HIRAM HOLLIDAY

PENGUIN BOOKS

Penguin Books Ltd, Harmondsworth, Middlesex, England
Viking Penguin Inc., 40 West 23rd Street, New York, New York 10010, U.S.A.
Penguin Books Australia Ltd, Ringwood, Victoria, Australia
Penguin Books Canada Limited, 2801 John Street, Markham, Ontario, Canada L3R 1B4
Penguin Books (N.Z.) Ltd, 182–190 Wairau Road, Auckland 10, New Zealand

First published by Michael Joseph Ltd 1939
Published in Penguin Books 1967
Reprinted 1986

Printed and bound in Great Britain by
Cox & Wyman Ltd, Reading
Typeset in Monotype Plantin

CONTENTS

CRISIS IN LONDON

'Who is Hiram Holliday?'

By the third day out, they were asking aboard the gigantic *Britannique*, Europe bound: 'Who is Hiram Holliday?' or: 'Has anyone seen this M'sieu Holliday?'

Politics and the coming war were of course the first topics of conversation in smoke-room, bar and lounge, but there is always room on a transatlantic liner, no matter how big it is, for speculation on the identity of passengers, particularly people of importance, though goodness knows there was nothing important about Holliday. He was there for all to see, but one of the curious things about the man was that he had a surface insignificance. You would never notice him either alone or in a room full of people until you knew him. And once you knew him well, you wondered how he had ever escaped you.

He appeared on the passenger list, cabin class, of the s.s. *Britannique*, as – 'Mr Hiram Holliday.' In the dining-room he sat at the Third Engineer's table along with a half-dozen dull and undistinguished people, and he spoke very little. The Third Engineer, who was reasonably observant, noted that M'sieur Holliday had eager, excited eyes behind steel-rimmed glasses, and that he seemed to miss little of what was going on.

Everyone is curious about everyone, but no one speaks to anyone on those huge four-and-a-half-day boats. The trip is over so quickly anyhow. And then with so many important people on board one does not like to run the risk of speaking to someone unimportant. It comes under the head of wasted social opportunity.

There was a famous adventurer-explorer-soldier-of-fortune-writer chap aboard the *Britannique*, and it was only natural that he should be expected to win the transatlantic pistol-shooting championship held in the shooting gallery on the promenade

7

deck. The explorer was over six feet tall and had piercing eyes and drew women like flies. The shooting gallery was jammed when he went to shoot his card, mostly with flappers. No one saw the rather stoutish little man – little compared to the explorer, though he was a good five feet ten and a half – with the unruly sandy hair and the bright blue eyes behind steel-rimmed spectacles, who stood on the far side of the gallery, shooting at a target with a ·22 calibre target pistol mounted on a ·38 frame.

The explorer shot with flair and flourish, and well. While he was performing to the admiration of all, the little man finished, brought his target back, examined it, said: 'Hmph!' signed his name across the bottom of it and went out after handing it to the steward in charge, who looked startled and pinned it up on the contest-board. The explorer then finished, and his target, a very pretty cluster for a rocking boat, was examined with 'oh's,' and 'ah's' of admiration. No shots were out of the black, and two were through the inner bull for a total of 56 out of a possible 60.

The steward said: 'But we are fortunate to have two such great shots on the same voyage. You, M'sieu, have won second prize.' And he then nodded towards the board where was pinned the target left by the stoutish little man. The black centre had been quite chewed out of it. The score, 59, was marked on it, and across the bottom was scrawled the name 'Hiram Holliday.'

'Now who the devil is Hiram Holliday?' asked the explorer with a grin, not of envy, but of admiration, because he knew shooting when he saw it. It created a small stir, because nobody remembered what he had looked like.

Then there was the matter of the injury to M. Lapol, the gymnasium instructor, the story of which also circulated around the boat, considerably magnified.

It seems that one of the passengers had approached M. Lapol and inquired whether he fenced. Now before M. Lapol had retired to the job of sports instructor aboard the *Britannique*, he had been, among other things, a good blade in his day.

8

It was rare that a fencer appeared on the passenger list, and while his interrogator did not give the impression of much sport to come, he said that he would be delighted. The passenger who gave his name as Holliday reappeared in an hour, canvas-jacketed and trousered, with mask, glove and *épée*, which is the three-edged, stiff-bladed, duelling sword. M. Lapol raised his eyebrow at the weapon and was pleased, and donned a short white cotton drill instructor's foils jacket.

Mr Holliday had come over and fingered the material, saying: 'Isn't that a little light? I like to use the *point d'arrêt*, you know. It makes it more exciting, more like the real thing.' He had said it, M. Lapol decided, apologetically, almost wistfully. Now, the *point d'arrêt* is a little blue steel button with three short, razor-sharp prongs which is fastened to the end of the *épée*. It will not penetrate mask, or tough canvas jacket, but it will catch and hold in the material, registering a well-made point. And it is no respecter of cotton.

M. Lapol had smiled tolerantly, and said: 'It weel be all right. I take the chance.' Mr Holliday adjusted his mask with some difficulty over his spectacles of steel, after the salute, and they faced one another on guard. M. Lapol was pleased to note that in spite of his somewhat pudgy appearance, the passenger's guard position was good, the bell of the sword completely covered his hand and forearm, and he looked as though in spite of his stoutness he might be light on his feet. Still, Holliday was not a figure to inspire too much respect in a confident swordsman. M. Lapol had the instructor's angle that the pupil or amateur must be put in his place quickly, so he devised a quick touch, a beat on the blade with a planned *pris-en-fer*, or envelope, to the reply to the beat with the lunge driving through to the inside of the arm. But somehow Holliday's blade was not there to receive the beat, it was driving forward through the attacker's enveloping blade, strongly held, the hilt pushing the attacking point outward, and M. Lapol's lunge finished the job of the stop-thrust to his own upper arm which shortly thereafter began to stain red on the white cotton.

'Ah! *Magnifique!*' cried M. Lapol, but the stout little man threw off his mask and ran to him, concern on his round features, but a tremendous excitement shining in his bright blue eyes. 'You are hurt,' he cried. 'I am terribly, terribly sorry,' but he looked at the spreading stain, and fingered the slit in the jacket in a sort of fascination, and murmured to himself: 'Just like the real thing. . . . What a way to start this vacation. . . . My dear sir, I beg your pardon. . . .'

'But it is nothing,' said M. Lapol. The ship's doctor later decided that it would improve the looks of M. Lapol's arm considerably if he took two stitches in the gash. 'It ees my own fault. Next time I am not so smart, and wear the proper jacket, *hein?*'

That story got around, and also one told by a lady from Iowa, who sat at the Third Engineer's table next to Holliday. She wore an unusual cameo ring, and it was passed around the table for inspection. Holliday handled it last, and returned it to her with a half absent-minded air. He said: 'That ring has been wept over.'

'It was my mother's,' said the lady from Iowa. 'My father gave it to her. She led a very unhappy life. She . . .' Suddenly she stopped and looked at Holliday in alarm: 'How did you know? But, of course, I just told you. No, I didn't. . . . It was *after*. . . . Oh, dear . . .' she began to flutter.

Hiram Holliday's round face turned quite red. He said: 'Forgive me. . . . I didn't mean to upset you . . . things sometimes . . .' he hesitated, flustered, grew redder and said: 'I am sure you will all excuse me,' and arose and left the table.

It became a sort of a joking byword amongst the faster set on that particular voyage of the *Britannique:* 'Look out, or Hiram Holliday will get you.' Then someone would ask, accenting the second word: 'And WHO is Hiram Holliday?' and then they would all chorus: 'He's the man with the radio eyes!' But not ten people on the boat knew him when they saw him.

One girl had taken the trouble to talk to him and walk with him a little. She was a buyer for a big department store, on her way to Paris, a pleasant-looking though not beautiful person who was travelling with her younger, prettier sister. They met during one of the afternoon horse-race sessions on deck, and he seemed so simple, and self-effacing and kind, that she felt sorry for him, and they walked the deck together and chatted, and even once had a coffee and liqueur in the smoking-room after dinner, though neither of them exchanged names. But somehow they talked to one another with the graceful freedom of people who are never going to see one another again.

The morning the boat docked at Southampton, the two girls were standing at the promenade deck windows watching the tiny tugs huffling and snuffling the gigantic liner into her berth. The younger sister said, half-indicating the direction with her eyes and head: 'Did you ever see a duller-looking man in your life? Has he been on the boat all the time? What do you suppose a man like that does in England? Something in shoes, I suppose.'

The buyer followed the direction indicated and saw standing at a window, too, Hiram Holliday, or rather, since she did not know his name, her casual last-day shipboard acquaintance. He was a little stouter, if anything, in a loose-fitting overcoat, and he wore a Fedora hat and carried an umbrella crooked over his arm, because, as always at Southampton, it was raining. He was gazing far out over the grey expanse of docks and the spare forests of masts and funnels.

'There,' said the buyer, 'is the most romantic man I ever met in my life. He was born five hundred years too late. I wonder what will become of him.' She sighed because of the thing Holliday had stirred in her that she did not understand.

Her sister's laugh tinkled like breaking glass against the deep bay of the *Britannique's* siren announcing that the voyage was over. 'You're getting dotty in your old age, sis.'

The buyer looked towards the man again, but he was gone.

Who Hiram Holliday Was

All men, more or less, lead double lives. They are as they know themselves to be, and also as their friends and associates see them and know them. Whether the line of divergence between the two existences is narrow, or wide, depends largely upon the knowledge and judgment of others and their opportunities for observation.

The lives of the insignificant-looking man marching down the drab Customs shed in Southampton to claim a modest allowance of baggage under the initial 'H', were as far apart as the two continents, and yet they had their curiously interlocking features.

What the testimony of certain passengers of the *Britannique* would have been with regard to Hiram Holliday has already been seen. And if you had asked a man by the name of Joel Smith, head of the copy-desk of the *New York Sentinel*, and who plays no further part in these stories, about Hiram Holliday, he would have said: 'Who, old Holliday?' (The 'old' was in itself revealing, because Holliday was not yet quite thirty-nine, it was just that he had been with the *Sentinel* so long.) 'Best copy-reader we ever had. But he's a stick-in-the-mud. He'll never be anything else. If you cut him, he'd bleed commas and semi-colons.'

Obviously there is a considerable gap. And this is how Hiram Holliday bridged it.

For fifteen years Holliday sat on the rim of the *Sentinel* copy-desk, correcting copy, writing headlines and checking up the work of men of action, the reporters and correspondents and feature-writers who went out into the world and got the news. The world passed beneath his fingers in the shape of words, typewritten on grey copy-paper, murder in a cheap Third Avenue rooming house, bombs raising clouds of tawny dust on the Abyssinian plain, an acid review of a new play, rolling floods that washed away lives and property, love on Park Avenue, love in Greenwich village, fire, tornado, war, exploration, heroism, such as it was, and Hiram had no illusions left, treachery, politics, national and foreign, arson, theft, rape and philanthropy, all of them were tossed at him sooner or later during the day or week by the man in the slot, during his eight-hour trick.

The *Sentinel* was a morning paper and Holliday's normal

shift was from three in the afternoon until eleven at night, with Sunday off, or perhaps a weekday, but he had done all the other tricks, the one from eight to four in the morning, and the lobster shift from midnight to morn. He was never late for work, and no one remembered him ever being ill. He appeared, removed his coat, opened his vest, pulled down his tie and opened his short collar, placed a half-dozen well-sharpened copy pencils and two fresh packs of cigarettes before him and waited.

When a story was floated at him by his chief he read it through, his mind forming the images of near or faraway places and things and happenings. He read it for libel, punch and clarity, he corrected errors. He brought up the point in a pithy headline, he initialled it, and floated it back to the head copy-reader. His lunch hour he spent in a nearby restaurant. He lived in two rooms in the village. When his time was up he donned his hat and coat and went away. And of what he did outside the office, or even of what he thought while he was there, no single soul on the huge paper had even the vaguest idea.

As far as his colleagues knew, he never went anywhere, never did anything, never saw anything, never joined in their activities, had no friends. He was liked by his chief and fellow copy-readers because he was pleasant, polite, willing and frequently showed flashes of biting, amusing humour. They didn't even know where he spent his vacations, or when the five-day week came in, his two consecutive days off. The only thing they did know was that for the past three or four years Hiram Holliday had been saving vacation time and money for a trip to Europe. Holliday had been forced by family circumstances to leave college in his third year. By the time his family obligations were lifted and he was free and alone in the world, he had been eight years at the desk. His ways were set. He had never married.

What no one knew was that outside office hours Hiram Holliday was a gentleman adventurer; that laboriously, with infinite pains and patience, he had in his later years acquired all of the outward attributes of the romantic hero. The inner ones he had always possessed. They were his inescapable antidote to the bitterness, the cruelty, the disillusionment, the harshness and ridiculousness of the world that is known to the newspaperman, the world in which there are no heroes, chivalry is dead, and the good deed is figured strictly on the percentage basis. The more idols that crumbled beneath the lead of his copy pencil, the more he learned of greed, selfishness and human rapacity, the more he yearned for selfless heroism, honesty and gallantry, the quest of beauty for beauty's sake, the love of humanity for its frailty, the cult of decency, the aura of fearlessness. The world was the most wonderfully exciting thing that had ever happened, the fantastic spinning ball that he was allowed to inhabit for his span of years, and his reading was devoted to devouring its history. He knew that if he could ever reach those far-off places where history had been made that the very stones and objects that had felt the touch of the people of the past would tell him things, would help to slake his great thirst to be one with, to understand this world which heretofore practically had existed for him only through the eyes of others.

He had known for many years of his extraordinary sensitivity to objects that had been in close connexion with people. It was simply a sensitivity magnified to a high degree, the same thing that enables a house-hunting person to walk into a dwelling for sale, or for rent, and say: 'This feels like a happy house. Let's stay here.' Hiram Holliday's life was a constant straining to co-ordinate and visualize the impressions of others. He had the true copy-reader's contempt for the careless or incomplete reporter, but in addition he actually suffered mental agonies at the lack of human insight in the stories he read, in the failure of this or that reporter to include the one touch that would make the event understandable to all. It was as if he had been given a book in which was all the information about the world in which he lived, only to find when he went to it for instruction or relief that half the pages were missing.

His physical attributes were even more amazing. He was, as has been said, a gentleman adventurer who would never go adventuring, but who played at it, instead, and let the play serve as an anodyne for his imagination, his longing and the dullness of a vocation into which he had been trapped by circumstances.

He learned to do the things that make men men, many old things they had had to do to survive, before the days when it was all done for them, and new things too. He went to fencing *salle* and shooting school and took lessons in foil, *épée* and sabre, pistol and rifle. He never forgot the thrill when his pistol instructor had told him: 'The first thing, if you've got to get into a gun fight, is to gain twenty-five yards. The average man with a pistol in his hand at twenty-five yards might just as well be holding a rock.' The very language enchanted him.

Because of starting late in life, and his physical attributes, he could become a champion at none of these things, but he learned to do them well enough to satisfy his own longings. Laboriously, an hour a week, because it was all he could afford, he mastered the art of flying a plane. He joined the National Guard and drilled once a week. He went to a gymnasium and learned to box, and even acquired a smattering of ju-jitsu. These were the escapes, practised in his time away from the paper which gave him the zest for living. When he faced an opponent steel in hand in the fencing *salle*, he was D'Artagnan at bay. Of these things no one ever knew. It was unto himself sufficient that he was a man and unafraid. It was here that Hiram Holliday and the average dreamer parted company. Imaginings satisfy the average amongst us. We can see ourselves performing romantic and dramatic deeds, and it suffices even though we know we cannot run a block without puffing and that in a hand-to-hand encounter of any kind we would not last two minutes. It amused Hiram Holliday to be able to put his dreams into practice. But he had never saved anyone's life, fired a shot at anything but a target, or raised his hand in anger against a fellow-man. His protective colouration was against him, his roundish face, his ruffled, sandy hair, his steel-rimmed spectacles, his slight tendency to corpulency and his bland manner. The thing was that people never looked at him

15

twice. If they had they might have noticed something besides the stubborn chin, the firm mouth and the eager, bright blue eyes. A man does not learn to shoot, fence, ride a horse, swim, box and wrestle and fly a plane, even badly, without its leaving a mark on him.

It was rather indicative of Hiram's life up to that point that his opportunity to fulfil his life's dream and visit Europe should have come about by virtue of a comma – eventually known as the $500,000 comma.

The *Sentinel* won a particularly nasty and dangerous half-million-dollar libel suit by virtue of the placement of a comma in the story in question. To have lost it would have cost the paper at least a hundred thousand dollars.

When the original copy was exhumed and examined after the trial, it was found that no comma had existed there when the story first arrived at the copy desk, but that a large, fat, and pointed one had been inserted with a firm stroke of the pencil by the hand of Hiram Holliday.

A grateful publisher, mellifluous under a victory that had saved him money and prestige, and willing once and for all to drive home to copy-readers past, present and future, the importance of well-placed commas, awarded Hiram Holliday a bonus of $1,000 and a month's vacation with pay. That, with the money he had saved out of his head-line prizes and the time he had coming to him, brought Hiram his trip. He sailed the next week on the *Britannique*.

Hitler was storming at Nuremberg, the French Government was tottering under strikes; the Russian bear was muttering to itself. Sudeten Germans were firing at Czech Customs guards and the Czech Government, too late, was offering concessions to the Sudetens. In England there was a quickening of something called A.R.P., and people actually began inquiring about getting gas masks. The poker-players in Downing Street squeezed their cards – behind them were out-of-date aeroplanes, insufficient aeroplanes, and anti-aircraft guns that had fought the last war, and an unprepared, ill-equipped army – and scratched the chins of lengthening and sallowing faces, faces

lined with worry. They were having to decide as they had
decided once before that if you are going to call a pat hand
that you think is a bluff you really ought to have better than a
pair of sixes yourself.

With mixed emotions Hiram Holliday went ashore at
Southampton, boarded the boat special for London and was
shunted down the vast dock, through Southampton streets,
out into rural England under rain, and headed for grey, sprawl-
ing London town. His race had been cradled in England. He
was there.

What Hiram Holliday Saw in London

The sulphurous black war clouds were piling on the horizon,
but at first they remained unnoticed by Holliday because he
was ranging London like a hound.

He drank in the city with his eyes and his ears, he took in the
unforgettable scent of London into his blood through his
nostrils, he soaked in the feel of the old, old city through his
finger-tips and the pores of his skin. He was feverish with the
turmoil of the millions of voices that called to him from every
crooked street and bowed window.

He left the smart West End with its glittering shops and
crested windows and walked down the grey, dusty alleys of the
back streets. He walked through the City and rubbed elbows
with the clerks and bank runners in their shiny silk hats. He
wandered through the musty Law Courts, down Chancery
Lane, and through Temple Bar, and felt, as he passed, all the
weight of the machinery of British justice on his shoulders.

He went down to the Pool on the Thames and stood amongst
the rusty ships and breathed in the heavy odours of tea and
coffee and a hundred spices and read the exciting names on
the bows of the vessels. He walked through Limehouse down
where the grey river bent itself into Limehouse Reach and
drank mild and bitter in the wonderfully redolent pubs. The
first night he climbed to the top of Hampstead Heath, ' 'appy
'Ampstead,' that he had read about and sat with the billion

beckoning lights of London at his feet and listened to the distant surf-roar of the city, and then walked for hours through quiet streets past the two-storied red-brick houses, and let his imagination play on what lay behind the shaded windows.

He learned the Strand and Fleet Street with its wonderful, intriguing old courtyards to be gained through narrow, grimy alleys, and tasted the tang and excitement of Regent Street and Piccadilly Circus. He sought out names that he knew, Paddington and Waterloo Stations, and went and stood there and smelled the English soft coal smell and read the names on the train boards – Torquay, Paignton, Plymouth, Land's End, Brighton, Harwich, Paris. . . .

Westminster Abbey, that fantastic jumble of the bones and relics of England's great, that charnel house of history, was almost unbearable to Holliday because of the sensations of ancient times that fought for possession of his body and his mind. He felt like a switchboard through which a million calls were thronging, but he could hardly tear himself away from the walks and old flagstones of the Tower of London because there he walked with a breed of men and women that somehow he felt had passed from the earth, and who still, he knew, were in their feelings and ambitions as of the people of his day.

The tiny tower that housed the globules of coloured light known as the Crown Jewels frightened him because of the passion and greed he felt draping the collection like a mantle, but he stayed for hours in the armoury of old weapons and let his fingers wander over the ashen shafts of ancient tilting spears and closed his hand over the pommels of the great two-handed swords, and felt the tough, truculent presence of the great, tawny men of centuries past who had had the strength and the will to swing them. He heard old cries and lamentations in the dungeons and once he passed through a zone of terror, and found that he was at the place where a girl named Jane Grey, Queen of England for but a few days, had waited to be killed.

One clear day, on an impulse, he drove out to Croydon and paid three pounds to a pilot to fly him over London. His fingers itched to be at the wheel, but he said nothing, and feasted his eyes on the illimitable meadows of grey stone, the threading grey worm that was the Thames and the green patches of the great parks. He saw the city below him built upon the mortar of centuries, a cement mixed of dust and blood, and knew that as all things pass, so this city must some day bleed and die again.

He thought, too, for the first time of bombers, and the coming threat of war, and looking down, he frowned a little and shook his round head, because he knew that while many might die or be mangled, and that much could be destroyed, it did not yet lay within the power of man to obliterate at one blow so vast a city.

There is something about flying that changes one's aspects. Literally, one gets off the earth, though still cloaked by its atmosphere. When he returned to the earth and London he was aware for the first time that fear was coming to the city. He saw it written on the faces of the people, but more, he felt it through his sensitive nerves.

He dined variously, in places high and low, at Quaglino's, at Frascati, at a little Italian restaurant in Soho, in an old pub off Curzon Street, at the Victor Hugo, at Simpson's, and at the Berkeley Grill, and the noisy Lyons Corner Houses. And it seemed that each time the clatter of dishes and voices had risen a note higher, and faces were paler and nerves more tightly strung.

Jonas, one of the men in the London office of the *Sentinel*, took him to the Monte Carlo Club one three o'clock in the morning, and Holliday, looking more neutral and insignificant than ever in a dinner jacket, sat in the close reek of food and perfume and bodies, in the long, narrow, red-furnished bottle-party club, and thought that he smelled fear the way a growling dog scents that a man is afraid of him.

A fat, red-faced man as squat and obese as a Texas toad sat at a table with his arms around two lovely girls. One had flame-coloured hair, and the other brown, with the fashionable streak of white dyed through it. Because the table cut them off, they seemed to Holliday to be naked except for coloured bits of silk across their pointed breasts.

'Who is that man?' Holliday asked.

Jonas looked. 'That's Lord Dregnath,' he replied. 'One of the richest men in England. Owns the *Gazette* among other things.'

'Lord . . . lord . . .' ran through Holliday's head. 'Master of men . . . giver of gifts . . . protector of the poor.'

A young fop was dragged past their table by a screaming girl, headed for the dance floor. His glasses had thick lenses and his hair fell in a bang over his brow. He had a woman's mouth and a receding chin. His clothing was awry and he was half drunk.

Jonas nudged Holliday and said: 'Sir Richard Riothlesley, Vanarvon's son. . . .'

'A knight,' Holliday said to himself, and then quoted *Canterbury Tales* inaudibly: 'He was a verray parfit gentil knight. . . .' A curious sort of grief suddenly clutched at his throat, and he said to Jonas: 'Let's get out of here. I want some air. . . .'

They went out and parted at the door, Jonas with the thought: 'What a queer, dull sort of duck.'

Holliday walked home through the deserted streets to the room he had found in a pleasant house on Bruton Street. The prostitutes in their silver fox capes were still hunting in pairs, standing in the doorways of New Bond Street and the by-streets, their eyes glistening in the lamplight. One of them, a pale, thin girl with black hair, spoke to him and said: 'Hello dear, don't you want to take me home with you?'

He would have liked to have talked with her, but in London there are no places where one can sit up and drink at that hour except the bottle clubs. He walked on. 'Oh, come on, dear,' said the girl, and gave a high, shrill titter, 'we may all be blown to pieces soon, anyway.'

'God,' said Hiram Holliday. 'Introduction to love . . .' and half broke into a trot to reach his room. . . .

Hitler gave his ultimatum, the field grey hordes began to

converge on the fortress of Czechoslovakia, and the waters of panic began to lap at England's feet. Chamberlain flew to Berchtesgaden, Chamberlain flew back to London. Holliday was abroad, night and day in the streets of London, looking, listening, feeling, trying desperately to choke down the thing that was burning him. The statesmen went to Godesberg to meet with Hitler. The handbills of the newsboys changed hourly and grew wilder, bigger and blacker. Tension appeared in the voices of the B.B.C. announcers. Then Godesberg failed. Chamberlain warned the Czechs to mobilize. And the panic took London by the throat.

At noon of Black Tuesday, the day the British Fleet mobilized, a stoutish man, wearing steel-rimmed glasses behind which blazed bright blue eyes, and with sandy hair wildly dishevelled, rushed into the already overworked London Bureau of the *New York Sentinel*. The Bureau Chief, red-eyed from lack of sleep, was trying to collect his material, rumour and fact, for his first lead, and looked up irritated. It was Jonas who came out from an inner office and recognized him.

He said: 'Hello, Holliday, what's up? Bill, this is Hiram Holliday. He's on the desk back home. Here on vacation.'

The Bureau Chief grunted something about 'Hell of a time for a vacation. . . .'

'Is . . . is someone sending the story?' cried Hiram Holliday. . . . 'Is . . . is anyone . . . ?'

Jonas looked amused. 'I'll say,' he said. 'This is the hottest we've had it yet. Roosevelt has cabled Hitler. Chamberlain is making a last speech. He may try to get in touch with Mussolini. The bombers may be over within twenty-four hours, m'boy. Got your hole picked . . . ?'

'No . . . no . . . !' cried Hiram Holliday, his voice rising. . . . 'To Hell with them. . . . That's a damned card game. The people, I mean . . . the story of the people . . . what's happened to them, what they're doing . . . the fear . . . the pitiful preparations. . . . I've been all over. I've seen . . . a city of eight million who think they're under sentence of death . . . the things they are doing, the greedy, pitiful, stupid, human things that mean the end of an empire, the finish of a great nation. . . .'

The Bureau Chief's nerves were ragged. He snapped: 'Oh, cool off, Holliday, and don't try to tell us how to run our business. Go get yourself a drink if your nerve is going, or get on a boat for home – if you can. . . . We'll pick up the colour as we go. Who gives a . . .'

'God damn it!' said Hiram Holliday, and his voice simply shattered the dingy office, rattled the desks and the wire trays and the papers. 'Get me a typewriter and some paper. I've been sitting on you birds long enough. I know you! Dictators, Prime Ministers, lands and armies! People want to know about people. . . . I'll write this story, and to hell with all of you. . . .'

He strode through the swinging gate so that it crashed. The one impression that Jonas had was that somehow he had added two inches to his stature and that his face had gone from round to square, that his mouth had hardened into the lines of a trap, and that he was ablaze with vitality and power.

There was a vacant desk with a typewriter. He sat down, ripped off his coat and pulled down his tie and slapped a pack of cigarettes down in front of him. He threaded a book of paper into the machine so that the ratchets of the machine gave forth a vicious noise, and then wrote at the top of the page something he had never written in his life before, and never thought he would see:

'By Hiram Holliday.'

His fingers at first were stiff because it had been a long time since he had used a machine, but as the story that was in him burst its bounds like a loft fire that finds a flue and leaps from its confinement, the clatter of the machine speeded up until the smoke of Holliday's cigarettes seemed to rise from its interior to wreath his embattled head.

'There will be no war,' wrote Hiram Holliday, 'because England is England no more.' (This sentence the managing editor of the *New York Sentinel* threw away and regretted it, two days later.) 'The head of the greatest empire the world has ever known has been blackmailed by fear. The very cabs of London crawl through the twisting lanes more slowly because of fear, the people shuffle the streets with leaden feet that bear leaden hearts and watch their workmen scratch the pitiful ditches through the public parks, ditches that would not even hold the dead, much less the living were death to rain from the sky.

'London is blackmailed, naked, and afraid. The people walk the streets as though they had no clothes on. The pride that once clothed England and Englishmen has been frayed too thin for shelter.

'England is an old man with an armless sleeve and ribbons on his chest, and an old woman with tattered hair, and a little girl, kneeling at the tomb of the unknown soldier, dust of a man who died for less a cause than this, praying for peace.

'England has lost its strength, its wits and its guts. It is like a prize-fighter who will bribe and buy and connive to hold the championship he once fought for tooth and nail. Its answer to challenge is tuppence-worth of sandbags, leaned against billions worth of property, and flight to the country.'

Then he began to tell of the exodus of the rich to their funk-holes in the country, the jamming of the roads and the railway lines, and the blocking of all telephone lines to the south, Devon and Cornwall, to Wales and to Scotland, with every real estate agent glued to the telephone listening to offers of twice and three times the value for vacant houses, or even rooms, in the more remote and safer sections of England, where the threatening bombers would not come.

He told the story of the queues of people lined up at the centres where the gas-masks were distributed, and the screams of frightened children that rang all the day because of that choking moment when the gas-mask was fitted and tested, and no breath at all was possible, and he wrote about the old man who was once a General in the British Army, digging a shallow trench in his back yard in Putney, and saying: 'There. Ours is done. Tomorrow we'll dig one for the maids,' and about the food hoarders who stripped the neighbourhood stores of canned goods, and drove the stuff out into the country and buried it, and then made maps to enable them to find the cache again for themselves, when the bombs should have blasted the city into starvation.

He wrote of the scene in the Haymarket where hundreds of panic-stricken Americans stormed the shipping offices and fought and begged and bribed to get as much as a cot or even deck-space on a west-bound liner, and the silent, half-crushed crowds that stood outside of the Downing Street Ministry, and Buckingham Palace – 'some in quest of news, but more for the comfort of gregariousness, and the thought that perhaps if they were somewhere near the great and the powerful, the talismanic mantle that seemed always to shield them would protect them too. . . .'

He told about the Zoo where shot-guns, rifles and chloroform were prepared for the solemn keepers who, at the first alarm, were to slaughter the animals dangerous to man – 'the poisonous snakes, the scorpions and spiders, the elephants and the carnivores' – the animals most dangerous to man, an irony so bitter, so obviously biting that no one thought of it as irony. The gentle deer might run the streets of London.

'There dare be no war because the Government has left its children as naked and defenceless as the day they were born. The people cluster around the few of the poor, cheap anti-aircraft guns, no more than five to four square miles, and like them, crane their own muzzles to the sky. All of the guns are obsolete and hopeless, as obsolete as the men who believed that force and lust for power has been legislated from the world.'

He wrote how all work had stopped because worry and apprehension had tightened stomachs, slowed the motions of the body and dulled the brain, and of how the rumours went racing through the streets and in and out of homes. Hitler was to send relays of planes over London for three days, until the city was wiped out – there would be no declaration of war – the planes might have left Berlin even now. . . . 'The pitiful things that were done, the ringing of trees shading the streets with bands of white paint, so that when London became a ghost city shuddering in darkness with only the fitful blue ghost lamps of the black-outs, Londoners should not walk into their trees and bump their heads. . . .'

He quoted the talk in restaurant and pub and hotel, the gallant talk of the people who could not get away: 'A direct hit, and of course you're gone. . . . Madrid has been bombed for two years . . . and look at Barcelona. . . . The shops are all out of gas-proofing material. . . . Thank God my wife and children got away to the country . . . have you any idea of what a 500-pound demolition bomb can do? They won't use gas. . . . It's the incendiary bombs . . . little ones no bigger than your head. . . . They'll fire a square block. Sand doesn't do any good. . . . What have they done about the British Museum? The stuff in there is priceless. . . .' And he told simple stories of service and gallantry.

He wrote as though he would burst if he did not. He drew the groaning city and its doom-ridden people through the mill of his machine and splashed the grindings in hot and brilliant colours on his paper.

When he had finished he threw the sheets on the Bureau Manager's desk, and said: 'File that! Or spike it. I don't care. I've done it.' He put on his hat and coat and went out. The Bureau Manager and Jonas looked at one another and Jonas made the wheel motion around his temple. The Bureau Manager glanced at the sheets out of curiosity, and then said suddenly to his assistant: 'Hey . . . c'mere. . . .'

How Hiram Holliday Met a Girl Named Heidi and Became an Adventurer

At nine o'clock that evening, Hiram Holliday went into Green Park opposite Piccadilly. It was threatening to rain, and he wore a mackintosh and carried his umbrella rolled and crooked over his arm. He was sensitive to wettings and colds.

There were others there, too, to watch the workmen reaming the wonderful old turf with their spades and mattocks, and throwing up the earth from their hurried entrenchment. They were working by the light of smoking yellow flares that gleamed from the shovels that were raised in a sort of slow rhythm from the gash in the ground. Hard by were piles of timber and scantlings. The flares were planted close by the trench work, and beyond were the deep shadows of the park. London was already experimenting with the protection of darkness.

The people stood quietly in huddled groups and Holliday could hear them murmuring to one another: 'Lot o' good that'll do ... think that's big enough for you to get into, Bert? ... I 'ere they've blocked up the tube, the part that runs under the river. What misses the 'ouses of Parliament will likely land in the river and smash the tubes.... Gord 'elp them that lives in Lambeth. That's too near the Government 'ouses. ...'

The long, thin fingers of many searchlights were stroking the under side of the coppery roof of the sky. Tomorrow was to be the deadline for the troops to march. Holliday looked about him at the groups of people and the individuals. Were there to be dead amongst these? He found himself like the others craning his neck into the sky. But when he heard a sudden movement near him he turned in that direction to see a girl standing a few feet away. In the darkness he could note no more than that her hair was pale. She was hatless, and when the damp wind threw a flare-flame in her direction, it shimmered. She wore a cape that fell from her shoulders to her ankles and was thrown back at the throat. And as he watched her he saw her slowly raise both her fists and shake them at the sky, and heard her say so clearly and deeply and thrillingly that it was almost like an actress speaking her lines:

'I am not afraid. I am not afraid of all of you.'

It moved something in Hiram Holliday so that he heard himself cry: 'Bravo! Bravo! Bluff and blackmail. Bravo?'

The girl turned a startled face to him, and she was lovely. But she saw only a stoutish, round-faced man not far from middle age wearing steel-rimmed spectacles, the collar of his

26

mackintosh turned up and a rolled up umbrella over his arm, and so she smiled a little, shyly.

'Forgive me,' said Hiram Holliday. . . . 'I . . . I am afraid I was carried away by the one brave voice that I have heard crying against bullies and blackmailers.'

He had moved close to her side and raised his hat to her, and they stood to one side, shaded by a tree, away from the nearest groups of people. And then he noted that she was not alone. An elderly woman stood near her holding a small boy by the hand. He could not have been more than seven or eight years old and was slim and fair. And that was all that he had time to note before the incredible began to happen.

Five men broke from the shadows. The woman with the little boy put her hand to her mouth and cried: '*Herrje!* Madame!' because the men were converging on her. Holliday heard one of the men say: '*Ja, ja! Los! Schnell,*' and knew it was German. The girl had whirled with blinding speed and gathered the child to her and opened her mouth to scream, but already one of the men had slipped behind her and held her with his hand pressed over her mouth, while another gagged and pinioned the woman. Two men were dragging at the child when Hiram Holliday lunged viciously with the ferrule of his umbrella at the ear of the one nearest to him, and drove it through his ear drum. The man fell forward on his face and lay still. It was over so quickly that the others did not even know what had happened and when they turned to see, they found only a bespectacled, guileless-looking man fencing rather ridiculously with a furled umbrella. They closed in on him.

Now, an umbrella is quite the silliest of all weapons except when in the hands of a competent fencer, then it becomes unpleasant and dangerous. The leader of the quartette suddenly found the steel tip menacing his eyes and made a grab for it with his hand, but it was not there, it eluded him and then was driven sharply against his mouth, smashing a tooth. The two women were free, but neither one of them screamed. They were watching as though fascinated. Something swished, and

Holliday felt a ripping blow on the side of his cheek. Suddenly he knew with complete clarity with whom he had to deal. A headline he had written flashed through his mind: 'NAZIS AND LEGIONAIRES IN YORKVILLE CLASH – Belt-buckles *v*. Fists as Six are Injured.' He saw an arm drawn back for another blow, and lunged straight for the eyes, and felt the point go home into something soft.

The man let out a roar of pain. People began to move towards them, and the men in the trench stopped their work and looked up. A voice said: ''Ere, 'ere! Wot's all this? Fetch a Bobby! Someone's 'urt!' The men fell back for a moment in indecision.

'Come on,' panted Hiram Holliday. One hand held the girl's arm, the other grasped the shoulder of the woman, who in turn held the child's hand. 'No, no. . . . Walk! Walk slowly with me. Don't run!'

They moved slowly away from the group and out into the flare-light, an innocent, middle-aged gentleman with an umbrella, a girl, a child, a nurse.

The group behind them around the man on the turf was static. Holliday felt it with the back of his head. 'Now a little faster . . .' he said. Under the urge of his hands they quickened their steps. . . . 'Steady . . . a little faster now. . . .' They were approaching the gate of the park. 'Now come on, with all you've got,' and they ran like rabbits.

There were shouts behind them and the drumming of feet. Hiram flagged one of the tiny, high-bodied London cabs that drifted by and thrust them in, followed and slammed the door. 'Get going, son,' he snapped at the driver. He looked back to see three of the men rushing from the park, one of them holding his hand in front of his mouth. They hailed a taxi.

'We're all right,' said Hiram. 'We'll find ourselves a cop . . . a policeman.'

'No. . . . Oh, no,' said the girl. 'Not a policeman. Please. . . . I . . . I am not supposed to be in England. . . .'

For the first time Hiram noticed that the girl spoke with a

slight accent, one that he thought he recognized. 'Oh, oh,' he said, 'you are German?'

The girl lifted her head. Holliday had never seen such a gesture before, but he knew that it was regal. She said: 'I am ... we are Austrians.'

'Ah ...' said Holliday. And then the absurdity, the utter impossibility of the adventure flooded him. This was the heart of London. ...

'But, my dear lady ...' he said, 'I cannot believe it. Here in London. ... No one would dare. No, it's too absurd. ...'

The boy suddenly began to cry: '*Tante Heidi. ... Ich habe Angst. ...*'

The girl took his chin in her fingers and raised his head up high.

'*Nie Angst haben, Peter!*' she said.

Hiram did not understand what she said, but the fierce pride in her voice reached him. She turned to him.

'Yes. They would dare. Because London is in the grip of fear. And they know it. They can do what they want in this crisis. The world is in the hands of evil.'

'What do they want? Why?' asked Hiram, although already he thought he knew.

'They want the child. For a hostage. You have already said the word. For blackmail. They will blackmail the world for money and power. I took him away after the *Anschluss* before they came. They have not found us – until now. If I can go to Paris ... at once ... to Paris ...' she stopped and laid her hand on Hiram's arm and shook her head. ... 'How can I? I know them. I know them. They will watch the airplanes and the trains. There will be an opportunity. See, they are following now. There are many of them here. ...'

Hiram looked back. A cab was keeping a steady pace behind them at a hundred yards. His eyes behind the spectacles were sparkling. Those endless mind trips he had taken over the map of Europe. He spread England and the Continent before his mind like a panorama.

'I will get you there,' he said, as calmly and matter-of-fact

29

as though he were offering to see her home. 'There is a third gateway to Paris which they will not think of because very few people ever do.'

The girl stared at him, at the round face and the slightly corpulent body. And then she saw the eyes behind the lenses and knew that they denied all that she seemed to see.

He smiled at her. 'No one will touch the boy. Or you. I have thought of something. But he must be brave and clever, and do exactly as you will tell him. And you, too, must keep your nerve, even if things look bad.' He leaned forward, and in a low voice said to the driver: 'Paddington. And open up if you can.'

'Where are we going?' asked the girl.

'Where there are people and confusion,' said Hiram Holliday, his heart singing inside him with excitement. And as the cab turned and headed for Paddington Station he told her what he wanted done, and watched her with admiration as she drilled the little boy called Peter.

The clock had been turned back twenty-four years at Paddington Station. So – with one exception – Hiram Holliday decided it must have looked in 1914 when England had last mobilized for war. The old railway station with its bowed series of roofs and long platforms was a jam, a crush and a bedlam of noise and steam and smoke, and rows of compartmented trains, and men in uniform, sailors, and Territorials, and hundreds of reservists in mufti answering the call, and excited citizens trying to get out of London. The one exception was that, forming the bulk of the fantastic throng, were hundreds upon hundreds of children, their clamour rising sharply above the shrilling of whistles of the guards, the panting of the green-painted locomotives, and the staccato shrieks of the engine whistles.

They were of all ages and sizes, in groups of from ten to a hundred, herded and chaperoned by efficient-looking females, hawk-faced women who bustled about them with lists in their hands, checking, assisted by men with arm-bands. London was evacuating its children to the country. That was what Hiram Holliday had remembered.

Some were simply clustered around the women in charge of them, others were centred around standards bearing the name of their school. Still others had as a centre a sign bearing the names of towns – Exeter ... Lyme Regis ... Torquay ... Newton Abbot, Totnes ... Polperro. ...

'Ah,' said Hiram Holliday, and began to push his way through the throng. It was even better than he had expected. And he noted the presence of the wonderfully efficient London Bobby, helping to maintain what order there was.

Hiram saw the three Nazi agents appear at a side gate and begin to search the crowd. They were young and powerful and pink-cheeked, three typical bully boys of the New Germany. Hiram noticed with a thrill of genuine pleasure that one of them held his handkerchief to his mouth, and that the handkerchief was red.

There was no time to lose. Hiram and his companions were by a group of some thirty children clustered around a standard reading 'Penzance.' At a word from the girl, the boy moved from her side, and in an instant had mingled with the other children.

But the three Nazis had seen them and began to press forward through the crush, and then stopped unbelieving for a moment as they saw Holliday and the two women deliberately move away some twenty yards and stand there, leaving the boy. The man with the smashed mouth, he was tall, and blond, with an eager, greedy face and a scar that extended slantwise down his cheek to his chin, nodded the other two forward, and they closed in again.

'Now steady!' said Hiram Holliday, and slipped his arm around the girl's waist. With the other hand he gripped the wrist of the trembling nurse. 'This may be hard. But no villains in the world can buck this combination.'

The girl gave a little moan because one of the three already had his hand on one of the boy's arms, and the man with the smashed mouth was reaching for the other, when the thing

31

happened. The woman in charge of the group was as lean and spare as a greyhound. She had the face of a bald-headed eagle, and a voice like a calliope.

'Here! I say! Stop that!' she shouted. 'What are you doing? How dare you! Leave that child alone. He belongs to me. Help! Police! Kidnappers!' A sailor, with *H.M.S. Courageous* on his hat-band, passing, stopped and took in the scene, and then suddenly hit the man with the smashed mouth a resounding thump with his shoulder, and said: 'Now then, 'Arry, not so fast. What's it all abaht? The lydy says it ain't your young 'un. Got a German look abaht you, ain't you?'

Two enormous blue-helmeted policemen began to move inexorably towards the scene. Hiram relaxed his grip around the girl's waist, but she remained pressed close to him. Three Territorials in khaki had stopped by the group and one said: 'Wot's this abaht Germans?'

'Help!' screeched the woman. 'They're trying to steal my child.'

'Oh, no they ain't,' said the soldier. 'Tyke the other two, boys, I'll tend to this one.' But the three had broken and were thrusting through the crowd headed for the exits, with the Bobbies, the soldiers and the sailors in pursuit. Whistles shrilled frantically. . . .

'Lovely, wasn't it?' said Hiram Holliday and chuckled. He did not notice that the girl was looking at him with misty eyes. 'Come on. They're moving.'

A man with an arm-band had taken the group in tow and was steering them into a carriage, eight to a compartment. Hiram noticed that the eagle-faced lady, flushed and triumphant, had Peter by the hand with a firm grip. Hiram and the girl waved to him, and he turned around and laughed back at them. Then Holliday and the girl and the nurse got into the car at the other end and stood in the corridor, Hiram keeping an eye on the platform. A uniformed guard challenged him. Holliday reached into his inner breast pocket and pulled forth the contents of envelopes and bills and folded papers, and said: 'It's all right. I've got all the papers for everyone.' The guard, satisfied, passed on. Far up front, an engine gave three maniacal shrieks, there was a terrific jolt and then the train slowly crawled out of Paddington Station, south-bound into the night, bearing its cargo of children towards safety.

There remained the retrieving of Peter, which was accomplished more easily than Hiram had expected. They waited until past Reading, and then invaded the compartment in which Peter and the eagle-faced lady were sitting. The girl was a magnificent actress and the boy was clever. It apparently was a meeting between lost child and mother. Hiram explained that they had become separated in the crush. The teacher was unwilling and suspicious because the girl and the boy were talking in German. 'Madame,' said Hiram, 'if you will consult your lists and make a count, I am sure you will find that you have an extra child.'

The check-up proved this immediately. The woman let him go, snapping a word of warning: 'You ought to be more careful, madame. Three men tried to make away with him while he was with me. . . .'

The girl turned astonished eyes on her, and for the first time Holliday noted that they were a deep violet in colour. 'How dreadful,' she said. 'Thank you so much for your care of my little boy. . . .'

They went back and actually found room in a compartment.

'What is your name?' asked Holliday.

The girl turned and looked at him gravely. He had time now to see how exquisite she was, fragile and dainty, with hair the colour of strained honey. She answered him.

'My name is Heidi.'

'Who are you, Heidi?'

She bent her head so that he could not see her face. She said in a very low voice: 'I . . . I am Heidi. Will you be hurt if I do not tell you more, you who have been so good and kind?'

'No,' said Hiram Holliday. 'No. I am happy, very happy. I have never been so happy in my life.'

Heidi suddenly closed her eyes and buried her face in

Hiram's arm. In a few minutes she was asleep with the child cuddled to her and the silent nurse sitting stark upright. Hiram, who had been consulting maps, woke them as the train slowed to come into Totnes. 'We get off here,' he said.

They followed him unquestioningly. 'We are still forty miles from our destination,' said Holliday. 'But I think we ought to leave the train. Just in case they have arranged for a delegation, you know. Though I rather think, being literal minded as so many Germans are, they will head directly for Penzance. Still . . .'

Heidi slipped her hand into his. 'We will go with you.'

They found a taxi to take them up the long hill into the little walled city where they found the Castle Inn still open, and an enraged proprietor complaining of the never-ceasing telephone bell – people from London calling up for accommodations. The backwash of the panic was lapping at the walls of the tiny South Devon town.

Holliday inquired the name of the best hotel in Plymouth and put a trunk call through to the night porter. When he came out of the booth, he was grinning. He consulted his watch. It was just after midnight. 'In five hours,' he said to Heidi, 'you will be on your way to Paris. The s.s. *Bordeaux* of the French Line was due to call at Plymouth, bound for le Havre at eight tomorrow morning. Because of the war scare, they've pushed her up. The tender leaves at four in the morning. We'll get a car and leave here around two. I want you to sleep until then.'

While the three slept, Holliday went out and woke the night man in the garage, and arranged for a car to drive them to Plymouth. It was one o'clock when he walked up the hill of the medieval town, passing beneath the old clock bridge, back to the hotel. He was nearly there when, with a rush and a roar, a huge car charged up the hill past him, and then with a scream of brakes pulled up in front of the inn.

'Oh, oh!' said Hiram Holliday, 'I don't believe it. It only happens in books.' Nevertheless he stepped into a shop doorway shaded by the overhang of an Elizabethan balconade.

34

'Hallo. . . . Hallo . . .' a voice cried from the car. . . . 'Iss anyone up ?'

The proprietor came grumbling to the door and peered out.

'Hallo!' said the voice. 'Are we on se road for Penzance ?'

'Well, now ye do be little off of it,' came the reply in broad Devon. 'Go straight on till ye get to Kingsbridge and take the Plymouth turn. Ye'll pick up the main road. But you do be still a hunder and twenty mile from where ye be goin'.'

The crash of gears and the revved engine rang through the sleeping town, and the big car leaped off and disappeared around the corner leaving Hiram Holliday shuddering quietly. There had been five men in the car. The street lamp had shone plainly on the man in the back in the middle. It was the German with the scar. He had a large piece of sticking plaster across his upper lip.

'That,' said Hiram Holliday to himself, as he waited until the sound of the car had died away, 'is what you get for being a dramatic ass and not leaving well enough alone. You had the game won, and then you had to pull the Escape from the Train, and the Midnight Flight through the Countryside. I will try to remember that. It is only the dramatic people who get into trouble. . . .'

He saw no need to inform Heidi of what had happened.

They drove, jammed together in a tiny Morris, through the high, twisting Devon lanes, on the back roads to Plymouth. Once Heidi had suddenly begun to laugh hysterically and cry. . . . 'Oh, no, no. . . . No. You fought them with your umbrella. . . . With an umbrella. . . .'

Holliday, embarrassed, glanced at the thing, still crooked over one arm, but the girl stopped laughing as suddenly as she had started, and said with the same wonderful tones in her voice that he had heard when she had defied the sky: '*Ach nein*. . . . No, no. It is not an umbrella. It is a shining sword.' And she took it suddenly from his arm and pressed her lips to the crook of the handle that was the hilt, with a gesture that Hiram suddenly knew was many, many hundreds of years old.

And once when he had told her his name she just sat and repeated it over and over again: 'Hiram Holliday. . . . Hiram Holliday. . . . Hiram Holliday. . . .'

And finally they drove up to the Southern Railway Docks in Plymouth, where the tender was preparing to leave for the s.s. *Bordeaux* where she lay in the Sound, beyond the Hoe, outlined by her own lights, and Hiram Holliday with a little catch in his throat because the adventure was ended, said: 'Goodbye, Heidi. And good luck in Paris – and everywhere.'

The girl stood for a moment with both hands on his shoulders looking into his round, old-young face. She said: 'Goodbye, Hiram Holliday. Thank you. I do not think perhaps our ways will ever cross again, but I at least have known a great and gallant man. There are not many left. Goodbye, my dear.' She slipped her arms about his neck and kissed his lips, and Hiram had his reward. Then she and the child went aboard the tender. But the thing that sent a little cold chill down his spine was the behaviour of the nurse. She came to him and took his right hand with her head bowed and slightly inclined. And as she carried it to her lips, she bent her knee to him in a quick, curious curtsy.

The tender emitted three sharp blasts and cast off. Hiram Holliday stood on the dock and waved to the three until they were out of sight, and then turned and walked slowly and wearily away, a very lonely, misshapen figure in a mackintosh and turned-up soft hat, with an umbrella crooked over his arm.

He went to the Grand Hotel and slept until nine and then caught the ten o'clock train back to London. He had bought some English magazines to read on the way back. He was looking at a copy of the *Sketch*, a periodical devoted to Society and sport, but left it open on his lap as the express roared through a station, and he caught the name – 'Totnes,' and all the fantastic, impossible happenings of the night before came flooding back to him. He had fought against Nazi agents in a park in London for an unknown girl, with an umbrella, helped her to escape something he was not sure he even believed, and had nearly run her right back into them again. . . . He sighed and shook his head, and turned the page and felt his heart stop. It was a full-length reproduction of an oil portrait, and staring at him were Heidi, and the boy Peter. She was seated in a high-backed, crested chair, with the boy curled at her feet.

He read the caption below: 'This charming portrait by De Brasse of the Princess Adelheit Von Fürstenhof of Styria, and her nephew Duke Peter, is on exhibition currently at the Sartor Galleries in New Bond Street, and was painted two summers ago at Castle Fürstenhof, Ober Zeiring. The Princess has not been in London since the *Anschluss*, indeed, there has been speculation in some quarters as to her whereabouts. Her many friends in London society have missed gay and gracious "Princess Heidi," as she is known.'

Hiram Holliday smiled a little smile to himself and leaned back in his seat and closed his eyes. Then he carefully tore out the page, folded it and placed it in his pocket.

When he got to London, the news of the accord in Munich was out. He had to shake himself to realize what had happened because he had been in another world. He took a cab and drove to his room in Bruton Street. There were two cablegrams waiting for him there. They had been addressed to him care of the *Sentinel* Bureau in Fleet Street, and sent on over. He opened one. It was brief and to the point. It said: 'Sorry. You're fired!' It was signed 'Joel Smith,' the head of the *Sentinel* copy-desk. He felt it slip through his fingers to the floor. He had forgotten about his fantastic performance in the *Sentinel* Bureau the day before. Of course, they had cabled New York about it. Probably thought he was drunk. Mechanically he opened the second cable. He looked at the signature first. It was 'Beauheld, Managing Editor, *N.Y. Sentinel*.' His glasses seemed to blur and he had to read it twice. . . . 'Congratulations. You're hired. I made Smith fire you. To hell with the copy-desk. You're writing for me now. Leave for Paris at once. Instructions there.'

Paris – Go to Paris. . . . He suddenly raised his arms and laughed a half laugh, half sob. Then he realized the umbrella was still crooked on his arm. He took it off and pressed the handle to his cheek. On an impulse he suddenly reversed it and examined the ferrule. There was a darkish stain on it. He fingered it half incredibly. It was indubitably blood. And this time his laughter rang gay and clear. . . .

SANCTUARY IN PARIS

How Hiram Holliday Left Paris

TWENTY minutes before the departure of the 10.48 Air France plane for Prague, the waiting-room of the Central Airport of Paris at Le Bourget was in something of a gay uproar. Grognolle, the great silent clown of the Cirque Antoine, Grognolle, *le Mélancolique (Il ne parle jamais)* who had taken all Paris by storm, was departing to fill an engagement in the capital of Czechoslovakia. 'Goodness knows, *ces pauvres*,' said one of the airline's officials, 'those poor people need someone to make them laugh. And we, too.'

The official was somewhat harassed, what with the gay crowd of laughing, voluble circus people from the Antoine who had come to see Grognolle off, the throng that had suddenly materialized in the waiting-room, as the magic of Grognolle's name spread, and the interminable police who were always looking for this one, or that one, and expected the overworked airline people to act as guardians of the portal, and produce wanted men like rabbits out of a hat.

This time it was an American by the name of Hiram Holliday who had disappeared under strange circumstances at a time, it seemed, when the police were rather anxious to secure his person for questioning. They had been watching the airport for days. Ah, these times, these bad times. Evil days and evil people, and Paris rocking again under the exposure of the great Vinovarieff plot, revealed, in an American newspaper, that pact of evil, unquestionably authenticated, involving Russians in Nazi pay, which had threatened the very existence of France and had again plunged Europe into political turmoil.

Ah, well – the official re-checked the list of passengers bound for Prague – Van der Aadt, a Dutch K.L.M. official; a Mrs Stoddart, an American lady with her two daughters; M. St

Cloud, a French racing man and his wife; Schmidt, a German business man travelling alone; Grognolle – ah, that funny man, two nights ago the official had been to the Cirque Antoine, and had laughed until the tears ran down his cheeks, and two Czechs. That completed the list.

He shrugged his shoulders and looked up, as the noise in the waiting-room redoubled and the crowd clamoured for a glimpse of the great clown.

It had begun with the arrival of the party in two cars. Someone had said: *'C'est le Grognolle !'* and the name had run like a fire around the vast steel and concrete hall. Everyone crowded to see, the porters, and the attendants, and the Customs officers, the passengers and the loiterers. . . .

'Grognolle, Grognolle!' they cried. . . . 'Bravo, Grognolle . . . see how modest he looks . . . the little dark one with him they say is his sweetheart . . . Grognolle, *regardez moi* . . . see, he never speaks, not even out of the circus. No one has ever heard him speak. *Au revoir*, Grognolle. . . . Give us your autograph, Grognolle . . . even in real life he looks sad . . . but so droll . . . come back to us soon, Grognolle . . . may we shake your hand, Grognolle. . . . Look at us in your funny way, Grognolle . . .' and then there would be a sudden wave of laughter ripple over the crowd, and the shuffling of feet on the stone floor as more and more people ran to see him.

The great clown really was not much to look at, he was even a little shabby, in the way of those of the circus when they don their street clothes, in a too big overcoat and a muffler wound around his neck, and a drab velour hat that seemed to perch on top of his head. He wore spectacles and seemed to be a little bewildered and shy of all the attention and excitement, but in spite of his appearance of being no longer young nor of good figure, he must really be the very devil of a fellow, for look how that small, pretty, dark-haired one clings to his arm, and see, there are tears in her eyes. Who is she ? Why, that is the famous Lisette Pollarde, the bareback rider, queen of the Cirque Antoine. These people are so difficult to recognize in their street clothes, are they not ?

So! Passengers for Rome! Passengers for Berlin! Passengers for London! *Enfin*, passengers please for Prague, at Portal four. Gendarmes here, hold back that crowd. They cannot all go through the gate.

The crush surrounding the clown began to move slowly towards the door leading to the field. Gendarmes in their blue capes fought valiantly to open up a passage. Grognolle shuffled with the mob, the girl on his arm with her pretty, frank face pressed to his shoulder. Once in a while, he would stare with sad eyes at someone in the crowd, a curious, pathetic, poignant stare that seemed to contain a world of yearning and desire, and the person stared at would break into shrieks of hysterical laughter which would spread until everyone was laughing, that is, everyone but Grognolle, and the girl on his arm, who was crying.

There were two men standing on either side of the door. The airline official knew they were detectives. They watched the passengers pass through. But they shook hands with Grognolle, and one of them, favoured with that strange, melancholy look, began to laugh, and they both clapped him on the back, and said: 'But, he is magnificent,' and permitted the girl to go through the gate with him, and many others squeezed through also, and so there was confusion and pushing, and shouting around the plane, and pilots and *mécaniques* from other ships came over to see the excitement. Grognolle was the last one on board.

He stood for a moment by the steps, a queer, silent, heavy-set, ungainly figure. He put his arms around the girl and leaned down and kissed her, mounted the steps, turned for a moment and lifted his hat to the crowd, and nobody laughed then. Instead, they raised a great cheer and hand-clapping, and yelled: 'Bravo, Grognolle. . . .'

Then the gendarmes drove the spectators back, the silver, Air France, stubby-winged plane roared its engines and moved off. All the people stood on the airport apron and waved their hats and their handkerchiefs as the ship raised itself from the ground and disappeared towards the east.

The flight was what might be described as routine and un-eventful, most of it being conducted above the clouds. Some of the passengers stared curiously at Grognolle, who dozed part of the way, or sat quietly and read out of a book. Five hours later they felt their way down through the cloud bank into rain and landed at the Prague airport. The travellers stretched themselves and climbed out of the ship. A Czech immigration official in khaki collected their passports as they descended the steps from the plane, and directed them to the waiting-room. The immigration official checked and stamped the documents quickly in his little office, the Dutchman, the French couple, the American lady with her daughters, the German business man, and the American by the name of Hiram Holliday. Because it seemed a curious name, the official thumbed through the pages – 'Hiram Holli-day – height, five feet, eleven inches; hair, sandy; eyes, blue; scar on right wrist. Place of birth, New York City, August 10, 1899; Occupation – copy-reader,' and then the picture of an inoffensive-looking, sandy-haired man with a round face, bespectacled and with a good mouth.

He stamped a page, pencilled his initials, stuck his head close to the little window and called: 'Meester Holliday?'

The man known as Grognolle started a little, and then said: 'Yes?' and moved forward to the window.

The official quickly checked the picture in the passport with the man who stood before him.

'Have you any Czech crowns with you, Mr Holliday?'

The man who had been Grognolle said: 'Three hundred.'

The official made a notation and then handed the little red booklet through the window, and said: 'Your passport, Meester Holliday. I hope you enjoy your stay in Prague. Proceed now to the baggage examination inside.'

'Thank you very much,' said Hiram Holliday, with something of a sigh. He went to the counter where a bored Douanier marked his bag with an 'X' in chalk, without bothering to open it. Then he went out, climbed into a taxicab and said: 'Ambassador Hotel.' He slumped back in the seat as the cab jerked forward. He noticed that his hand was shaking a little.

How Hiram Holliday Came to Paris

It all began, the whole, absurd, fantastic, unbelievable adventure, in the smart, glittering Dunhill shop at the top of the rue de la Paix, where Hiram Holliday exchanged apologies and umbrellas with the large man with the spade beard, the morning coat and striped trousers and a bowler hat, a pleasant and polite gentleman with kind eyes shining behind gold pince-nez attached to a black ribbon, rather a fatherly sort of character, and the last person in the world Hiram would have suspected of being capable eventually of trying to kill him.

Or perhaps the unseen strands of the dangerous web began to weave about him much earlier, even shortly after he arrived from London, to report for orders at the Paris Bureau of the *New York Sentinel*. For, Hiram Holliday was not exactly received with open arms by his colleagues in Paris.

Clegg, the Paris Bureau Chief, was a tired man of some twenty-three years of experience in the French capital, and he was having troubles of his own, when Holliday arrived and asked for orders. A new man on a foreign beat is practically worthless the first two or three years until he begins to get the hang of things and makes contacts and friends. Also, Beauheld, the managing editor of the *Sentinel*, had been little less than vague in his instructions for Holliday. Truth to tell, now that the first enthusiasm over the remarkable story Holliday had filed from London had died down, the editor was slightly at a loss as to how exactly to use him. He was even in some doubt as to whether Holliday could do it again, as indicated by his cable to Clegg:

Sending you Holliday who filed a knockout story from London stop used to be on our copy-desk stop may have makings of a reporter if it wasn't an accident stop turn him loose on anything you think he can do.

BEAUHELD.

43

Clegg said: 'Ha . . . hmmm. Holliday ? Oh, yes. Holliday. Beau cabled me about you. Damned if I know what to do with you. Nice story you had out of London, but it's a little different here. Matter of fact we're busy as hell on a tough yarn and I'm afraid you wouldn't be much good on it.' He said it in a manner that left no doubt that what he actually thought was that Hiram would, if anything, be very much in the way. 'Why don't you just sort of take it easy and take a look around the town; there's a hell of a lot to see, and meet some of the boys, and maybe you can do some sort of a piece on the city a little later. Come in here and use the office any time. Glad to have seen you. . . .'

For all his somewhat extraordinary nature and accomplishments, Hiram Holliday was a shy man, and his fourteen years on the copy-desk of his paper, reading and correcting stories written by others and writing the head-lines there, had not made him less so. But by virtue of his work and his newspaper associations, he was a very practical man.

He understood the attitude of the Bureau Chief in Paris. Indeed, he was a little at loss himself as to what his line of action was to be. What he had done in London had grown out of himself, the product of the terrible tension under which the city had lived for days. Paris, he already knew, was different, and he felt useless, and even more so after he had inquired politely and in the manner of the shy neophyte as to the nature of the story that was adding grey hairs to the heads of the seasoned veterans in the Paris Bureau.

For, it was one of those nasty, difficult, less than half tangible political intrigues, hints of which only reach the newspaper offices and bureaux guardedly and in roundabout ways. Its existence could not be admitted at any of the embassies, or the French Foreign Office, or the Prefecture. No one knew anything, and everyone had heard, or suspected something. The intrigue centred around a purported deal between the Germans and the White Russians whose headquarters were in Paris, to involve the Ukraine. It threatened the safety of France, the friendship and protection of Soviet Russia, the destiny of Poland, and the peace and security of Central Europe, such as it was.

It had come to the surface in the murder of a Soviet under-secretary Mikoff, shot down in his home in Paris by an unknown assassin, and through the mysterious disappearance of General Grigor Vinovarieff, former Czarist officer and erstwhile leader of the White Russians in Paris, but repudiated by them when he became suspect of selling out to the Nazis. When the French secret service began to take an interest in him with a view to deportation, he vanished without a trace. But in the meantime it became apparent that he was still giving orders, and that they were being carried out. There had been an attempt on the life of the Soviet Ambassador, there was inspired unrest on the Ukrainian border, traces of German money in Russian hands were found. . . .

Hiram shook his head and sighed. These were insidious and dangerous world politics that took a lifetime to understand. His colleagues, he knew, might nibble away a little of the crust of the conspiracy, but the heart of the plot would remain the secrets of the nations involved, buried in their archives and dossiers or locked in the cold meat of the corpses of the men who knew too much or had been too careless with what they knew. As a veteran of the copy-desk he knew that from half to two-thirds of the real news in any sensational story is never published.

He felt lonely, superfluous and unhappy. The exhilaration that had been with him since the London adventure had left him.

'Thanks,' said Hiram Holliday. 'I won't be bothering you. I'm at the Hotel Voltaire if you want me for anything.' He donned his hat and coat and went out, a curiously undistinguished figure.

'Whatever possessed Beau to send us a cluck like that?' said Bureau Chief Clegg when the office door had closed. 'He must be getting senile,' and promptly forgot about him. Nor did he think about him again until three days later he was rather forcibly called to his attention when it developed that an

American by the name of Hiram Holliday had vanished into thin air in Paris, and in his stead had left in his wildly disarrayed and battered hotel room the silent and rigid person of a well-dressed, unidentified Russian gentleman. The Russian gentleman was rigid and silent because he was dead of a broken neck. He sat on the floor with his back against the bedstead. In his right hand he clutched a nickel-plated pistol of which one chamber was discharged, the bullet being found in the wall. But of what became of Hiram Holliday no one found out; not certain foreign gentlemen of nobility who shook in their shoes for every second that he was missing, not certain members of the Soviet Government who would have given many roubles to have known, just as a group of worried and enraged members of the German secret foreign service would have paid thousands of gold marks for his person, not the French police, who, after all, had a duty to perform, even though after they had identified the person of the rigid Russian gentleman they were very, very glad that he was dead.

In London, Hiram Holliday had never been free from the strong impressions of tradition. The dust of the ancient English, and before them the Romans, and even before them the Britons called to him up through the very streets that he walked. In Paris he was conscious only of modernity. And this was, he felt, because Paris was never really at any time ancient. The people who had lived there had never been anything but modern.

He felt more cheerful walking the thronged, noisy streets and boulevards, the Madeleine, the Capucines, the Italiens, and the crooked side-streets with the fascinating names that led from them, or near them, Maturin, Auber, Caumartin, rue de la Paix, streets whose names had such a familiar ring that when he turned into one of them it was almost with a sense of home-coming.

Mainly, he was impressed with the complete femininity of the city and immediately it set up a curious nostalgic yearning in him. He was a man and lonely in a city of women, a city where every woman dressed exquisitely from the poorest shopgirl upwards, a city where when one walked on a great boulevard like the Champs-Élysées or the Capucines there was always the strong scent of perfume in the air, a scent that was ever changing as woman after woman drifted by, each with her own.

He noted with pleasure how beautifully the little children were dressed, like dolls in the windows of toy-stores around Christmas-time. He went to none of the places indicated by the guide-books, but sat in the lemon-yellow sunlight in the park at the end of the Champs-Élysées between the Rond Point and the Place de la Concorde, and saw the children ride the little wagons drawn by goats, and on ponies and on a tiny carousel, and watched the women go by, the women with which Paris adorned herself. He felt that Paris wore her women like gay flowers in her hair or lovely jewellery.

He observed how Paris turned the autumn to her own account. Like all good things of age she took to herself a patina. Her trees turned into no patchwork of autumn colours. They bronzed quietly until all Paris was the shade of the late after-noon sun, the shade of the old buildings and the brown river. Even the still bright flowers in the patterned beds of the Tuileries were paler and seemed eager to join the autumn blend of bronze.

Sitting there, his mind turned to thoughts of the Princess Adelheit von Fürstenhof and the little Duke Peter, her nephew. Heidi, she had called herself during that fantastic adventure in London. There would never be an adventure like it again, he thought, at least not for him. He wondered whether she was still in Paris and whether he would ever see her again. He realized that if she were she would be with friends, per-haps in hiding, and that there was little hope of seeing her. And what if he should? Grim forces had swept them together in London and in the heat of the struggle she had leaned on him for a little. Well, the crisis was over now and perhaps it was best that he did not see her again. What was it she had said: 'Good-bye, Hiram Holliday. Thank you. I do not think our ways will ever cross again, but at least I have known a great and gallant man. There are not many left.'

Hiram shook his head. It was not good to be greedy. That adventure had ended with the accolade of Heidi's kiss. He put her out of his mind.

That night he dined by himself in a little restaurant near the Church of Saint-Germain-des-Prés, and then, because that was the kind of man he was, he called a cab and drove over to Montmartre and the streets of bals and the cabarets, the broad, garish, fragrant, noisy Boulevard Rochechouart where the big electric signs glittered, and the restaurants and amusement places sat shoulder to shoulder with tiny bistros, and oyster and mussel bars. There, he walked for a while and then, with no more than a glance at the showcases of nude photographs outside the cabarets, he bought himself a ticket in the front row of the Cirque Antoine, 'Le Cirque de Paris,' and went in.

The cabarets failed to attract him, not because he was insensible to the flesh, but because he felt there was no romance in the blatant tawdriness of these places. It was all cut-and-dried like a slab of roast beef ordered in a bad restaurant, sex turned on like a cheap song purchased with five cents inserted into an automatic phonograph. But all circuses were romantic and the men and women who peopled them romantic characters and of another world, a world so much their own that it had always fascinated him. In that dream sphere of adventure and daring in which he lived during the hours away from his work, the circus had always figured.

The Cirque Antoine enchanted him. He sat with his knees pressing up against the side of the ring which was the centre of the building, and the completely circular rows of seats rose steeply like the sides of a funnel, almost to the roof, a roof supported all the way around by tall, red pillars, and from the top of which hung the exciting paraphernalia of the acrobats and aerialists. On the wall between the last row of seats and the roof were painted frescoes of circus acts.

The bill was good, Paolo, a magnificent young juggler, and Coco, an amazing parrot, and the Six Cossacks who performed magnificently on horseback – Hiram wondered why they were called 'Six' when there were really seven, though the seventh, a great, bearded giant of a man, did no riding, but signalled the changes with cracks of a great whip. He quite lost his heart to the gay, lovely dark-haired little circus queen, Lisette Pollarde, and her white horse, Capitan. She introduced each act with a gay little speech, and later performed beautifully on the back of her trained horse. He shuddered to see that the aerialists worked under the circular roof-top without any net. He watched the work of the clowns, and while he could not understand them when they spoke, he studied their pantomime, and deplored again to himself the passing of the silent clown who told his story of comedy and pathos with pantomime, the universal language. He noted also that the auditorium was no more than half full.

But most of all, Hiram was charmed with what took place during the intermission. He followed others of the audience through the huge curtain that screened the door through which the performers made their entrance, and there, behold, was the bar, and, not far, the stables from which came the pungent odour of horses and elephants, and most of the performers were there, the clowns and the acrobats and the jugglers, and Lisette, all holding court for their admirers and worshippers. Some of the clowns were sipping drinks at the bar with civilians, and others were leaning over talking to little children, and there was the warm, friendly hum of conversation and the smell of cigarette smoke and animals and grease paint and perfume, and Hiram Holliday suddenly felt happier than he had at any time since he had come to Paris.

He went over and stroked the nose of the white horse Capitan because he was hoping desperately to be able to talk to Lisette, the girl looked so fresh and charming. She had chestnut hair and fine dark eyes framed in a broad face with high cheekbones, and she had a large, frank, red splash of a mouth and fine white teeth. It was Lisette who broke the ice. She said suddenly: 'Capitan, shake hands. Give the hand to the American gentleman. So. Quick!'

49

The horse raised his right foreleg and placed the hoof in Hiram's hand and arched his neck so charmingly, that Hiram suddenly leaned over and kissed its velvet nose, and the girl laughed in confusion almost as though he had kissed her and said: 'Oh . . . but you Americans are always so impulsive.'

'Gee,' said Hiram, 'you speak English. You . . . you are simply charming. Would . . . would you have a drink with me, Lisette?'

'I have been to England, often,' the girl said, and then bowed her head and added: 'Thank you. I will have a lemonade please, and Capitan would like very much a piece of sugar.'

They went over and sat at the bar, and made friends and talked about the show, and Hiram noted and mentioned that the Cossacks did not seem to be in evidence. The girl tossed her dark head and said: 'Oh. . . . Those Russians. They keep by themselves. They are not like us. I love people.'

'Look,' said Hiram Holliday. . . . 'Maybe this is all out of order. I mean I'm an American and don't know what your customs are. But would you come out with me a little after the show? You see, I am a stranger and lonely. And I do love your business very much. . . .'

The girl was silent for a moment and then studied him. She saw a man, no longer a youth, with unruly sandy hair and a round, innocent face. He had seemed to be a little stout, and yet she had noticed how well he moved when he had approached the horse. His steel-rimmed spectacles gave him almost an owlish air, but there was something in the large, bright blue eyes behind the glasses that made her wonder. The eyes did not belong with the face, the body or the manner. They were the eyes of men who did things. And there was an expression in them that made her want to smile warmly. This funny, innocent American who was so obviously charmed with her. She laughed engagingly and said: 'After the performance I am always very hungry. I have the enormous appetite. You may have permission to take me to supper. I shall meet you right here.'

Thus they met, after the performance was concluded. She

came dressed in a skirt and sweater and a camel's-hair polo coat and no hat, but a dark red ribbon in her hair. And arm-in-arm they walked away from the bright, garish lights and blatant, tinny noises of the Boulevard Rochechouart, up the hill of the Mount of Martyrs through crooked streets, past crooked houses, and the dark pile of the Église du Sacré Coeur to a tiny restaurant in the rue Nicolet where the tablecloths of red and white checkered stuff were clean and fresh. The chef came forth from the kitchen to be introduced, and because he too seemed to have been caught by something in the eyes of the plain man with the little circus queen, he announced that he, Manuel, would with his own hands prepare them an onion soup to be followed by an omelette *aux fines herbes*, after which they should have *les rognons*, kidneys with the sauce of his own soul and being.

While they waited they went to the door and looked at the wonderful, crouching shape of Paris that lay at their feet, the fantastic, shadowy roof-lines and the jewelled blanket of lights that lay over the city like a downy covering that followed every contour.

It was Hiram who talked mostly during the wonderful supper. He spoke of the beauty and the tradition of the circus, and particularly of clowning. He said: 'Do you know, Lisette, I would rather be a clown than priest or president. Strange that only the brutal men of the world are remembered and not those who make us laugh, the Marcelines and the Grocs. Groc was a great clown. I saw him once. He never spoke a word, but the audience would laugh so hard that it cried. Can there be anything more beautiful in this grim, troubled world than to make people laugh, or as you do, to delight the eye and the senses and the feeling of rhythm? Never mind the mechanics of it. But certainly, when an arena is rocking with the laughter of human beings, God is more surely there than in the gloomy caverns where we choose to visit Him. . . . Oh, dear,' finished Hiram Holliday, 'now whatever made me talk like that . . . ?'

The circus girl watched him with her dark, shining eyes and

51

suddenly reached across the table and patted his hand. She said: 'You are a strange American. The outside . . . yes, it is American. But inside . . .'

Later they walked on to the rue des Portes Blanches where she lived, and he thanked her gravely for her kindness. The girl looked up at this man who was not handsome or the figure of a hero, but who seemed to have such strange fire inside him, and said: 'Please do you kiss me good night, Hiram.'

He bent down and kissed her and said: 'Thank you, Lisette, for your great kindness. May we be together again?' and turned and went away. He wanted very desperately to stay, and she might have let him, but then he was more a romanticist than an opportunist. The curious, searching tenderness of the girl's kiss had set a period to the evening. And besides he had no illusions about himself. He felt that he was hardly the figure for conquest. He was never able to know how much that which was within him blazed through his plainness, how much he was a man.

How Hiram Holliday Killed a Man and
Created Laughter in Paris

The next afternoon occurred the absurd episode of the exchanged umbrellas. It had drizzled in the morning and there were low-hanging coppery rainclouds over Paris. Hiram went forth in his mackintosh with his umbrella hung over his arm by the crook of the handle, the handle that in England had been kissed by a princess named Heidi. In the late afternoon he stepped into the Dunhill shop at the top of the rue de la Paix to leave a pipe to be repaired. He left the bowl with his name and the address of his hotel, and selected a new briar, paid for it, turned to go and ran plump into the rear extension of the well-dressed, fatherly-looking gentleman who had been bent over a showcase and was peering into it through gold-rimmed eye-glasses fastened to a black ribbon. There was a thump and a clatter as two umbrellas fell to the marble floor.

'Oh, my dear sir!' said Hiram. 'I beg your pardon.'

'But no! A thousand pardons. It was my fault. How stupid of me to stand so.'

'Permit me . . .' said Hiram, and prepared to reach for the floored umbrellas. But the affable gentleman with the spade beard, striped trousers, morning coat, and pleasant, fatherly demeanour, was before him. 'No, no. . . . Permit *me*. It is all my fault.'

He bent down quickly, pounced upon the umbrellas and handed Hiram his. The two men lifted their hats to one another and Hiram went out of the store and stepped into a taxi, and said: 'Notre Dame!' to the driver. He wanted to see it in the gloom of the cloudy twilight and in possible rain. He fancied as he drove off that he heard a shout: '*Hola! Hola! M'sieu!*' but then, Paris is full of shouts and cries and squawking and braying of auto horns, so he paid no attention and was driven off. It was not until they were crossing the Pont Neuf that he noticed that he did not have his own umbrella, though the one he had was so similar, in fact, almost identical, that it was not surprising a mistake should have been made. But it felt different, and looked different. And when he suddenly opened it and examined the steel ferrule he was certain. Because it was clean and shining and there had been a stain on his, a stain that he cherished greatly, since it had been acquired when he had driven it through the mouth of the unpleasant Nazi with a scar on his face, in London.

Hiram thought first of returning to the shop, because his umbrella had become very dear to him, but, of course, the gentleman with the spade beard would long since have gone. He was irritated at his loss, and gave the handle of the umbrella an exasperated twist so that something clicked and came loose, and he held in his hand the wooden crook and eighteen inches of sword steel, razor sharp, needle-pointed and channelled down the centre. It was discoloured slightly, and Hiram noted with a sudden catch of his breath that it was the same kind of stain that was on the ferrule of his lost umbrella.

'Now what the devil,' he said to himself, 'would a nice,

polite old gentleman like that be doing with a pretty thing like this?'

He examined it with more interest. He had heard of French sword canes, so why not, indeed, sword umbrellas, too? It was a terrible weapon. He tried the temper of the blade and fingered it carefully. He was unaware that the driver had drawn up in front of Notre Dame and had stopped and was waiting stolidly, because he was interested in the way the blade was set into the handle, and holding it carefully he twisted and pulled gently near the top. It gave a little, so he pressed and twisted and it came away smoothly and showed the haft ingeniously embedded in a ring and socket. He thrust his finger up into the hollow wooden handle and found it entering what seemed to be a small cardboard cylinder that was loose and came out when he pulled. The cylinder had a double wall with the inside one loose, and it came away when he tugged at it gently. Inside there was a roll of a half-dozen sheets of delicate onion-skin paper covered with fine writing, but he was unable to read it, as it was in a language that was quite foreign to him. He judged it to be Russian, though part of it seemed to be in German. There was also a long list of names, and at the end a signature that struck him as vaguely familar, not in writing, but in the name.

'Oh, no. No,' said Hiram Holliday to himself. 'It is not possible. It doesn't happen. The papers ... the secret compartment ... the deadly weapon. ...'

'C'est Notre Dame, m'sieu,' said the taxi-driver.

'Yes, yes,' said Hiram, but sat with the sheets between his fingers. The signature, 'Vinovarieff.' Where had he heard ... ?. The light broke. It was the Russian general who had disappeared. And Mikoff, a name that appeared in one of the lists. ... The Soviet under-secretary who had been stabbed to death in his home by an unknown assassin. Vorolich – the Soviet Ambassador upon whose life an attempt had been made. The stain on the blade? Was that all that remained today of the murdered Mikoff? What was in those papers? At which point Hiram Holliday folded them and put them into his pocket. He returned the empty cardboard cylinder into the hollow of the handle and snapped the blade back into place, and then returned it to its sheath in the shaft of the umbrella. The obvious thing to do was to find out.

Now there is one thing that working on a newspaper for many years, no matter in what department, does for a man. It makes him intensely direct and practical when it comes to finding things out. From another pocket Hiram pulled a small guide-book and directory of Paris and consulted it and gave an address to the taxi-driver in the rue des Jeûneurs. When he arrived there he told the man to wait.

There was a large sign painted across the upper windows of the building: 'Demoisson School of Languages.' Hiram went upstairs and inquired for Professor Demoisson.

When the professor, a portly gentleman with a bald skull, appeared, Holliday wasted no time. He said: 'Perhaps you will be able to help me. I came upon some curious papers by accident. They seem to be mostly in Russian. Is there anyone here who could translate them for me?'

Professor Demoisson adjusted a pair of spectacles. 'It will be a pleasure to assist monsieur. I myself am quite fluent in Russian.'

Hiram handed him one of the sheets and watched him as he read; watched him turn first pale, and then crimson, and saw the globules of perspiration rise at the top of his bald skull, and his hand begin to shake, and hear him murmur: *'Mon Dieu! Mais non! C'est pas possible. . . . Bon Dieu!'*

When he turned to Hiram again he was completely shaken and unstrung. 'M'sieu!' he said, hardly able to speak. 'Is it possible that you do not know what you have here? I . . . but we must inform the police at once. At once. . . .' He hardly noticed that Hiram had gently removed the sheet from his trembling fingers. . . . 'It is incredible. I will telephone the prefecture at once. But at once. They must have this immediately. I go to telephone.'

He rushed from the front office. When he was gone, Hiram sighed, refolded the sheets, put them into his pocket and quietly went out, down the stairs, got into his taxi and drove off. If the stuff was that good, he wanted to be in on it before the police. Nor was he sure how the French authorities would accept his explanation of how they had come into his possession.

And then he did a rash thing, a thing he later very much regretted. It was an intensely simple and practical thing and the idea seemed a good one to him at the time. He dismissed the taxi and walked until he came to a post office where he secured a stamped envelope. At the desk he wrote a short note on a telegraph blank, and placed it in the envelope along with all of the thin sheets of paper removed from the umbrella. Then he sealed it, and wrote the address: 'J. R. Beauheld, Esq., Managing Editor the *New York Sentinel*, New York City, N.Y., U.S.A. *Personal*.' He consulted a sailing list on the wall, marked the envelope 'Via s.s. *Normandie*,' purchased the requisite number of stamps, added them to the envelope and dropped it through the posting chute. He was no more than a block from the post office when he found himself wishing he hadn't done it.

It was nearly seven o'clock when he returned to his room on the fourth floor of the modest little Hotel Voltaire in the rue Jean Goujon. His heart was banging, somehow, as he turned the key in the lock. The place had been hit by a cyclone. It had been ransacked, and by an expert. Nothing had been overlooked, furniture, bedding, bureaux, luggage. . . .

The telephone bell tinkled and the porter said: 'A gentleman is on his way up to see you. He has been here several times already.'

The knock on the door coincided with the click of the replaced receiver. Hiram opened it. It was the pleasant, fatherly gentleman of the Dunhill shop, with his umbrella.

'Ah, m'sieu!'

'Come in, come in,' said Hiram. 'Excuse the mess. Somebody evidently thought I was rich enough to rob. How did you know where I . . . But, of course, I left my name and address at the shop. I'm sorry you've been put to all this trouble, but I'm damn glad you found me, because I value that old umbrella of mine a hell of a lot.'

He was watching the pleasant gentleman as he babbled on, and it struck him that he was pale and his eyes kept staring behind Hiram.

'So stupid,' said the gentleman. 'And all my fault. It was I who made the exchange. Well, now here is yours. There is mine, and the little comedy is happily ended, eh?'

Hiram said to himself: 'But is it? What a damned fool I was.' And then aloud: 'Sure, and much obliged. Wouldn't like to have a drink on it, would you?'

The man with the spade beard made his excuses. He was already late. Again he was obliged. M'sieu would, of course, report the robbery to the concierge. Then, *au revoir*. They shook hands, and the gentleman departed.

Hiram looked at the closed door. 'He may have a kind face,' he said to himself, 'but he had a damned clammy hand. Now I wonder what is going to happen?'

He said nothing about the battered room to the concierge, but arranged it quietly himself. Then he went out and dined uneasily, because he felt that he had been a fool. He had meddled with something that did not concern him and was dangerous. And above all, he had done something that was irrevocable, and which was almost certain to bring unpleasant consequences. It was nine o'clock when he went back to his hotel to face them. He hurried back because he wanted them to begin, to be brought out of the dark of his imagination into the light of reality.

They were waiting for him in his room in the form of the fatherly gentleman in the striped trousers and the black beribboned eye-glasses, who was sitting quietly on the edge of a chair with his hat on his lap and his hands folded over the crook of his umbrella handle. He arose courteously when Hiram let himself in the door with his key and said: 'Hullo, what are you doing here?'

'Forgive me that I chose to wait for you here,' said the fatherly gentleman. 'But I thought we could talk better. I felt sure that M'sieu Holliday could enlighten me. This umbrella that you have returned to me. It is not exactly, how shall I say, as you received it from me. There is something missing. You have it perhaps, and will return it to me, I am sure.'

Hiram tried one bluff which he was certain was not going to work, but he wanted time. And besides the gentleman with the spade beard and the kindly eyes did not look dangerous. Hiram had forgotten about the clammy hands. He looked at him blankly and then at the umbrella, and said: 'Eh? Missing? Damned if I know what you're talking about. I gave you your umbrella. That's mine over there in the corner. You can look it over if you want to. But you've got a nerve coming into my room.'

The man sighed patiently, and said: 'That is a pity, M'sieur Holliday. I had hoped that I was mistaken.' He then reached inside the breast of his frock-coat and produced a small nickel-plated pistol, which he fired at Hiram Holliday without further warning.

Simultaneously with the sharp little 'spang,' Hiram heard the bullet smack into the wall behind him and threw an ash-tray at the man's head, and then a magazine, a book, a sheaf of papers, a mineral water bottle, a glass, anything and everything he could lay his hands on.

He did these things as a reflex, but it was an old idea stored away, something he had been told by his pistol-shooting in-structor at the Armoury in New York, a grizzled sergeant who had said: 'If you're ever in a jam in a room with a fellow who has a gun and you have none, throw everything at him you can lay your hands on, and keep on throwing until you can get to him. It will spoil his aim. The average man, if he is excited, will miss you at ten feet. Things flying through the air at him will make him duck instinctively. . . .'

The little gun did not go off again, the bottle had scored a direct hit, and the fatherly gentleman stood there weaving a little. Hiram brought him down with the simple trick known to every ju-jitsu pupil, he slid for his legs, and with his own feet tripped the other's out from under him, one foot hooked be-hind, the other applying pressure from the front. With the same movement, he scrambled up and over and behind him

58

and brought his left forearm across the man's throat, his hand holding his own right shoulder. His right arm he brought over the man's shoulder and then back behind his head, and then with his right hand pushed the head slowly forward against the bar-lock of his own left arm.

Now, ju-jitsu practised in a gymnasium with a clever and benevolent instructor is one thing, and the same art as applied to the person of a potential killer is quite another. When the ju-jitsu student or exponent feels himself caught in a grip that is too much for him or is threatening to break a limb if the pressure is increased, he pats the nearest part of his opponent that he can reach and the bout is over. Also it takes a genuine expert to apply holds so as not to injure a man. Holliday was no expert. The man struggled and threshed with his legs. Hiram increased the pressure. The man did not reach up and pat him to signify submission. He continued the pressure until the man gave a sudden convulsive shudder and relaxed and lay still. It was not until long after that Hiram realized that he had applied the wrong hold.

It was over. And Hiram Holliday knew that he was badly frightened, that in fact he was no longer Hiram Holliday. For the first time he realized the truth of the many interviews with persons who had committed acts of violence, that passed through his fingers on the copy-desk; that what they had done thereafter seemed like a badly remembered dream.

He did not know whether the man was alive or dead. He only knew that he wanted to get out, to people, to his own kind, to keep on going. He was still wearing his hat and coat. Incongruously he snatched up his umbrella, hung it over his arm by the crook and hustled out of the room. Any moment people would come, attracted by the shot. He must get to the *Sentinel* Bureau and see Clegg at once and tell him everything. Miraculously the tiny, self-operating lift was waiting at the landing when he reached it. He got in and pushed the button for the ground floor. The windows were of frosted glass, but as he descended he saw the shapes of men passing on the way up, and heard their feet pounding on the stairs.

There were five or six men standing in the lobby by the porter's desk, and Hiram held himself to walking past them slowly. But one of them suddenly cried out in German: *'Das ist er. . . . Hallo. . . . Halt !'* – and made a grab for him. Hiram ducked and ran through the door and turned left up the street with the men streaming after him. He was frightened at the forces he had invoked, and driven very close to the panic of the hunted when there came a sound like a back-fire from behind him, and something went 'Pht' past his left ear. It was a long street, a full three hundred yards more before he would reach a turning. He wondered what it would feel like to be hit. Then he was conscious that a car was running close beside him. A good-humoured voice said in French: 'Taxi, m'sieu ?'

Hiram made the running-board with a leap and flung himself inside. Through the rear window he saw the men piling into a car. He had forgotten about Clegg and the *Sentinel* Bureau. He was hunted and he wanted a warren in which to run to earth.

'Montmartre! *Vite !*' he gasped to the driver. He had remembered the twisting, crooked streets. He also knew that German agents were now aware that he had abstracted papers that concerned them vitally, and that he was in deep trouble.

Because all Paris cabbies drive like mad, Hiram kept some two hundred yards in front of the following car. He knew that if they caught up with him they would kill him. And then suddenly he acted purely on hunch and instinct. He saw the lights of the Cirque Antoine, the huge electric sign advertising its glories. He stopped the cab, handed the driver a twenty-franc note, bought a ticket and went inside. He had a wild idea that he could lose himself in the audience. But as he went through the door, he saw the pursuing car draw up and the men piling out.

He no longer felt that there would be any security in the circus crowd. There was a deadly and uncompromising implacability in the pursuit. He hustled around the encircling corridor to the rear, to the only friend he knew.

She was standing outside the door of her dressing-room with her white horse, waiting for her cue to go on.

'Lisette,' panted Hiram Holliday. 'I'm in a jam. They're trying to kill me. Is there anywhere I can go? Lisette! Quickly!'

Anyone but a Frenchwoman would have screamed, or stopped to ask questions, or wasted time. Lisette simply said: 'Oh, *mon Dieu!* Hiram!' opened the door to her dressing-room, drew him inside with her and slammed it shut.

The men ranged the back-stage area like wolves, over the protests of the doorman through whom they had brushed without the formality of tickets. They searched the stables and behind the bar, the men's room, the property room, and began to walk unceremoniously into dressing-rooms. In the arena, the Six Riding Cossacks were performing to the pistol-like cracks of the whip of the huge seventh Cossack, reports that would cover and justify the sharp spang of a pistol. And they came eventually, two of them, big men, young, powerful, rosy-cheeked, yellow-haired, arrogant, to the gold-starred door of Lisette Pollarde, Equestrienne Queen of the Cirque Antoine. They burst it open.

'*Hola*,' said Lisette in French. 'If you please! At my door it is the custom to knock.'

The men stood framed in the doorway. One of them had his hand in his pocket. They stared at the lovely circus girl in her short, spangled costume of white and silver, and the sad-eyed, sad-faced, trampolin clown who sat with her at her dressing-table, putting the finishing touches to his white and scarlet face.

He wore the ragged, tattered garb of the classic tramp clown, reminiscent of Joe Jackson, the out-at-the-toes, too big shoes, the battered derby hat, the patched baggy pants and grotesque shirt-front. His nose was shining red, and his mouth painted over the white face was a scarlet inverted 'U' of misery, and two great dark rings accentuated the pathos of his eyes. Strands of a ragged, wispy, red-coloured wig stuck out from beneath the battered derby. He was clutching a ragged and torn umbrella with one hand.

From the arena came a long-drawn finishing chord, and then a burst of a gay, saucy music.

'*Allons*, Grognolle,' said Lisette. '*C'est à nous!*'

Without another glance, she moved between the two hot-eyed men in the doorway followed by the grotesque, pathetic, shuffling clown. It was thus that Hiram Holliday, erstwhile copy-reader for the *New York Sentinel*, found himself in the middle of the Cirque Antoine in Paris, centred in a white pool of light behind which lurked some thousand gleaming eye-balls, rising tier upon tier, and heard Lisette say, as she leaped to the·back of the cantering, snow-white Capitan:

'*Mesdames et Messieurs – Il me fait grand plaisir de vous présenter, mon oncle Grognolle. Il ne parle jamais!*'

Hiram Holliday's legs were weak. He felt frightened, sick and dizzy. He shuffled across the ring dragging the remains of his umbrella and sat down limply on the raised edge, his hands folded over the crook of the umbrella handle, his head hanging dejectedly. And a woman sitting close by laughed.

Hiram looked at her reproachfully and the woman cried: '*Oh, le pauvre drôle,*' and laughed again. Hiram moved a little so that he could observe her better and turned his mournful gaze full upon her, and the woman let out a shriek of mirth that was taken up by her neighbours. He was a little resentful of the laughter at first. And then he suddenly remembered the mournful mask with which the quick, experienced fingers of the circus-girl had endowed him, in those fearful few minutes in her dressing-room, when he had told her what he could of his adventure, and she had hidden him from all eyes beneath the chalk and vermilion of the circus clown.

A change came over him. He began to experiment with the laughter of the woman in the audience, a stout, motherly soul with a hair mole on her face. He sighed, she laughed more loudly. He looked at her with·a steady gaze and her shrieks increased. He now set himself to imagine that she was the most beautiful creature in all the world and that he longed for her hopelessly. He turned away in despair and walked a step and then whipped around and sat down again, his eyes yearning for her face. The woman was screaming with joy. Her laughter was incendiary, and one by one the candles of mirth were kindled until the whole section in which she sat was ablaze. Hiram turned his face upon a good-looking young girl in the third row, and she immediately became convulsed. He turned his gaze back to the first woman and sighed to show her that he had not forgotten her and she shrieked louder than ever, and the audience catching the connexion and the by-play shouted, and cried: 'Ah . . . ah, Grognolle, remember your first love . . . she is the one for you.'

Hiram tried something else. He decided to pretend that it was suddenly raining and that he must put up his battered umbrella, the umbrella that he had fought with in London, the umbrella that Lisette had torn and broken, at the last minute in the dressing-room, to make it a thing of comedy.

Of pantomime, of the art of clowning, Hiram Holliday at that time knew nothing, though he learned with amazing rapidity. But this he knew. He must himself believe with all his soul and being that it was raining, that he was afraid to be in the rain, and that he must somehow open his bent and tattered umbrella to seek shelter from it. Thus, he worked slowly, and with infinite care and patience, studying with deep grief and dejection each broken strut, and torn bit of black linen, widening the rents, breaking it further, until the thing that he finally elevated over his head with infinite misery, despair and sense of utter failure, was a tangled, hopeless wreck of steel and cloth. His reward was peal after peal of laughter that seemed to rock the slim, circular building and which brought fat, moustached Papa Antoine, impresario of the Cirque, rushing from his office to stare in amazement at two things. The first was gendarmes ejecting a half-dozen men who had apparently rushed through the gates without paying, and had been breaking into dressing-rooms. The other was a new clown of whose existence he had not even known, and who had the ancient Cirque shaking to such peals of joyous laughter as it had not heard in his lifetime.

Long after Lisette and Hiram had taken their bows and were closeted in Papa Antoine's office, and the next act was on, the arena was still ringing to cries of 'Grognolle! . . . Grognolle! . . . We want Grognolle. . . . Come back, Grognolle!'

Much, much later, when the show was over, and the Cirque dark, Lisette and Hiram Holliday appeared at the stage door opening on to the boulevard. They were still in make-up and costume, except for coats thrown over their shoulders. The clown signalled to a passing taxi while the girl chattered angrily at the injustice of having to perform at a benefit when she was so tired. A few passers-by stopped to watch them. The cab drew up behind a car in which there sat a silent group of men. Hiram and the girl got into the cab.

'Club Schéhérazade in the rue de Liège,' said Lisette, still grumbling, and the cab drove off. But after they had driven for five minutes, and made sure that there was no pursuit, the girl suddenly tapped the driver on the shoulder and gave him the address in the rue des Portes Blanches, where she lived. There they dismissed him and went inside together.

It was the next day when Lisette read and translated for him from a newspaper that he learned that, as Hiram Holliday, he was wanted by the French police to explain the presence in his hotel room of a gentleman with a broken neck, and that as Grognolle, he had become famous overnight. 'Lumière,' the famous French commentator, had happened to be in the audience the night before, and had written two columns in *Le Figaro* on the art of the clown, and particularly Grognolle, the new sensation at the Cirque Antoine.

And so Hiram Holliday was no more, and nightly, Grognolle packed them into the formerly half-empty Cirque Antoine until the inspector of buildings had to be bribed so that still more could be permitted to squeeze inside. Papa Antoine rubbed his hands at the shrewd bargain he had driven with Lisette's uncle. His talents, it is true, had been called to his attention in a rather queer manner, but since the silent man – it was indeed queer that he never spoke beyond nodding or shaking his head, and always had his little niece present at conferences – was coining money for him, what then was the purpose of being too nosey? *Vive* Grognolle!

Hiram Holliday ceased to exist, even to himself, and in his stead there was Grognolle the silent clown. Those were unforgettable days and nights, but when in later days and years he remembered them, it was as though he was recalling and remembering something lovely and wonderful that had happened to someone else, a poignant story that he had read or heard with which in some way he had come to identify himself.

It was Grognolle and not Hiram Holliday who lived in the little flat in the rue des Portes Blanches, overlooking Paris, with Lisette the circus queen. He spoke only to her, and only when they were alone, because she insisted that for his safety he maintain the fiction that he never spoke, off-stage or on.

She looked after him and arranged a set of simple signals whereby when interviewers came he learned by watching her whether to shake his head in assent or negation. They had but the one performance at night – Le Grognolle now had to appear in both halves of the programme, and out of her ancient knowledge of the circus, her family having been circus people for six generations, she rounded out his performance, taught him new bits of business, developed his strange talent.

They kept house together, carefree like two children, rarely leaving the neighbourhood of the Montmartre, even when the hunt for Hiram Holliday seemed to have died down. They went together to the lovely little church of the Sacré Coeur, and the ancient one of Saint-Pierre-de-Montmartre on the site of an old Roman Temple to Mars, and in whose crypt, according to legend, Ignatius Loyola founded the order of Jesuits. Together they ranged across to the great Cimetière du Nord where they stood before the grave of Heinrich Heine, and on other stones read the names of Berlioz, Offenbach, Renan, who wrote the *Life of Christ*, and Théophile Gautier. They did their shopping in a wonderful old market, a miniature replica of the ancient Halles, where all the vegetables were scrubbed and shining, and the autumn flowers turned the stands into solid banks of lovely pastel colours.

They lived resolutely in the wonderful, glamorous present, and battened their minds against the future, because of the knowledge of the truth that was locked in the heart of each, that some day the dream of the clown and the equestrienne must end, that they must go again their separate ways in the angry, bitter world that was so wrong, but from which somehow they had snatched together the few moments that were right. Only once, before the end, did Grognolle become Hiram. It was on a morning when he read a short item in the American paper, the *Paris Herald*, that Lisette had brought him. He read it and re-read it, and was moody and silent for the day, and that night his performance lacked its usual life and sharpness. But the mood passed and he became the great Grognolle again, the sad, silent clown Parisians flocked to see, each hoping to be the recipient of the long, love-lorn stare which would send them into the maddest peals of laughter.

And Grognolle he remained, to all, to Lisette, to himself, until the storm burst from overseas, the storm for which the person who had been Hiram Holliday was waiting.

How Paris Laughed at Hiram Holliday for the Last Time

The *New York Sentinel* began the publication and exposé of the great Vinovarieff plot, documented and authenticated, the story of a group of White Russians who had sold out to the Nazis in a plot against their own fatherland, as well as against France, the country that had adopted and sheltered them. It was a clear, well-worked-out scheme to foment trouble in the Ukraine, and provide for Germany the opportunity to carve out her huge slice of the rich granary. It gave the murder list of the plotters – Mikoff, the man already stabbed to death, and others marked for liquidation to advance the scheme, Soviet diplomats, loyal White Russians, even French officials, and named the men from the German Embassy involved in the plot. It named the trigger man of the syndicate, Sujureff. He was, Hiram suspected, when Lisette translated the tremendous scare heads and stories from the French papers, the man whose neck he had broken so many ages ago in his little hotel room.

The story set Paris and half Europe on fire. And Hiram was glad to note that in accordance with the warning he had sent with the papers, Beauheld, his managing editor, had not involved him.

The exposure drove the French police and secret service into a tornado of energy. One link was needed to complete the tale – General Grigor Vinovarieff, the leader in the plot. And for the first time Hiram realized that the finding of General Vinovarieff was of vital importance to himself. Because in his hands lay the identification of Sujureff, the man who had been sent to murder Hiram Holliday.

He had now become two men again, Hiram Holliday by day, Grognolle at night. Lisette saw and understood. Was the idyll drawing to a close? There was no surface change in her, but that was because she was a Frenchwoman and a performer with a tradition.

In his daytime hours Hiram hatched a hundred wild imaginings of how he would find the missing man, all of them impossible, he knew, because a French paper had wondered whether there was any connexion between the plot, the missing American, the dead, unidentified Russian in his rooms, and the curious story told by a certain language professor. The hunt for Hiram Holliday was on again. He took to keeping to his room by day. At night, muffled, he drove with Lisette to the Cirque Antoine and was safe as Le Grognolle who never spoke, but only made people laugh until they cried.

But how safe?

It was on a Saturday night that the police suddenly invaded the Cirque Antoine.

The little Cirque was packed to the last available inch. People sat in the aisles, and stood jammed up under the roof. Remi Ventura and his talking parrot Coco held the arena when Papa Antoine, pale and perspiring, burst into the dressing-room where Hiram and Lisette had just finished dressing and making up.

'*Bon Dieu!*' he cried. '*Mes enfants. Les flics* ... detectives ... the police. They have come. They are here. Everywhere. All of the performers must line up for inspection. They wish to see all .. all. ...' He paused for a moment and then looked at them cunningly. He had suddenly remembered the circumstances under which Le Grognolle had come to him. '*Mes chers enfants,*' he said. .... 'Is ... is there anything you wish to tell Papa Antoine before it is too late?'

Hiram's stomach turned over. He had understood the word police. But what it was about, Lisette could not translate for him in front of Papa Antoine. A man with a moustache stuck his head inside the door and cried: '*Allons, allons, vite!* Come out ... come out!'

They filed out of the dressing-room. All of the performers in the show except the man in the arena who could be examined later were lined up in the space before the bar. Hiram and Lisette walked slowly to the end of the line by the Cossack act, and Hiram stood next to the bearded giant, with Lisette on his right, the last one. She herself had placed herself thus so that she could whisper in his ear that the police were there, and that detectives and secret service agents had commanded the line-up of performers, that there was no escape, that it was the end.

There were many gendarmes about. From the arena behind the curtain came the absurd voice of the parrot, singing a chansonette with his master. And three men in plain clothes began a slow march up the line-up of performers, pausing to gaze at each one. The leader was a little man with keen eyes behind gold spectacles.

All time and thought had stopped for Hiram Holliday. Somehow they had discovered, or had had a tip. ... They would reach the end of the line. There would be a tap on his shoulder. ... No one would believe his fantastic story. He could feel himself sweating beneath his thick make-up. Now the men had reached the centre of the line, passed it, moved slowly on, they were passing the riding Cossacks. ... In a moment they would reach him. ...

It was Lisette whose nerve broke. With a half-cry, half-sob, she threw her arms around Hiram's neck: 'No! No, no! My Hiram. I will not let them take you. . . . Oh, Hiram, Hiram. . . . '

But curiously, the three men seemed to pay no attention to her outburst. They had stopped in front of the giant Cossack ring-master and the little man with the gold-rimmed eye-glasses was looking at them curiously. Then with a movement that was too quick for the eye, he suddenly knocked off his hat and twitched away his big and bushy black beard. 'Eh bien,' he said, or rather began: 'General Grigor Vinovarieff, I . . .'

He never finished it. The Russian leaped back with a roar like a bull and a gun flashed in his hand. It exploded, but it was Hiram who had knocked his arm up. It exploded again, but this time it was aimed at himself, and slowly, the huge man folded to the ground where he lay a heap of crumpled, gaudy clothing, while in the pandemonium Hiram Holliday struck himself on the forehead and cried: 'Fool! Fool! Will you never learn? Fool! Complacency! To think that you would be the only one taking sanctuary in a circus! The seventh Cossack! He was there all the time for you to see. And now the only man who can clear you is dead. Hiram Holliday, the great adven-turer. . . . Idiot! Fool! . . .'

The little detective had taken a quick hand to restoring order.

'Vite! Vite!' he cried. 'Attention! There must be no dis-order. No one must know. Go on, go on!' Ventura and his parrot had just made an exit. 'Oh! Go on! Here you, Gro-gnolle! Go out there quickly and make them laugh. . . .'

Hiram Holliday felt himself pushed and hustled through the curtain and out into the pool of white lights and thousands of shining eyes that was the arena. He was greeted with a wild burst of applause, and a great shout of laughter, laughter that sounded to Hiram more mocking and bitter than anything he had ever in his life heard before.

But that night, in their home, it was Lisette who faced him bravely and clear-eyed and told him that he must leave Paris.

69

'My Hiram. My strange, beloved American. The next time it will be you. You cannot stay here. They will find you as they found . . . the other. It was I nearly who gave you away tonight, because I loved you. I would have killed myself, Hiram, if it had been so. Something of me will die when you go, but that I can bear because what we have had has been so beautiful. But if they take you I could not bear it. Hiram . . . Hiram. . . . All beauty does end. Let this end so that I know you are safe – safe, somewhere.'

They clung desperately to one another and Hiram knew that she was right. Later he said: 'But how can I get out? Every avenue will be watched. They will check my passport and find – Hiram Holliday.'

Again it was Lisette who said: 'No, no! You are not Hiram Holliday. You are Grognolle, the great clown who never speaks. They will not ask for the passport of the Great Grognolle. You will see. It will be made known at the airport who it is that is leaving. You are more famous in Paris than the President or the Prime Minister. No one will ask.'

'I . . . I will fly to Prague,' said Hiram Holliday, and then hid his face in his hands and tried to blot out those inner messages that came to him from the deep well of his being and told him those happy, gay, wonderful days were over and that this dark, brave, shining companion whose heart had been his, he would never see again.

High in the air, in the silvery plane carrying him to Prague and safety, the quiet man with the round face and the remarkable blue eyes behind the steel-rimmed spectacles, who was known to the other passengers as Grognolle, took a clipping from his wallet and re-read it. It was a brief cutting from a column of news and gossip he had taken from the *Paris Herald*. It stated in effect that the Princess Adelheit (Heidi) von Fürstenhof of Styria, once a well-known figure in Paris society, was now rumoured to be living in Prague.

The man sighed, replaced the clipping, and leaned back and

closed his eyes, and the gay, lovely face of the girl of the circus filled every cranny of his mind, and in his ears once more rang the shattering peals of laughter pouring over him in waves from the packed arena of the Cirque Antoine.

ILLUSION IN PRAGUE

*How Hiram Holliday Sought a Princess and
Found a Man with a False Beard*

HIRAM HOLLIDAY saw the man with the false beard for the first time in the lobby of the Hotel Ambassador, situated in Prague on the broad, stately Václavské Náměstí. He had returned there shortly before nine o'clock, tired and depressed after another day of his curious and wholly illogical search for the Princess Adelheit von Fürstenhof of Styria.

What surprised Hiram and gave him pause was not that the man should be in disguise, but rather that the appendage should be so obviously false, and that he was wearing it so badly. Hiram had already become accustomed to the bizarre character of the lobby of the Central European hotel with its inevitable scattering of mysterious and slightly sinister characters which peopled the collection of little tables behind potted palm trees from early morning until closing time, obvious conspirators who leaned with heads together and talked endlessly, men who sat the whole day through and watched the revolving entrance door; Czechs, Jews, Germans, Yugo-Slavs, Slovenes, Russians, sitting over tall glasses of Pilsener, an atmosphere redolent of suspicion and intrigue. They belonged, somehow, to the gloomy, dour, rainy, medieval Prague that Hiram had discovered in his lonely wanderings through the city, a city that had been doomed to death from the air and which had not yet emerged from the shock of the reprieve.

Hiram was at first startled and then inclined to smile when he saw him (though at later times when he encountered him, he did not smile at all), because, to begin with, the beard material was not of the same colour as the hair, and then it seemed to have been put on crooked. The unmasking, or rather de-bearding of the renegade White Russian leader, General

Vinovarieff, by the French detectives in the Cirque Antoine was still fresh and vivid in Hiram's mind, and it had been somewhat of an education to him in what may be done with effective disguise in the hands of an expert. The man who stood at the desk, conversing with the blue-coated *portier* in the Czech language, was obviously the rankest kind of an amateur at the game.

Holliday studied him while he waited his turn to query the *portier* as to whether an expected cablegram from New York had arrived for him. The man was of medium height, elderly as indicated by the sprinkling of grey in his brown hair. He had dark eyes sunk deep into shadowy sockets, thickish lips half concealed by a moustache that was obviously as false as the beard, and he wore a rusty black frock-coat and a black Homburg hat.

But the hair of the beard was a reddish brown, almost rust-coloured, apparently coarser, and it was on askew. The hair line on one side of the face was lower than on the other, and in itself was plainly detectable. In shape, the appendage was square and bushy, and reminded Hiram of similar ones he had seen to be purchased for twenty-five cents in any of the trick and joke shops that lined Forty-second Street between Lexington and Third Avenue, shops that specialized in sneeze powder and stink bombs.

The *portier* made a motion with his head, indicating apparently that he had something confidential to say, and the man leaned across the desk to bring his ear closer to his mouth, and for one horrible moment Holliday entertained the notion that the beard was about to fall off, and he cringed a little with anticipatory embarrassment. This, however, did not happen. The beard merely waggled as the man nodded in response to the *portier*'s words. He then turned and went out into the street through the revolving door.

The *portier* handed Hiram a cablegram. It was from Beauheld, his Managing Editor in New York, and read:

'Congratulations relieved you are safe 500 bonus awaiting you stop suggest you lay low until our men square Paris rap stop expect results from there shortly stop contact Wallace Reck our man in Prague stop further instructions shortly.'

Hiram smiled, and for the moment the depression that had gripped him since he had arrived in Prague lifted. He was remembering the days on the copy-desk when a two-dollar bonus for a cleverly written headline was money. He went to a vacant table in the lobby lounge and ordered a tall glass of Pilsener, and sat sipping it, a quiet, inconspicuous figure in a raincoat and a crushed felt hat. Men and women at nearby tables glanced at him and then returned to their whispering. Here and there newspapers were lowered. Eyes speculated upon him. The newspapers were raised again. There were a half-dozen secret agents of various nations in the lounge. They noted the attire, the round face with what seemed to be washed-out blue eyes behind steel-rimmed spectacles, the bland expression, and marked him down as a dull and harmless American tourist.

No one could possibly have suspected that this undistinguished, colourless, close-to-middle-age fellow was a man pursuing a stubborn and unreasonable quest, the results of which were to have repercussions in a grey building in Berlin's Wilhelmstrasse and cost a traitor his life.

For in Hiram Holliday's wallet there burned the clipping cut from the *Paris Herald*, a brief notice to the effect that the Princess Adelheit (Heidi) von Fürstenhof of Styria, well known in Paris, was thought to be living in exile in Prague.

And Hiram had hunted for Heidi in Prague. He had looked for her high and low, but the search had been conducted by him according to his own nature, his recent weird experiences in London and Paris, and also in terms of the gloomy, rain-spattered, hag-ridden, romantic old middle-European city. Before Paris and London he probably would have acted a great deal differently. He would have gone to Wallace Reck, or any of the three big Press service correspondents in Prague, and asked whether they knew of any such person, and if so, where she was. And one or all of them might have told him.

But he had been touched by the purest adventure in Paris and London, and Hiram Holliday was a man who never had known physical adventure before. Even to dream about such things as had actually befallen Hiram is dangerous and heady stuff. He had been thrown into bizarre and dramatic events too suddenly, and it had affected his balance and disturbed the cold, even detached mental attitude of the veteran copy-desk man who reads everything set before his eyes, and accepts or believes nothing. When he had first arrived in Paris he had not yet been able to evaluate the physical adventure that he had lived through in London. He had regarded it as a bizarre accident and had been content to consider it as such. He had put aside the temptation to try to see Heidi again.

The days as Grognolle in the Cirque Antoine had altered him. The climax to that adventure had tipped the scales and he suddenly saw life as from an orchestra seat, extravagantly and theatrically. It became inconceivable to him that he should ever again encounter this Princess he knew at first only as a girl named Heidi, in any but romantic circumstances. She was, he told himself, in danger. The idea grew into a conviction fed only by his imagination, and out of that conviction grew a stubborn determination, to find her, to be there when she should need him again. And thus as he ranged the cobbled streets and twisted alleys of the ancient baroque city, his eyes were searching constantly for the small, brave, white face, and his ears were ever attuned to catch the sound of her faint cry for help.

The plane that brought him from Paris to Prague had descended through rain and mist to land, and it had rained ever since. Rain lay over Prague in an enveloping cloak, glistening from the streets, enhancing the mystery of the towered churches and fortresses, changing their shapes, making them loom larger and more menacing and mysterious, just as the curtain of romanticism had fallen over his own mind. Sometimes the spiny towers of the old Týn Church on the Market Place, opposite the still more ancient City Hall, vanished into the grey, boiling mists, and then his imagination was uncapped, and he visioned them as topless and ever rising.

After the wonderful bronze and copper shades of Paris and

her pastel flower-beds and pale blue autumn skies, Prague was grey, and drab, and heavy, and depressed. The shapes of the more modern houses reminded him of barracks, and the massive masonry of the medieval piles weighed him down. Windows were slits in ancient walls three feet thick, and iron-barred. It was the face of Heidi that he kept envisioning behind them. For all its modernity Prague was a city of fairy towers and ogre's dungeons, of old walls, and dormers, casement and embrasure, of postern, wicket- and lych-gate. Arthur Rackham, or Edmond Dulac, who had illustrated the fairy tales Holliday had read as a child, might have conceived it. And Heidi was a blood Princess, and in that other world into which he was leaning too much, princesses languished in towers.

Hiram felt gloomy and depressed in Prague because he was so acutely sensitive to the gloom and depression of the inhabitants. Searching around in his mind for a comparison, he decided that all the people in Prague somehow resembled the rag-tag of the off-streets of New York, like First and Second Avenues. There was no colour or life in them, or in their clothing, or their bearing, or very little hope either. A little taxi-driver who spoke English said to him: 'What is the good? They have give us our lifes and take away our freedom. The German, he can liff without a soul, but not we Czechs.'

Yes, Hiram had felt, that was the difference. London and Paris sprang back into gaiety, lights, laughter, dancing, music, and joy, when the cloud had passed. He thought he understood, perhaps for the first time, why men are willing to die for freedom. Later, when he reviewed in his mind the things he did in Prague, and the absurd passage with the Man with the False Beard, he could realize how profoundly disturbed he had been by the weight of misery and the emotional drag that lay over the city. Because his antidote, more than ever, had been his queer, coloured imagination that yearned for the high and gallant adventure that transcends all the cheerless misery of truth.

He had climbed to the great grey fortress on the left bank of the Moldau, the Hradčany, and there wandered through rain and fog down the Street of the Alchemists, an old, old, tired alley with tiny, tired houses, built into the masonry of the fortress wall, houses that leaned to one another for support, the aged leaning upon the aged. With his mind he peopled them with the fusty-bearded alchemists at their cauldrons and crucibles, and the bare, deserted, rain-drenched streets he dressed with spurred and belted bravoes trailing their long swords. He himself felt as though he wore at his belt the long, basket-hilted rapier of Toledo steel, and once at a window, a tiny dormer under a roof so low he could have touched it with his hand, he was sure he saw the lovely, hunted face of Heidi, and heard her cry: '*À moi, Hiram, à moi.*' But there was nothing at the window but rain streaks on the pane, and no sound but the old grating and creaking of the hanging lamps and metal signs outside the houses.

Lost in his thoughts, Hiram heard his name called over the noise of the lobby and looked up from his beer to see Wallace Reck threading his way through the tables. Reck was the Prague correspondent for the *Sentinel*, a thin, preoccupied man who worked eighteen hours a day in a messy hotel room littered with newspapers and reports, and who was eternally telephoning. He had been far too busy to do more than acknowledge Hiram's presence civilly. Hiram had understood and had stayed away from him.

He waved a hand and said: 'Hi! How you getting on ? Sorry I haven't been able to be around with you more. There's been some sort of a row on the Hungarian border. I had a wire from Beauheld. Said he'd think up something for you to do shortly. Pretty soft.'

Hiram grinned and waved to a chair. 'Got time for a beer ?'

'One,' said Reck, and slid into the seat. 'I've got to meet a guy in ten minutes. What do you think of our little town ?'

'Dead,' said Hiram. 'Up here, I mean. Or here,' and pointed first to his head and then to his heart. 'A guy came into our office once. He had been in the death-house up the river for six weeks and then been pardoned. The other guy confessed. He was alive, but he was still dead, if you know what I mean.

The eyes . . . and his gait. He wasn't walking free yet. It's like that.'

'Mmmmm. Yeah, and a lot worse,' Reck said. 'It's as though the day after the guy was freed they grabbed him again and gave him a life sentence. The people, many of 'em don't realize it yet, but the worst is yet to come. The Gestapo has moved in already. All the under-cover guys are coming up out of their holes. See that guy over there?' He indicated a slight, wispy-looking man sitting at a table with two others. 'He was around here with us before Munich. Working for some Belgian paper. He seemed like a nice guy and used to join us at the *Stammtisch* at midnight when we'd gather to have some beer. He disappeared while the row was on. We just thought he'd got scared and beat it. He's back now with the other two. They're all Nazis and Gestapo men. You never know who is who in this town any more, so you just don't trust anyone.'

Hiram thought suddenly of the Man with the False Beard, and it was on the tip of his tongue to tell Reck about it, but he checked the impulse because he was shy. Instead he said: 'I never felt so much . . . so much despair in a city. . . .'

Reck grunted. 'Despair . . .' he repeated. 'These people were resigned to die for their freedom and they wouldn't even let them do that. Now they're in for it. Not immediately, but it's coming, the beatings and the kidnappings and blackmailing, and the concentration camps and the persecutions, and worst of all the loss of their liberty. Their pals, France and England, abandoned them to THAT.'

Hiram's nostrils expanded. . . . 'God,' he said. 'To have seen that happen. To get it on paper. . . .'

Reck moved irritably. 'You don't see it happen, you *feel* it happen. And you can't write what you don't see. The tunnelling and spying was bad enough before Munich, it's ten times worse now because they've got a free hand. Hitler's going to move in and take over sure as you're sitting there. There's a lot of damned good Czech patriots still, but what can THEY do? They're all on the list. The nation and the Government is still intact, but they know what's coming, what's in store for

78

them. They go on as before, but their hearts are dead. Like your pardoned guy. . . .' He looked at his watch suddenly. 'Oh, nuts. When I start to talk shop I lose track of time. Got to beat it. Thanks for the beer. See you later, maybe.'

He arose and left, but at the door paused suddenly and came back. 'Say,' he said, 'just thought of it. Would you like to come to a party a little later? Be a hell of a good gang there. You know, diplomats, Government officials. . . . I've got to talk to a guy who's going to be there.'

Hiram said: 'Thanks, Reck. . . . I don't like to bother you. I guess I'll have another beer and turn in.' He did not want particularly to see people. Now, more than ever, after his talk with Reck, he wanted to keep his rendezvous with Heidi, to walk those dark, mysterious streets, past the heavy, iron-bound doors and barred windows behind which seethed the intrigues of a dying nation, to be at hand when and if she called. . . .

'Sure,' said Reck. 'Suit yourself. I thought you might like to meet some of those people. They'll be mostly from the legations. Good to know if you're planning to do any work here. Come over if you change your mind. I'll be there from nine-thirty on. The address is the Wilson House, Podebradova, Number Thirty-five. It's one of those new modern apartment houses. Any cab-driver knows where it is. The name is Schoenau, third floor. Ask for me when you get there. Hope you change your mind.' He smiled and left.

When he had gone, Hiram sat thinking for a long time. He realized that the few minutes with Reck had been good for him because he had been lonely in Prague and also that it was important for him to make all the contacts possible. He knew he should have agreed to go to the party.

But Hiram had fallen into a strange mental and romantic trap. There were moments when he caught himself wondering whether there was not something faintly comic in the figure of a man close to middle age in mackintosh and umbrella questing the streets of a strange city for an Austrian Princess in exile. But stronger still was the fear that if he relaxed his search,

79

sometime, somewhere in Prague the call from Heidi would come, and he would not be there to answer it. It was as though the time he had already put in called upon him to do more, seek further. He remembered what a famous and successful reporter had once told him about his methods. He had said: 'The trick is to keep moving. Pile up action. Nobody ever got a story sitting on his tail in a hotel lobby. If you keep moving about from contact to contact and from source to source you've got a better than even chance, mathematically, of being around when something comes off.'

Hiram sighed and looked at his watch. It was nine-thirty. He signed for his beer and got up. It wouldn't hurt to go for a walk before going to bed, to prowl a little – perhaps down to the old Ghetto section. Many eyes followed him as he went out through the revolving door. It was still misting heavily.

How Hiram Holliday Sought the Man with the False Beard and Found the Princess

Hiram stood on the pavement in the cool, damp air, for a moment, undecided. He heard the door revolve again behind him with the quick 'plock-plock' of someone in a great hurry, and when he turned to look out of idle curiosity, he saw that it was the Man with the False Beard. He was carrying a sort of briefcase under one arm, and wearing a long, dark overcoat. He hurried across the walk to the taxi rank at the kerb, and Hiram heard him give an address in Czech. But two words of it he understood. They were 'Wilson,' or rather 'Veelson,' and 'Podebradova.' It was the address that Reck had given him. 'Oh, oh,' said Holliday to himself. 'That's funny. Or is it?' His mind flashed back to what Reck had said: ' ... important people ... mostly from the legations ... you never know who is in this town. ...' And it *was* a false beard. He was sure of it. The wind had snatched it for a moment, and Hiram had fancied almost that he had caught sight of the chin beneath it, though of course in the dark this was not possible. But he made up his mind instantly, a mind that was still crammed with the memories of those fantastic happenings in London and Paris. He entered the next cab in line and said: 'Wilson House, Podebradova thirty-five,' to the driver. He was not more than a block or two behind the Man with the False Beard. And there was a curious beating excitement in his breast.

The Wilson House was one of the modern type apartment houses that had been going up in the newer section of Prague, a six-storey, flat-roofed building, in cream, steel and red with what seemed to be almost a solid front of large casement windows. There were some two dozen cars parked in the street outside. Holliday paid his driver, went in through the heavy glass door and found himself in a lobby that still smelled of fresh cement. On the right there was a panel of post boxes with name-plates on them. Further on, the lobby widened into a large central well with two staircases and two self-operating lifts, a larger one in front and a smaller one in back. The rear staircase and lift were obviously for service. Near the name-panel was a glass door and the sign 'CONCIERGE' above it. Holliday merely glanced through it long enough to see that the concierge was sitting with his back to the door, reading a newspaper and drinking beer, when his attention was caught by two figures ahead of him. One was the Man with the False Beard, and the other was a woman. They had their heads together and were talking earnestly in Czech, the woman with her lips close to the man's ear. They were moving away from him. In the glimpse Hiram caught of her, he saw that she had thick, almost greasy, black hair and a small mouth that had been painted into a startling crimson bow. Her face too was heavily rouged and her eyes, dark and protruding, were heavily shadowed, and the lashes thickly laden with mascara. The pair passed on into the lift, closed the door, pushed a button and ascended smoothly from sight. After a pause he heard the humming of the machinery stop, but had no way of telling at what floor it had paused. It did not start up again.

'Oh, well,' Hiram said to himself, 'I guess that is that.' He consulted the name panel and found 'Von Schoenau,' and the apartment number, '3A.' He pushed the button to recall the lift, entered it, went to the third floor where he found himself on a corridor that made a square around the central well that housed the two lifts and staircases. To the left and in the corner was a door with '3A' on it in bright steel numbers, and from behind it came the crashing chatter of conversation and noise of glassware and dishes, and isolated patches of laughter that indicate a party. He rang the bell.

A maid opened the door, and the talk and noise and laughter leaped at him in a crescendo. He said to the maid: 'Is Mr Reck here? Will you please tell him that Mr Holliday has come?'

'Ah, *ja*, Herr Reck,' said the maid. 'One moment, please, I will get him.'

She returned with the lean correspondent, who was frankly glad to see Hiram. 'Hello,' he said. 'Changed your mind. Fine. I was hoping you would. Come along, I'll introduce you to your hostess.'

Hiram saw that he was in a small vestibule that from one door which was ajar led down a hall from which opened rooms, and guessed that the apartment was laid out in the American style. The other door led into a huge drawing-room that was full of noise, and smoke and people, most of them in dinner-clothes or full dress, and who overflowed into a large dining-room that connected with the *salon*. He caught no more than glimpses, impressions of people, lovely women, decorations, a uniform or two as he threaded his way through the crush, closely following Reck towards a group occupying and standing about a settee near the broad casement windows in the corner.

He heard Reck say: 'Princess von Fürstenhof, may I present my friend Hiram Holliday. . . .'

And then he found himself in front of Heidi, Heidi who was sitting on the low divan and who now held her hand out to him and said: 'Hiram, my dear friend. How glad I am to see you again.'

'Hah!' said Reck. 'You've already met. . . .'

There she was. She wore a simple white evening dress, and at her waist was a bunch of violets, the colour of her eyes, and her pale hair was piled high on her head. Her hand was cool and smooth, and she was surrounded by friends. And once she had slept in a railway carriage with her face pressed against his shoulder. The windmills of Don Quixote were turning in his head.

'In London,' Heidi was saying coolly, and volunteered no more upon the subject, except to say: 'We are old friends,' and then: 'Hiram, may I present Count d'Aquila, my fiancé – Hiram Holliday ... and Captain Ovenecka, and Dr Virslany....'

The windmills were whirling faster and rocking his world with the flapping of their arms. Absurdly a sentence rang through his head, a sentence he had heard spoken by a teacher of literature in school, he even for a moment saw the man plainly in every detail standing on the podium, and saying: '... Cervantes's story of Don Quixote delivered the *coup de grâce* to the already dying chivalry of Europe, and reduced it to absurdity....' And so this was the end, too, of a fool's romantic quest for a Princess held in durance vile.

He knew that he was bowing acknowledgement to the introductions, and he forced himself to see the people whose names had barely filtered through his consciousness – the Count, a small, dapper man with slick, black hair, a narrow face, tiny black moustache, the kind he somehow had always connected with shoe salesmen in New York, and small teeth that were extraordinarily white; Dr Virslany fantastically fat and shaking with apparent jollity, and Captain Ovenecka, quite the handsomest man he had ever seen.

A woman came over and joined them. Startled, Hiram recognized her immediately as the one he had seen in the lobby of the building a short while before, with the man he had been following. Heidi arose and put her arms around her neck and kissed her, and said: 'Lola dear. It was so good of you to come. So good. Hiram, this is Madame Strakova, my dearest friend. Lola, dear, you are just in the right time. And you, too, Hiram. We were talking of going upstairs to call upon Madame von Ovenecka, Captain Ovenecka's mother, and you shall come, too....'

Mother . . . captain . . . fiancé . . . Heidi . . . 'how glad I am to see you again.' Lola, dear . . . small, white teeth . . . enormous, round, bald head, endless chins, twinkling eyes and rumbling chuckle . . . frightened white face behind a barred window, and a call for help in the night: *'À moi! à moi!'* violets worn at a slender waist, lights and laughter, and people, and the sound of a piano . . . thoughts, and sounds, and faces went racketing through Hiram's brain, and loudest he seemed to hear at that awful moment the un-sounds, the not-clashing of non-existent rapiers. . . . With a harsh, physical effort Hiram wrenched himself back into the world that was, and to what Heidi was saying even while he wondered whether she was deliberately creating a diversion to keep him from referring to their fantastic, bravado adventure in London.

But even that did not seem to be so. He caught up with Heidi's words: ' . . . and the most fascinating woman in Prague. Imagine, eighty-seven, and she still cooks. She baked me a cake for tonight. We shall have it later. We always go up to call on her. She is simply marvellous. I adore her. She lives up on the next floor. Shall we go now?'

The handsome Captain glanced at his wrist-watch, and said: 'It will make my mother so happy. You are so kind, Your Highness. She loves you as though you were her daughter. Now, or perhaps a little later. It is still early,' and he glanced at the throng in the *salon* through which they would have to thread their way.

Heidi caught the glance, and said: 'Now. Come, we will go this way.'

She took Madame Strakova by the hand and led her through the less crowded dining-room, followed by the enormously obese Virslany, chuckling, grunting and puffing, the small, lithe, dapper d'Aquila, Hiram and the Captain.

All reality had again fled from Hiram. He did not seem to be walking, but instead objects were passing him – a door, the long corridor he had seen before, down which they turned, another door at the end of the corridor through which they passed, that opened to the outer hall, obviously a service en-

trance to the apartment, a flight of steps up to the next floor
... another door at which they paused and rang, and a sharp
voice that called out in German from within: *'Wer ist da?'*

The Princess replied, almost in song: *'Heidi, Heidi ...
Heidi ist hier.'*

There was a moment of silence and then the door was
opened by a tall, angular woman in the neat, black dress of a
companion nurse, and they all trooped in.

Madame von Ovenecka was seated at a little table under a
lamp, drawing on a pad with a crayon pencil, with bold, broad
strokes, but she set them down when they entered, and Hiram
thought that he had never seen age look so lovely, or an old
woman so sweet.

Her hair was snow white and piled on top of her head in the
same manner as Heidi's and held there with an amethyst clip.
She was still slender and wore a trailing lavender gown with
long, loose sleeves that ended in lace almost to her finger-tips,
and a high collar that came up beneath her chin, and her face,
though lined and wrinkled, was ageless. Hiram had never seen
a *grande dame* before, and for the moment he was fascinated by
the extraordinary sweetness and charm of the old lady, and
when he was introduced to her, he felt impelled to bend over to
kiss her hand, but she withdrew her fingers and instead, patted
his cheek with the gentlest gesture, and said: 'An American,
the only place where there is left the real gallantry,' in soft
English, only slight accented.

The conversation was carried on sometimes in German,
sometimes in Czech, and sometimes, through the Captain's
forethought and politeness and deference to Hiram, in English.

To Dr Virslany she said: 'Anton, did you really lift yourself
the whole flight of stairs to see me?'

The fat doctor roared, and rumbled and chuckled, and
heaved, and made her a bow that was astonishingly graceful for
so gross a man, and said: 'Madame, I would climb the steps of
Santa Maria di Aracoeli vor a loók vrom you. ...'

The stalwart Captain bent over and kissed the top of his
mother's head, and said: 'Madame ... were I not your son ...

85

I would suspect you of devil's arts. Each time I see you, you look younger.'

The old woman looked at her son with delicious mischief on her bright, aristocratic face. 'Petrus, you are a fool. The arts by which an old woman makes herself look younger have nothing to do with the devil. Thank God for Paris.' To Heidi she said: 'Don't let Petrus eat too much of the cake I baked. He always does.'

Somehow Hiram was conscious that the tall, angular companion had whispered to someone: 'Madame must not be tired too much. . . .'

They began to take their leave. Hiram found himself next through the door after Heidi. Without turning her head, she said quietly: 'Later, we shall find time to talk, Hiram. Lola, my dear, where are you? Come.'

Hiram suddenly realized that he disliked Madame Strakova intensely, with her thick, shiny black hair, protruding eyes and tiny painted mouth. The Count moved forward to Heidi's elbow with a mincing step, and Hiram added him in his dislike to Madame Strakova. He dropped back and descended the stairs with the cheerful, chuckling Virslany and the powerfully-built Captain, and then they were back in the throng and clatter of the party where Hiram immediately sought out Reck and found him by himself, eating a plate of chicken salad.

'I've just met the most wonderful old lady,' Hiram began by way of introduction.

Reck smiled with a mouth full of salad, and said: 'Mmmm. Madame Ovenecka.'

'Who . . . who are all the others?' Hiram asked. 'The little guy who looks like . . . like a gigolo. . . .'

'Gigolo?' said Reck, and then grinned. 'Oh, you mean Count Mario d'Aquila. He's the first secretary of the Italian Legation. The fat chap is Dr Anton Virslany. He's a Czech. Officially he isn't supposed to be anything more than the Czech correspondent of the *Amsterdamer Handlesblat*, but unofficially he's probably the most powerful man in Prague.

86

Europe's full of guys like that. Knows everyone and everything. He's the best source I've got here. . . .'

Hiram searched the crowd for the huge figure of the Doctor. He was standing not far away, holding forth in English to an amused group. He was an enormous blob of a man who must have weighed in the neighbourhood of three hundred and fifty pounds. His huge, round head was hairless and sank, via a series of chins, directly into his body, a body that was always shaking with laughter. Even through the noise Hiram could hear his rumbling bellow: 'Oh-ho-ho-ho. . . . The Czechs haff been goot rewanched on Austria. Last nide, the Czech Catherina Myslikova danced in *Die Fledermaus* ballet. Oh-ho-ho-ho. She is the worst dancer in the world. Der Strauss iss still in his grave abinning. So she danced it . . .' and he suddenly, with all his three hundred and fifty pounds, went into the most absurd pirouette in the world. Hiram watched him with a grin as he actually completed a turn and ended in a grotesque burlesque of the offending ballerina.

'. . . Madame Strakova,' Reck was saying, 'is the widow of the former Minister of the Interior. He was a great man. She's a bigger power in the Government now than he was.'

Holliday saw Count d'Aquila cross the room in response to a glance from Madame Strakova, and noted that he moved like a cat.

'The tall, good-looking chap,' Reck went on, 'was Captain Petrus Ovenecka. He's really the political head of the Czech Army. You know how those things go sometimes. He's quite a guy. He's fought five duels, rode in the last Olympic Games . . .' Holliday looked for the Captain, but did not see him. He had been powerfully drawn to the tall, magnificently built, blue-eyed man with the lean, square jaw and lean mouth and the charming manner. He had the looks and carriage of a hero.
'. . . is afraid of nothing and could head a revolt in the Czech Army any day he wanted,' continued Reck. Before he had finished speaking, Hiram noticed that the Captain was again in the room and part of a group.

Reck looked at his watch, and said: 'I've got to blow and see a guy and check on something I heard here. Why don't you stick around? They'll be thinning out soon. Funny your having met the Princess before. Well, maybe we can have lunch tomorrow.'

Alone, Hiram browsed through the party. One thing he had ascertained. The Man with the False Beard who had gone up in the elevator with Madame Strakova apparently was not there. Soon there was another departure. Madame Strakova suddenly complained of feeling ill. Hiram was instantly certain that she was lying, and watched the scene. Over Heidi's protestations she persisted in going home. Dr Virslany, who was nearby, offered to take her, but it was the Count d'Aquila who insisted and won out. They left together. Hiram had a sharp sensation of a definite plan, something that had been cooked up between the two. A few minutes after they had left, the Count returned alone. Madame Strakova had left a small, diamond-encrusted vanity case. He found it on the sideboard of the dining-room and departed again through the dining-room exit.

Hiram was desperately miserable, let down and uncomfortable. But he could not leave until he had spoken to Heidi, to reassure himself that all was well and that the fears that had begun to grow in him again in spite of the shock of his disillusionment were groundless. The guests began to thin out until there were only Virslany, the Captain, and a half-dozen others. Heidi came over to him after having bid some guests good-bye and said: 'My dear Hiram, at last we can be together. Come and tell me everything. We shall sit over there and talk.' She led him over to a settee in a corner and they sat down and looked at one another. Hiram was the first to speak.

'Heidi ... Heidi ...' he said. 'Are you safe? Is everything all right?'

She took his hand in hers and said: 'My dear, good, kind friend ... yes, yes. ... I have been so happy here. It was not safe in Paris. When Mario – that is the Count d'Aquila, my ... my ...' she hesitated for a hardly perceptible fraction, 'fiancé, was moved to Prague he suggested that I come here. I have been able to live again, Hiram. I have such good and strong friends. They are so good to me.' Perhaps she noticed the shadow that had passed on Hiram's face, for she added quickly: 'And now you are here, too!'

'The boy . . . Peter . . .' said Hiram.

'Safe and well,' said Heidi, proudly. 'He is sleeping in his little room,' she indicated the direction with a nod of her fine head, 'with Johanna. Do you remember Johanna?'

Hiram nodded and said: 'Yes. I remember Johanna. She . . . she kissed my hand when you left.'

Heidi nodded too, and said: 'Johanna does that only to a Royal personage. Or to a personage with a Royal heart – such as yours.'

'Tell me, Heidi – do you think they still want the boy? The Nazis, I mean. . . .'

The girl looked grave. 'I . . . I am afraid so, if they could. My brother, Prince Joseph, was a wise and far-seeing man. Before he died he had placed most of our fortune in English and American banks. If they held Peter as they are holding old Baron Rothschild they could force us to bring it back. But they would not dare here. Besides Count d'Aquila, who is a powerful man in Italy, I am also under the protection of Dr Virslany and Captain Ovenecka. And Madame Strakova is high in the Czech Government. I am really safe. Tell me now of yourself, Hiram. Did you know that I was here?'

'Not until I saw you, Heidi. I knew, somehow, that I would find you in Prague, but . . . well . . . not quite like this. Reck asked me to come to a party and gave the name Schoenau.'

Heidi smiled mischievously and said: 'Schoenau is one of our family names. Shall I tell them all to you: Fürstenhof of Styria, von und zu Schoenau und Blankenburg Hohenlohe Altmark, and then there are ten more. You were wonderful when you met me, Hiram, your face never moved. I was so proud of you. Oh, you should have been a European. No, no. I so much prefer to have you an American.'

They talked a while longer, Hiram with only half his mind

and heart. He wanted to go some place where four walls could enclose him alone with his nakedness. He was sore and raw and hurt, and the pain was not lessened by the knowledge that he had been a fool and the victim of his own imagination. There had been no lack of sincerity, sweetness or graciousness on Heidi's part. She had been genuinely happy to have found him again. But the man that was within Hiram was strong and honest enough to tell him that he had no place in this new and secure world of hers. He prepared to leave.

'Would ... wouldn't you like to see Peter for a moment before you go? He has so often spoken of you and asked for you.'

'Yes,' said Hiram Holliday, 'I would very much, Heidi.' He was the last link between Heidi and himself and their other days when she needed him, this quiet, brave boy of eight, with the brown hair and light blue eyes.

Heidi rumpled up her nose deliciously and crooked her finger at Hiram. 'Come. We will go to see him. Johanna will scold that we wake him until she sees who I have brought and then she will be glad, too.'

She led him down the long corridor that he had already once traversed that evening and opened a door and stepped through into the darkness and Hiram followed her. He heard Heidi's fingers searching the wall for the switch, and the lights came on.

Hiram saw the nurse, Johanna, in a woollen nightgown, turning on her elbow at the sudden awakening, in her large bed in the corner. He saw the smaller one nearby, empty, with the top bedclothes still shaping the small body that had been within. Then came Heidi's dreadful, mortal scream:

'*Johanna! Herr Gott! Der Peter!*'

'*Herrje! Hoheit!*' Johanna answered the scream and was out of bed, a grotesque, staring figure with two grey braids of hair hanging down her back. Then with a leap she whipped through a door that led apparently into a bathroom, and they heard her half-inarticulate cry there. Another door banged, and then she was back with nearly all sanity gone from her

face as she flung herself on to her knees crying: '*Jesus, Maria*
. . . *Er ist nicht da . . . Jesus, Maria. Oh, Gott, Oh, Gott!*'

Heavy feet pounded down the corridor and it was Captain
Ovenecka who first burst into the room, eyes blazing, one hand
at his gun pocket, followed by the puffing, wheezing, elephantine
figure of Virslany. '*Was ist hier los?*'

Heidi was sagging at the wall, and Hiram quietly went to
her and slipped his shoulder under her arm. 'The boy,' he
said, 'the boy is gone. We came in here to see him, and he's
gone.'

'*Tausend Donner!*' cried the Captain in a thundering voice.
'He must be here. Look everywhere. It is impossible.'

The remaining half-dozen guests had come, and they scattered and searched the apartment, the kitchen, the maid's
room, the bathroom and Heidi's room adjoining, the closets,
every nook and cranny. Hiram did not wait. He was already
through the service door and out into the hall. It was deserted.
Going down the stairs three at a time, he noted by his watch
that it was half-past eleven. The light in the concierge's little
compartment was still burning, but the man was asleep at his
table, his head on his arms. A thousand children could have
been carried past him. Hiram ran on out through the great
entrance door. The street was dark, quiet and deserted except
for three waiting cars with their chauffeurs slumped snoozing
at their wheels.

Thirty yards away, its tail light diminishing, a cab was moving off. It passed beneath a bright street lamp and then out of
the lighted area, but not before Hiram had caught a glimpse
through the rear window of the absurd appendage, the coarse,
crinkled hair jutting out from the chin under the Homburg hat
of the person he had come to know as the Man with the False
Beard.

With a yell he started to give chase. A wild sprint, all out, with
every ounce of power and he might catch it. But he had started
just too late. The cab speeded up, rounded a corner and was
gone.

Hiram turned and roused the sleeping chauffeurs. 'A child

has been stolen,' he shouted. 'Did you see anyone . . . ? Has anyone come out with a child? Did you see a woman with a child, or a man with a beard?'

They stared at him stupidly and then at one another. It was obvious they did not understand a word. 'Oh, God damn it!' cried Hiram. 'The fools. . . . And the concierge asleep! They can be miles away with the boy.' He went back into the house and roused the sleeping concierge, but he too spoke no English. He ran back up the stairs and into the apartment, where he found that the Captain and Virslany had taken charge and Heidi was at the side of the hysterical nurse.

'There's nothing below,' said Hiram. 'The concierge was asleep and so were the chauffeurs. And I can't make them understand me.'

'The border is closed,' said the Captain in a voice like the clashing of steel. 'I have closed it. Not a person can get through.'

Dr Virslany was at the telephone, talking harshly and sharply in Czech.

His great, bubbling merriment had left him. His eyes were stormy and the flabby lines of his face hard and bitter and he looked to Hiram like a veritable mountain of vengeance. 'The Inspector will be here in an instant,' he said.

'Heidi,' Hiram cried, 'what does Johanna say?'

There then was the white face and the frightened eyes he had seen so often in his mind.

'She heard nothing. Absolutely nothing. She put out the light about ten o'clock. Peter was there. She went to sleep.' She turned to Virslany. 'Anton, call Mario. Tell him to come.'

Dr Virslany's voice rumbled and rasped. 'The telephone in se home of Count d'Aquila does not answer.'

They went back into the nursery. There was a white teddy bear at the foot of the empty bed.

'*Gott verdammt!*' roared Dr Virslany, and Hiram saw that there were tears in his eyes. 'Se bear that his Uncle Anton gafe him! The poor child. *Gott verdammt!* They cannot get away . . .'

Uniformed men poured into the rooms, soldiers and police. Captain Ovenecka was spitting orders like a machine-gun. Dr Virslany had a worried police inspector by the lapels and was thundering at him. Doors were banging down the hall from other apartments and from floors below, and there was the constant sound of boots on cement flooring.

Hiram stood in the centre of the room, shaken by his thoughts, admiring as the two powerful men set into motion every agency of pursuit and arrest. If the kidnappers could be stopped they would stop them. And he thought he knew who had stolen the child and how it had been done. But there was nothing he could say or do but stand there, ignored by all, all that is except Heidi, who suddenly and swiftly crossed the room to him and threw her arms around his neck and cried: 'Oh, Hiram, Hiram! Help me. Help me. Find him, as you helped us once before,' and then clung there shaking and wept all her heart out into his arms.

How, Because He had Looked upon the Beard, Hiram Holliday was Blind

It had then been to him that Heidi had appealed for help in the time of her trouble. And Hiram Holliday had never in his life been quite so helpless. He was a stranger in a foreign country with an impossible language. When French or German was spoken Hiram knew enough from his schooling to make out the general sense of what was being said, but Czech was pure gibberish to him. And he was no detective. He was a man who had spent a third of his life on a newspaper copy-desk. And that which he needed to recover the child, knowledge and experience and power, he knew he lacked. A Virslany, steeped in the intrigue of Central Europe, might, or a Captain Ovenecka, politician and fearless professional soldier, but not a Holliday, and the thought drove him close to desperation. He could not even, in honour, confide in Reck, who might have helped or advised him, because the Captain had bound all of those present to strict secrecy. If the news were published the boy might be destroyed. His only source of information was Heidi, and it was last of all to Heidi that he could go with his suspicions – suspicions that amounted practically to knowledge. For there was no doubt in Hiram's mind but that Count d'Aquila and Madame Strakova had abducted the child. Somewhere into the picture fitted the Man with the False Beard, exactly how Hiram had not yet been able to determine. But the Count was Heidi's fiancé, and a well-known diplomat, and Madame Strakova her best friend, and a power in the Czech Government. HE COULD NOT TOUCH THEM.

Irrespective of Hiram's instinctive dislike of the small, sleek man with the too small white teeth and sneering face, and the large, painted woman with the protruding eyes, the pieces fitted, and he saw so clearly in his mind how it had been done. Madame Strakova and d'Aquila had left the party together shortly after half-past ten when the nurse would have been in her deepest sleep. D'Aquila had returned for Lola's case and had gone out through the dining-room door into the corridor. He then had walked down to the nursery, entered and taken the sleeping child without waking Johanna. Hiram remembered his cat-like tread.

And he ran absolutely no risk. If the child awoke, he would be in the arms of the fiancée of his aunt, someone he knew and probably liked. And if the nurse awoke, again, it was Heidi's fiancée who had come, perhaps to take the child into the *salon*. But neither had happened. He had simply let himself out of the service door and walked down the service steps where he had rejoined Lola and possibly the Man with the False Beard. The latter might have taken the child. Hiram had not seen him since. And the later actions of d'Aquila and Madame Strakova had not been satisfactory. Hiram had found them out from Heidi. Neither had been reached by telephone until after three o'clock in the morning. Lola's story was that upon returning home she had taken a sleeping drug and it was not until three that she had been roused by the ringing of the bell. The Count, after he had taken Lola home, had gone to the

Italian Legation, let himself in with his night key, and had worked over some papers until a late hour.

Hiram was helpless to attack either of their stories, or them. It was the Man with the False Beard, he told himself, who was the key. Who was he? Hiram racked his brains. Had he been among the guests at the apartment? Would he have recognized him without the beard and moustache? But there had been close to fifty people there, constantly moving about. He might have walked calmly beneath Hiram's nose. He seemed to recall vaguely that there had been a man among the guests with deep sunken eyes. He knew that if he went to Virslany or Ovenecka with his story they would laugh at him. D'Aquila and Madame Strakova were above suspicion. He would be set down as a meddling busybody and a fool. No place, no place, no place for him. The cry rang through his head. Five days had passed since the kidnapping. He saw himself in his mirror. Hiram Holliday, the great adventurer. He did not look capable of finding a lost dog, he told himself, with his round, plain face, steel-rimmed spectacles, and stoutish frame, he looked like what he was, a copy-reader for the *New York Sentinel* who ought to be sharpening pencils and preparing to mark up the copy of men who by their brains and ingenuity and strength and daring went out into the world and wrested its secrets.

His telephone rang, and when he answered it, it was Heidi. Her voice sounded terribly strained and frightened. She said: 'Oh, Hiram. Can you come to me? I must talk to you.'

Hiram said: 'Coming!' It was nine o'clock in the evening. In the cab on the way to Podebradova Street, Hiram noted that it had stopped raining, and that the sky over Prague was copper-coloured from the city lights, the same coppery colour that had been in the London sky the first night he had ever laid eyes on Heidi.

She was alone in her apartment, very small and white, and she had been crying.

'Hiram. . . . Oh, Hiram, my friend,' she cried, 'they have Peter. They have him. . . .'

Holliday felt his heart sink. He said: 'Heidi . . . how do you know . . . ? Have you heard anything?'

'A man came,' said Heidi, her tone dull and despairing. 'I know him. I know who he is. One of them here in Prague. He was very polite. He said very little. He only suggested that perhaps now was the time to begin to discuss the return of the Fürstenhof moneys, *Devisen*, as he called it, to Germany, where they belonged. . . .'

'Give it to them . . . for the child . . .'

Heidi shook her head sadly. 'It would be no use. I know them. They would not give him up. He is in the line to the Austrian throne. Oh, Hiram, cannot you get him back for me?'

'Have you told Captain Ovenecka?'

Heidi nodded. 'Yes. He swears that the boy could not have been taken over the border, that he will get him back. But in the meantime . . . if they should kill him. . . .'

Through Hiram's mind passed a picture of the stalwart, capable, splendid-looking Captain with the lean jaw and flashing eyes, and his own insignificant figure as he had caught it in his mirror, and suddenly he broke, and cried: 'Oh, Heidi, Heidi, he will. The Captain will find him. Heidi, I can do nothing. I am a fraud and a fake. I can't go on this way. You must see the truth. I'm just what I look like. Nothing! A fat fool. Don't you see? You cannot build on me. Honestly, Heidi, I would die for you, but that wouldn't get us Peter. I'll go back where I belong. I . . . I can't help you, Heidi. . . .'

She had sighed quietly, patted his cheek and said: 'No, no, my dear friend. You must not say that. There . . . there are forces of evil let loose upon this earth, somehow beyond the control of human beings – yet . . .'

But in the cab, returning to his hotel, Hiram had made up his mind. It was ten o'clock, and he stopped at the *portier's* desk and demanded a telegraph blank. On it he wrote:

'Beauheld, Sentipapers, New York – resign present job is copy-desk still open Holliday.' Finis to adventure!

Hiram was preparing to hand the cable to the *portier*, when he was aware that there was a man standing close beside him. Instinctively he looked up and saw that it was the Man with the False Beard. And without an instant's hesitation he reached around with his right arm, secured a firm grip with his fingers in the coarse, reddish hair, and yanked.

Later on he realized that a thousand thoughts had spun through his head between the sight of the man and his deed. There had been his memory of the despair on Heidi's face, his own helplessness, his deep-rooted conviction that this man held the key to the mystery, the notion that, unmasked, he *might* recognize him as one of the guests at the party, even the wild, desperate thought that the stripping of the absurd *crêpe* beard from his chin might at least start a chain of circumstances that would lead to the vanished child. Or perhaps mostly there had been in him the terrible aching necessity to DO something. . . .

That which then happened he never forgot as long as he lived. He had a momentary vision of the man's face lurching violently forward towards his own, his outraged, frightened eyes nearly popping from their deep-shadowed sockets. And Hiram was in the grip of such horror as he had never known before. For the big, bushy beard so loosely and wrongly applied and which should have come off and revealed the face beneath, had resisted the powerful pull of his fingers. 'Oh, my God!' rang through Hiram. 'It isn't false. *It's real!*'

The next moment he had received a buffet on the side of the ear delivered with the flat of the hand that spilled him to the floor on his back and sent a thousand bells to clanging in his head, and the man was standing over him blazing with wrath and indignation, releasing a torrent of Czech and waving his arms wildly.

Suddenly Hiram cried out, but not from pain. It was as though the blow had burst something, a thick, opaque, rubbery veil that had lain clamped over his mind, rent it through and let in a light so bright and terrifying that he hardly dared look at it. But look at it he must . . . alone . . . away from the noise and clamour of the now excited lobby. Oh, if this fool's gesture had involved him in something that would hold him back, keep him from pursuing that bright and dazzling light. But now he could think again. He raised himself, swaying to his knees and shouted to the *portier*: 'Drunk . . . 'm drunk. Terribl' sorry. Never had any of that dam Slivowitz liquor before. Tell him 'm drunk. 'Pologize. Make any restitution. Never happen me before. Humble 'pologies. Tell him for Gossakes . . .'

The *portier* seized the man by the arm and Hiram saw him lean his mouth close to his ear and speak to him. The man seemed to calm down a little, and still muttering and waving his arms, he went on through the lobby and disappeared in the rear.

'Mm drunk, porter,' Hiram said, rising to his feet, or pulled there, rather, by the tremendous power of what had suddenly been born within him. 'Mus' excuse me. Not used to that stuff. Who . . . who is he, porter? Mus' send him a li'l present.'

Amusement was fighting with indignation on the *portier's* face. He said: 'That was Dr Otto Chirpaty. He is a dentist, a very respected one. He has an office here in the rear of the hotel. Do you not think you had better go to your room, sir?'

'Yes . . . yes . . . go my room . . . sleep dam' stuff off. For Gossakes, porter, one thing more. Is the Doctor a little deaf?'

'Yes, yes . . .' said the *portier*, anxious to be rid of him. 'He is hard of hearing.'

The light waxed and grew until Hiram did not think he could stand it any more. He suffered himself to be led by the arm by a bell-boy, and not until he was safely in his room with the door closed did he realize that in one hand he held the unsent telegram to his managing editor, and in his other some strands of coarse, reddish hair.

Then he ranged his room like a man gone mad, now at his desk scribbling on a pad, now pacing around and around, tugging at his hair as hard as he had pulled at the red-brown beard, and crying out:

'Fool! Fool! Romantic, forsaken fool! Idiot! The beard! The beard IS the key! You thought all the time that it was false, *but it was real*. Appearances ... appearances, you deluded, romantic fool! You've been thinking in terms of the beard. You looked for Heidi barred in some old dungeon and found her safe in a modern apartment house. Because a man's beard was a different colour from his hair you concluded it was false because your head is full of damned romantic nonsense. False ... true.... True ... false.... Oh, God, help me to think clearly now. I must ... I must ... I can feel it. It's there ... the truth, if I will only see it. Steady, Holliday, steady. You must be steady now or it may be too late. Now again. If that which is false is true, then that which appears true may be false....'

He dashed back to the desk where he had written a number of names on a sheet of paper: 'Madame Lola Strakova.... Count Mario d'Aquila ...' He began to shout again....

'Great God, Holliday.... Because the Count looks like a dancing-partner and has slicked hair and white teeth and a little moustache, and the woman black hair and a painted face and popping eyes, and both look like movie villains, you've *made* them villains. Now .. now ... apply the test of the beard to them. The beard looked false and was true. They looked evil, therefore we will set them down as good. What have we? Wait ... wait ... start from the beginning.... The Man with the False Beard has a real beard and is an innocent and respected dentist who is a little deaf – remember the incident of the porter who leaned close to talk to him the first time you saw him. What was he doing at Podebradova 35? He was answering a night call from a sufferer from which you also saw him returning. He encountered Madame Strakova bound for the party and inquired a direction from her, and because he was deaf their heads were together. And because she looked like a casting director's idea of a villainness.... You fool, you fool.... And you've been working on a picture-paper for fourteen years and seen photographs of hundreds of murderers and murderesses who looked like kindly, innocent people, and celebrity after celebrity who might, if dressed badly, be taken for a thug. Wait . . . wait now. False is real. Finish it, Holliday, finish it. The Count and Madame Strakova are decent, innocent people. And they were TELLING THE TRUTH! She was ill. And because she was Heidi's best friend, and the Count was her fiancé, he WOULD insist upon seeing her home. She *did* take a drug. He *did* work at the Embassy. They had nothing to do with the stealing of the child. *Nothing!* Then who . . . WHO?'

He began to pace the room again, hitting his forehead with the heel of his palm. . . . 'Who? Think, Holliday, think. . . . If evil can be good, good can be evil. Why not? Why not? But does it fit? The Count who looked evil is good. Then. . . . Ah! The Captain! The Captain! The handsome, heroic Captain! And. . . . Oh, God, wait! That jolly Virslany! The child was taken by someone who was familiar to it and to Heidi, and who could move like a cat! Virslany! Virslany! That dance burlesque you saw him do. For all his weight, he was as light on his feet as a girl. Fat men usually are. But were they both ever out of the room together . . . ? But they wouldn't have to be. Or would they? There were times when I saw only one or the other. Or I *thought* I always saw one. . . .'

He suddenly in his room paced off the distance he remembered the hall had been, and then suddenly yelled: 'Of course! Of course! Fifteen seconds would suffice if they time it. *Fifteen seconds.* Virslany, of course. Can move as quietly as a puma. He leaves the room and goes down the corridor. The Captain begins to count. Virslany removes the child. If Peter awakes he is in the arms of his Uncle Anton who gave him his white teddy bear. Nor would the nurse be alarmed if she were aroused and saw him with the child. Well then. A step to the service door. At the count of fifteen, the Captain has gone there and is waiting, *outside*. Virslany hands the child over and in a few seconds is back in the drawing-room. It fits! . . . It fits! . . .

'But then what? Where to? How? The Captain was never gone long enough. Never! The chauffeurs out front saw no one – nothing. . . . And yet he got the child away. The link. . . . The link is missing. . . . I have it, but I haven't it. I'll go mad. . . .'

His wanderings brought him back to his papers where above the names he had printed in large letters: 'FALSE IS TRUE – TRUE IS FALSE – EVIL IS GOOD – GOOD IS EVIL. . . .'

'Apply the beard, Hiram . . . that damnable, outrageous beard that nearly landed you in a Czech jail . . . the . . .'

And then the truth burst upon him, came, as it were, in a sudden picture that formed itself in his mind, a vision of enchanting sweetness and loveliness, and he was out of his room hatless, coatless, and running down the stairs as though possessed, and out through the lobby. He heard someone cry: '*Verdammter besoffener Amerikaner,*' and then he was out the door and into a cab. Of the ride to the Podebradova he remembered nothing except that he continued to urge the driver to greater speed. And then he was pounding on Heidi's door out of breath, wild-eyed, dishevelled, and when it opened, he found himself in the room with Heidi and the dapper, pale little Count d'Aquila. The two stared at him.

'Heidi! D'Aquila!' Hiram cried, 'I know. . . . I know. . . .'
They ran to him. 'Hiram. . . . Oh, tell me! What? What?'

'Where the boy is! Or where he *was*! If it isn't too late. Where they took him. . . .' Behind the steel spectacles, his eyes were wild and his knees were shaking.

It was the little Count d'Aquila who went to him and placed hard and friendly hands on his shoulders. 'My friend,' he said, 'is this true? . . . Heidi has told me what you did for her in London. I am here to help you. . . . Be steady. . . .'

Hiram recovered under the soothing grip. 'Yes . . . yes. . . . But come at once, for God's sake, at once. It mustn't be too late. Both of you come. . . .'

They were out of the door after him, bewildered, but infected by his rush. He ran down the outer hall and up the service staircase, three at a time to the door of the apartment of Madame von Ovenecka. The other two arrived there panting.

'Knock!' whispered Hiram to Heidi.

'Are you sure? You are mad. You are out of your mind, my friend,' said Count Mario d'Aquila.

'No ... no, no,' said Hiram. 'I cannot be. I was mad, out of my head before, but I see clearly now. He must be. ... He must be.'

Heidi knocked.

'*Wer ist da?*'

'Answer, Heidi,' said Hiram.

'*Die Heidi, die Heidi, die Heidi ist da,*' sang Heidi, as she had done on that other night.

'*Bedaure, Madame darf nicht gestört werden.*'

'She says Madame Ovenecka cannot be disturbed,' translated Heidi.

Hiram made a curt motion towards the door with his head, and said sharply: 'We go through,' and it was the little Count who hit it first. For all of his slight size he must have been as hard as iron, for the door trembled under his charge, and the shock of Hiram's following impact completed the job and they burst through.

The tall, dour companion and Madame von Ovenecka were both standing at the fire-place, their faces black with anger. Hiram did not even stop to look at them. 'Come on,' he shouted, and ran through to the series of bedrooms down the corridor. In the second they found the boy Peter on the bed, obviously in a drugged sleep, thin, pale, but otherwise unharmed. ...

It was Hiram who picked him up in his arms, and said: 'O.K., skipper. And I guess that's that.'

But when they returned to the drawing-room, Hiram still carrying the unconscious child, they found that the broken-in doorway had filled up. It was blocked with the enormous, overwhelming girth of Dr Anton Virslany, who stood there puffing and wheezing and grunting, his little eyes gleaming merrily, and inside the room stood the magnificent figure of

Captain Petrus Ovenecka, and in his hand there was a small, graceful gun.

'So,' said the Captain. 'This is indeed most unfortunate. But first perhaps I suggest that you give me the child.'

Heidi's cry in German rang out to wake the dead. Once, twice, three times: 'Help! Help! Police!'

Without the slightest compunction or change in the bland and almost noble expression of his handsome face, the Captain turned slightly and shot at her – and missed. And then the slim and dapper little Count was at his throat like a raging animal.

Hiram was burdened with the boy, and hesitated. He had an impression of the little man with the trick moustache and the slicked back hair fighting like one possessed, and apparently gaining, and the angular companion picking up a heavy vase from the mantel, when Heidi hurled herself upon her, a small, desperate ball of fury, and they went to the floor together.

The odds were even now, except for old Madame Ovenecka, who could be discounted. Hiram swung around, set the child down on a couch and started for Dr Virslany. Here was battle at last. But the tremendous Nazi agent in the doorway never moved. He stood, huge, obese and motionless, still wheezing and puffing, the merry look in his eyes, his flabby chins climbing out of his collar. He did not stir or raise a finger. Hiram heard the Captain's gun explode twice more at intervals. And then he was conscious of a swift, hard rustling behind him. There was no time to turn his head more than to catch out of the corner of his eye, an impression rather than an actual sight of the sweet and benign old lady standing over him with her arm raised. He did try to duck as the lavender silk of her arm flashed towards him, but it was too late. Something seemed to tear loose the lining of his skull, after which there came nothing but a great and enfolding darkness.

He awoke to noise and confusion, and the presence of many people, and too, the sound of weeping. He was on a couch with a stranger bending over him, apparently a doctor. With his head splitting, and the room still rocking, he struggled to a sitting position. The place was full of people, police, men in plain clothes and some soldiers. Two of them held the raging figure of the angular companion-nurse between them. A form was stretched out upon the floor, half-covered. It was the handsome and heroic-looking Captain Ovenecka. He was dead. Close by, propped up in a chair with Heidi kneeling beside him, sat the Count Mario d'Aquila, deathly pale. The left side of his coat and clothes had been cut away, and arm and shoulders were wrapped in fresh bandages that showed a faint seepage of blood from his wound. The weeping was coming from Heidi. As Hiram sat up, she heard him and turned her head. She arose and came over to his side and took his head in her arms, and held him there, and he felt her tears dripping on to his cheeks. An agonizing fear took hold of Hiram. . . .

'Heidi . . . Heidi . . .' he said. 'Where . . . where is Peter ?'

Because of the way he had said it, she hardly dared tell him. She said first: '*Danke dem lieben Gott* you are alive, Hiram. You and Mario. Peter . . . Peter is gone. The police came too late. The woman was choking me. When . . . when the police came, Virslany was gone and Peter, too.'

Hiram sickened so that he thought he would lose his senses again, because now he knew another truth. But he managed to ask: 'And Madame von Ovenecka . . . Where . . . where is she . . . ?'

'She was gone, too. . . . Both were gone with Peter. But Hiram. . . . It did not seem to be. . . . It was not Madame von Ovenecka. . . . It was a much younger woman who was like her, but . . .'

A terrible cry of agony and remorse burst from Hiram, and he shook himself loose from Heidi, and again struck his now aching skull with the heel of his hand as though by increasing the pain he could make restitution. 'Oh, dear God! Yes, yes! I knew. . . . I knew, and again I didn't think far enough. It's my curse. I'm cursed with it. And the child is gone, and a fine, brave man nearly lost his life. False was true, and true was false. I merely assigned to Madame von Ovenecka an evil role.

That was right. But it wasn't enough. And it was all there for me to see. There never was an *old* Madame Ovenecka. The crayon with which she was drawing when we came in upon her that night of your party before the usual time when you were expected, it was an actor's lining pencil. You will find it with the rest of her make-up. Great God, she said it herself. "The arts by which an old woman makes herself look younger have nothing to do with the devil...." No, but she and her supposed son WERE devils. The same arts will make a *young woman look old!* And she hid her hands from me, because young hands are hard to disguise. It was all there to see if I had not been blinded by my own vanity. Heidi ... Heidi.... I cannot look at you, or at d'Aquila.... I wish to God that she had killed me....'

Heidi held his head until the sobs that gripped and tore him had abated, and somehow Mario managed to leave his chair and come to his side and place an arm around his shoulder.

And when the strange, stoutish man, with the plain, round, bespectacled face now pain-racked, blood-flecked, dishevelled, and looking older and sterner, finally raised his head, there were the two, one on either side, and on their faces were love and sympathy and understanding. Hiram managed to speak then, softly at first, almost as though he were talking to himself. He said:

'I will get him back. I WILL get him back. I will get Peter back for you, Heidi, somehow, some time. I promise you, and I promise you, too, Mario. I promise you both that I will bring him back. I can. I will. I WILL do it. You must both trust me and be patient, but I will do it. When you know what a fool I have been, you will see that I must bring him back, and you will believe me.'

The amazingly strong fingers of the little man with the small, white teeth and shining, slicked back hair and absurd little moustache, took his hand in the grip of comradeship of men who are not afraid to adventure, and held it, and for the second time in his life Hiram Holliday felt upon his cheek the gentle kiss of Her Highness the Princess Adelheit von Fürstenhof of Styria, von und zu Schoenau und Blankenburg Hohenlohe Altmark. And to him there returned for the first time since he had come to Prague, a small measure of peace.

DEATH NOTICE IN BERLIN

How Hiram Holliday Was, but Was Not in Berlin

LATE in November the city of Berlin, capital of the expanding German Reich, harboured a mystery, still unsolved, and the Gestapo, as the *Geheime Staats Polizei* is known, is not fond of mysteries that occur under its nose, especially when one involves the death of so exalted and prominent a personage as Dr Heinrich Grunze, the little hunchback who was *Minister für Auslandspropaganda*, or Minister of foreign propaganda and the Number 4 Nazi, though some claimed he stood even closer to the top than that.

The mystery then involved the passing of Dr Grunze – it was officially announced that he had died in bed at home of heart failure, but this was not true – the disappearance of one of the most famous beauties in Berlin, and the execution in the courtyard of the grim and famous old Moabit prison of one Hermann Weide, a traitor and Communist, for *Landesverat*, which is the equivalent of high treason. Dr Grunze remained dead, and the beauty continued to be missing, but Communist Weide, although his bandaged head rolled on to the cobbled ground at the flash of the axe in the hands of the white-gloved, top-hatted executioner and thereafter, by special order, was immediately cremated, apparently never existed, even though he was officially listed as dead in the German archives.

It was many months before those working on the case began to have even an inkling of what might have been the truth, and by that time those who could have shed the final light on the affair were either dead or safely out of the country.

It was the morning of November 21, a Monday, in Berlin, that the famous People's Court was in session in the grim grey building that housed it. The three elderly judges sat at a table at the far end of the large, bare, whitewashed room with barred windows. At another table covered with brief-cases and papers were the prosecutors. At a smaller table, alone, was the advocate assigned by the court to defend the prisoner, who sat on a bare bench to one side, manacled, and between two black uniformed, black-steel-helmeted S.S. men. Near the door, and ranged at intervals around the wall were more S.S. men, armed with rifles. The prisoner himself was unrecognizable, because his head was wrapped in bandages that left free only his eyes, but a pair of steel-rimmed spectacles were on the place where his nose would have been, the two shafts worked into the crisscross of the bandaging so as to hold them in place. He sat erect and silent between his two guards.

The case was a cut-and-dried one. The prisoner was a Hermann Weide, age forty, a German citizen who had been brought up in the United States. He was a member of the Communist Party, and had come to Germany to take part in the subversive underground propaganda against the Third Reich and its leaders. He had been apprehended in his room in the Adlon Hotel. Incriminating documents were found among his effects, including plans for setting up an illicit broadcasting station to send out treasonable material to the German people.

The trial was conducted with the utmost simplicity and in German, which the prisoner apparently did not understand. After the reading of the indictment, the evidence, a mass of documents and the passport of Hermann Weide were placed before the judges, who studied them, frowning.

Finally the first judge looked up and inquired: 'Has the prisoner been identified?'

The chief prosecutor, a large man with grizzled, brush-like hair, arose and adjusted a pince-nez, and read from a paper.

'He was identified, Your Worship, at the time of arrest, by Frau Johanna Reuche of No. 3 Alt Graben Strasse. She is his aunt and remembered him from several previous visits he made to the Reich. She is an innocent woman and knew nothing of his activities. She can be produced immediately if Your Worship wishes it.'

'Not necessary.'

An S.S. man gave testimony as to how Weide had been taken when he returned late one night to his quarters in the Adlon. He had fought desperately, and in the capture had been so injured that the bandaging was necessary. The three judges conferred, whispering, and examined the documents again. The first judge then said: 'What is the defence of the prisoner?'

Although the prisoner did not understand the language the import of the nod of the judge's head in his direction was plain. He half arose, struggling to speak through the bandages, when he was pulled back to the bench by the two S.S. men, one of whom said: '*Schweige!* It is not permitted to talk. Your advocate will speak for you.'

The prisoner's lawyer arose. He was a small, nervous man with his coat buttoned too tightly. 'With the permission of Your Worships,' he began. 'It is the contention of the prisoner that he is the victim of a plot. He maintains that he is not Hermann Weide but that his name is Hiram Holliday, that he is an American citizen and a newspaper correspondent with connexions in New York, and respectfully begs that the American Embassy be advised of his predicament.'

The judge looked in the direction of the prosecutor and said: 'Who is this American that the prisoner claims to be?'

The prosecutor arose again. 'He is an American newspaper correspondent, Your Worship, a harmless one. May I read from my record. A Mr Hiram Holliday arrived in Berlin from Prague on Tuesday, November 8, and registered at the Hotel Adlon. He engaged in no subversive activites as far as could be determined, but spent most of his time sightseeing. On November 15, the day before the arrest of the prisoner Weide, he ordered an air ticket to Paris. I have here a statement from the *portier* of the Hotel Adlon. He left by cab at eight-thirty in the morning. The previous day he had notified the American Embassy by telephone of his intention of leaving for Paris. He took the nine-thirty plane for Paris. I have here the records of the Lufthansa agents at the Tempelhofer Flughaben. He occupied seat Number Five. His passport and *Devisen Schein* were examined and stamped at Cologne at eleven o'clock. I have here the records of the Grenze and Devisen Polizei at Cologne for that day, and also the cancelled *Devisen Schein* (money declaration) given up by Holliday there. And finally, he left at the Adlon, as his forwarding address, the Hotel St Régis in Paris. If Your Worship desires, we can attempt to contact him there through one of our agents for purposes of verifi . . .'

The judge interrupted curtly and sternly: 'Not necessary. The evidence is clear and sufficient.'

There was very little more. The three judges conferred a short while longer. The first judge then said: 'Hermann Weide! You have been adjudged guilty of high treason against the Third Reich and are hereby sentenced to be executed the morning of Wednesday, November 23. The next case, please.'

The prisoner was on his feet and a protest half-uttered when one of the S.S. men guarding him slugged him on the shoulder with his pistol butt and knocked him back to the bench again. Others from the side of the room leaped forward and helped secure him. Stumbling, Hermann Weide, under sentence for high treason, was hustled from the room and back to his steel and stone cell in Moabit prison.

Except that the man hidden by the close bandages was not Hermann Weide. His name was Hiram Holliday, correspondent for the *New York Sentinel*. And he was being led away to certain death.

How Hiram Holliday Saw a Pogrom in Berlin
and Met a Woman with Red Hair

It was in the early afternoon of November 9 that the telephone rang in Room 32 in the Hotel Adlon, Unter den Linden, Berlin, and Hiram Holliday went to pick up the receiver. He had arrived there the day before from Prague in obedience to instructions from a cable from Beauheld, Managing Editor of the *New York Sentinel*, which read: 'Vom Rath Garmen Embassy Secretary shot in Paris by Jew if dies suspect trouble in Berlin suggest go there immediately cover if can enter without trouble.'

Holliday had flown to Berlin at once. His passport was checked in at Dresden with no trouble whatsoever, because it bore the visa granted by the German Consul in New York collected, among others, when Hiram had prepared to go on the first European vacation. If the authorities in Germany were advised of his curious activities in Europe since his arrival no news of it had apparently reached the Grenz-Polizei in Dresden. They had smilingly wished him a pleasant stay in Germany, and two hours later he was registered at the Hotel Adlon.

The voice out of the receiver said: *'Herr Holliday? Einen Moment, bitte.* Herr Biederman wishes to speak with you.'

Hiram's lip curled a little as he waited for Biederman, the Berlin correspondent of the *Sentinel*, to come on. He had not much respect for him. For years, at the copy-desk of the *Sentinel*, he had been reading and headlining the dry, newsless, Government-biased despatches of the man, and his meeting with the wizened, self-important old fellow the day before had not improved his opinion.

'Hello – Holliday? Biederman speaking. I thought you might want to know. Von Rath is dead. May be some trouble. I'd stay off the streets tonight if I were you.'

Out of natural politeness Hiram tried hard to keep the contempt out of his voice. But he said: 'What the hell for? If anything happens, I'm supposed to be there to take a look at it.'

Biederman made little impatient, testy noises at the other end of the phone. '. . . It won't do you any good, and you're safer in your room. You can't send the story out of the country, anyway. If anything happens, you can get a statement from the Foreign Office afterwards. You can do as you like, of course. I'm just telling you for your own good. Beauheld knows very well that if anything of importance takes place he can count upon me to cover it for him.'

'O.K., O.K.' said Hiram. 'Much obliged. . . .' He wanted to be rid of the whining voice at the other end.

'Oh yes, and Holliday – you remember our little talk about Dr Grunze, the Foreign Propaganda Minister. Hm . . . ah. . . . You weren't serious about trying to interview him, were you?'

'Of course I was,' said Hiram sharply.

'Well . . . ah . . . you must forget about it, old man. No one has done it yet, and if I haven't succeeded no one can. You'll just get yourself into trouble. Beauheld is always sending rash young men through here with crazy orders and then I have to get them out of trouble. We'll be lunching at Baarz tomorrow. Come over and join us if you can.'

Hiram hung up the receiver, and made a face. Anything he hoped to accomplish in Berlin he knew he would have to do alone. And there was the matter of the pledge he had given the Princess Heidi. He had been glad when he was ordered to Berlin. Somewhere, somehow, in the Nazi stronghold he hoped to come upon a clue to the whereabouts of the kidnapped boy. He realized now that he must not even mention the affair to the Berlin correspondent.

He put Biederman out of his mind and went down to the famous Rococo Adlon Bar and had himself a Scotch and soda for which he paid an outrageous price. The bar, with its friezes and bas-relief panels and nymphs and fauns frescoes, was deserted, as was the little lounge that opened off it to the left. The bar-tender studied the big, stoutish man with the bland face behind steel-rimmed spectacles, and the nondescript tousled hair, and decided that there was no mischief in him. It is surprising the confidences a bar-tender will sometimes receive, and he made regular reports to certain officials in the Wilhelmstrasse. Hiram knew that he was being weighed, and it amused him, and when the bar-tender said: 'You like Berlin, yes?' he put on the breezy air he had learned from travelling Americans and replied:

'Oh yeah, sure. Great town. Clean. That's what I like about it. Say, how do you fellas tell a store that's run by a Jew from any other store?'

The bar-tender was caught off guard. Before he knew that he had said it he replied: 'The name of the owner must be on the outside on the window in big white letters.' All the help in the hotel were under strict orders not to discuss the Jewish question with foreigners, not to admit even that it existed.

'Well, well, well,' said Hiram fatuously, 'isn't that interesting. I declare.' He paid for his drink and departed, leaving the bar-tender lulled. He went out to the gold-braided doorman and said to him still in the American style: 'Get me a cab, and tell the feller to drive me around the town a little and show me the sights. . . .' He was beginning to feel the contempt that all Americans in Berlin do eventually for the clumsy, heavy-handed Nazi police spy system, but he felt that the role of fatuous American tourist suited him, and that it might come in handy.

The chauffeur dutifully drove him around Berlin and showed him the palaces of the former Kaisers, the Friedrichstrasse, the Charlottenburger Chaussee, the famous Siegesallee and the Tiergarten, the Kurfürstendamm, the night-life and shopping centre, and when he had concluded the principal points of interest, Hiram kept him at it with: 'Just drive around through the streets for a while. Boy, I sure get a kick seein' how clean everything is.' By the time he had the driver deposit him at Horchers in the Lutherstrasse, where he proposed to dine, Hiram Holliday had a good knowledge of the layout of the immediate city, the location of the principal synagogues as well as a mental map of the distribution and situation of most of the important Jewish-owned stores in Berlin. For he had a hunch that if there was any trouble to come as the result of the death of Vom Rath in Paris it would be centred at those points.

At Horchers he dined on the curious coppery-flavoured Dutch oysters, and saddle of deer with cream sauce. The decor of the place reminded him of '21,' in New York, and he listened to the guttural babel of German spoken all about him, with occasional snatches of French. There were, he noted, some stunning women dining there, large, clear-skinned, tawny-haired, animal-like creatures, and he suddenly felt excited and stimulated, more so than he ever had in Paris. In Paris the women had been light and airy and unconcerned about the business of being women. Or rather, he felt they concerned themselves so much with it that the results were wholly natural and undisturbing. In Berlin he already felt the powerful under-current of smouldering, suppressed passion, the despairing, heavy-scented passion of a people who had been commanded to love for the sole sake of procreating, and who yearned re-belliously, and torturedly, so that one could almost smell it through the pores of their skin, to love for the sake of loving. Somehow, he felt that there was more attraction in one of these great, clean, chatteled bodies doomed to breed for the State than in all the painted, febrile women of Paris at liberty to love as they choose.

After he had eaten, Hiram walked over to the Kurfürsten Damm and mingled with the crowds that paraded the pave-ments of that broad street, passing the shops and cafés and beer restaurants, and felt again that curious excitement that had gripped him while dining, and he noted too that he had a nervous constriction at the throat. The feeling was yet new to him, but later he was to know it as a warning.

He stopped in front of a famous antique store, its windows full of lovely and graceful *objets d'art*, in porcelain, marble and bronze. There was a priceless head by Dürer, some little gems of Bokhara prayer rugs, a small, blue vase in whose slender form lay the limitless and ageless art of ancient China, and there was too a graceful, polished harpsichord at which Mozart had once sat. Hiram wished that he might go inside and lay his hands upon its smooth surface and feel what it had once felt of grace and light and inspired beauty. But the store was closed, and Holliday noted on the window in large white lettering the name of the proprietor: 'Herschel Jacobsen, Berlin, Paris, London, New York. . . .' Something made him shudder and he turned away and continued to walk. He was still walking the confines of his mental map at three o'clock in the morning when the streets of the grey city were all but deserted except for an occasional cruising green, high-bodied taxi with the checkerband design.

He walked briskly and tirelessly, his coat collar turned up against the November damp, his hands stuffed into his pockets. Once he stopped at one of the big *Litfass-Säulen*, a sort of a cylindrical public advertising board that stood on certain street corners with announcements of theatres, or music, or Government decrees. He studied a large, blood-red poster affixed to it, and the black lettering thereon. He had heard about them, but this was the first time he had seen one. It was the famous, gruesome, death notice of those whose heads had rolled on to the stones of the old Moabit prison courtyard for treason. Even Hiram could translate the wording, or at least gather the import. It was to the effect that Johann Grosch and Herta Vieralt had been executed the morning before for *Landesverat* – betrayal of country.

Hiram shuddered and touched the poster with his fingertips as though the contact with the glossy surface could somehow bring him closer to the torment of the poor souls who had walked out into the grey morning to face the terrible apparition in the frock coat, the high silk hat, and white gloves with the shining axe. But it told him nothing.

He looked at his wrist-watch. It was four o'clock of the morning of Thursday, November 10. He heard the chimes of the clock in the Gedächtnis Kirche at the nearby Auguste Viktoria Platz strike the hour. At the fourth stroke a crashing explosion shook the pavement beneath his feet, followed by another and a third and fourth, mimicking almost in rhythm and spacing the strokes of the clock tower. Hiram Holliday knew where they came from. The Fasanenstrasse was only a half-block away and on it was a huge, ornate synagogue. He ran and turned the corner and saw four columns of smoke pouring up from the roof of the edifice, and two of them were already laced with shoots of bright orange flame. Simultaneously, Hiram heard for the first time the sound that was to ring through Berlin for the next twelve hours, the high-pitched crashing of shattering plate-glass to the accompaniment of the cry: *'Judah – Verrecke!'* 'Perish, Jewry.' ...

The sleeping streets awoke at once to the roaring of motor-cars and motor-cycles and fire apparatus. Crowds materialized out of the darkened houses. Hiram recognized the brown uniform of the famous storm-troopers, and the black and silver of the S.S. men, the Elite, or Black Guards. Police, with their small, coal-scuttle helmets, appeared magically. The crowds were silent except for a venomous rustling, the scrape-scrape-scrape of their feet, so that it seemed to Hiram as though some great, shadowy serpent was abroad and uncoiling through the streets. From distant quarters of the city came like kettle-drum beats, the 'Poom ... poom ... poom ...' of other explosions.

The curving dome of the synagogue began to throw orange flame in large boiling gouts. Someone had started a bonfire in the middle of the street and men, booted and leather-jacketed, kept running in and out of the great central door. They carried out with them books, and scrolls, and trappings, desks and benches, which they heaved into the blaze in the street. Fire-men, their brass helms gleaming in the double firelight, went into action with their hoses, but Hiram noted that the streams were not directed into the flames but on to the houses adjoining the burning church.

With a sudden pang, he bethought himself of the antique store in the Kurfürsten Damm, and threading his way through the growing mass of people he went back to it. He had to shoulder his way through another crowd to reach it, but here his harmless and nondescript appearance again stood him in stead, and they let him through. He reached the inside of the circle just as the first wooden club, in the hands of one of the dreaded Roll Kommandos, battered in a section of the huge plate-glass window.

There were seven in the Roll Kommando, or wrecking crew, and Hiram noted that they all wore the so-called *Räuberzivil* uniform, or 'bandit mufti,' consisting of short leather jackets without identification marks, worn over uniform trousers and boots. Hiram saw that two of them were young boys who wore knickers beneath their jackets.

The air shivered and danced to the ring of breaking glass and a deeper crash announced that the door had been smashed in, and then came the sharp clinking sound of porcelain and china and cut glass swept off shelves to shatter on the ground. A little man with grey hair ran out of the door from somewhere into the bare circle made by the police who kept the crowd back, and he held both hands to his head, and cried: *'Oh Gott, Oh Gott! Nein ... Nein!'*

One of the wreckers immediately struck him on top of the head with his wooden batten and he fell to his knees, moaning and weeping, a dark strain showing in his white hair. Two or three voices from the crowd shouted: *'Jude ... Jude.... Gib's den Juden. ...'* Two storm-troopers in brown uniforms yanked the man to his feet and held him while a third slugged him with his fists, so that his head bobbed from side to side.

In Hiram Holliday there was already a desperate sickening that had begun with the spiteful destruction of the beautiful things that lined the shop, and his stomach turned again as he watched the storm-trooper beating the helpless man, the more so because he was using his fists the way a woman does, and screaming hysterical imprecations in a cracked falsetto voice. It was so foul that he had to turn away to fight off the nausea, and when he shifted his glance it fell full upon the cruel, magnificent, fantastic breath-taking woman who had forced her low-slung, lavender-coloured nickelled sports car to the kerb and was standing up in the driver's seat, her hair flying in the wind that had come up.

Her background was the fire glare from the burning syna-gogue, but her hair was redder than any of the shoots and tongues of flame that boiled up out of the coal black and sulphur yellow smoke, and it poured and swirled and ascended from her head as though she, too, were on fire. The dead white, oval face beneath it, lit green and red by two staring emerald

117

eyes, and the crimson cut of her mouth made Hiram Holliday think of an Egyptian temple urn he had once seen, and her hair was the votive flame rising from the top.

She was large – Hiram judged her to be as tall as himself – and she was dressed in a glossy mink coat, and a white scarf was wound around and around her throat until it seemed to him that her appallingly beautiful head rested not upon her neck, but floated disembodied upon a white cloud. And when the wind that fluttered her hair turned back the edges of her coat, he saw that beneath it she wore nothing but a nightdress.

The uproar and the terrible night was catching up Hiram's soul, and bending and buffering it, and he saw the girl thus the first time to the evil music of destruction, the 'thop-thop-thop' of the blows of the storm-trooper, still striking the now unconscious man, the near to inhuman screams, the wild clanging of the fire bells, and the wrenching and cracking of splintering wood. He was conscious of two impulses, and they shook him so that he felt that he was near the end of his control. The one was to rush to her and bury his face in her breast, and the other was to get his fingers into the white fluff of silk beneath her chin and grope until they found the flesh, and then throttle her until those staring green lamps of eyes went out for ever.

It was Walpurgisnacht, and she the Red Witch upon the Brocken, and the Brocken was her cream and lavender car, a colour that deadened her face and brightened the pyrotechny of her hair. She stood on her car with both hands to her breast, a weird, wonderful, compelling figure of a woman, with her mouth half-parted, and a curl to her lower lip, and Hiram could not tell whether she gazed upon the maudlin, obscene sight being enacted before her with love, or with hate, but he knew that he, Hiram Holliday, was looking upon this woman that he had never seen before with such longing and hatred combined that they were well-nigh unbearable.

The air was full of the pungent, acid smell of smoke, but in Hiram's nostrils was nothing but the scent that his tortured imagination pictured as coming from her, the distant waft of the rising perfume of hell, smelled at the gates of heaven. The spell was partly broken, but only for a moment when she gave a little cry, but again, he could not tell whether it was of horror or of glee, and when he turned his head back to the scene of riot and ruination, he saw that three of the wreckers had dragged the lovely maple harpsichord out of the window on to the street. A man yelled: '*Ha, Junger Volksgenosse, spiel uns etwas auf dem Judeninstrument. . . .*' One of the young wreckers in knickers and leather jacket, bare-headed, adolescent fuzz on his broad, flat mouth, pulled up a spindly French chair and sat down at the instrument, and began to pound out a military march and the poor, pathetic, tinny, tinkling sound that it gave forth suddenly brought half-blinding tears to Hiram's eyes. . . . It cried to him with its whispering, ancient, cultured voice that rang down the corridors of the decades from civilization to savagery: 'Mozart . . . Mozart. . . . Help me. . . .' The crowd took up the tune and began to chant it, and stamp their feet, and the other wreckers came and beat the time upon the polished case with their hardwood billets, and each beat gouged and scarred the surface. Hiram stole a look at the tall girl in the car, and with horror saw that ever so faintly, her head was moving, hardly perceptibly, to the rhythm of the beat.

And then the thread that held Hiram Holliday in check was snapped. The last wrecker came out of the shattered shop. He was a tall, powerfully built man dressed in a raincoat, and his trousers were stuffed into huge, military boots. He timed himself with his running jump so that his leap into the air coincided with the fall of the boy's hand playing the finishing bar of the tune, and with the chord his boots went through the top of the harpsichord, with a wrenching, tinny, tearing sound through the slender wires of the harp; the delicately carved legs splayed outwards and gave way, man and instrument crashed to the ground, and a roar of laughter went up from the uniformed men watching, though now the crowd was quite silent. The head of the girl was thrown back and her face was turned towards the orange-coloured sky, and Hiram thought that it was in silent laughter. He could stand no more. He must kill her, but kill her he could not. Yet act he must, or not care to live to see himself mirrored, ever again.

The storm-trooper who had been beating the proprietor of the store had relinquished him, and was standing looking down at the mess of man and wreckage tangled on the pavement, and laughing in a silly high-pitched shriek. Hiram Holliday walked over to him, and because he was on the other side of the circle, he had to go some fifteen steps, and everybody saw him and watched him, and he knew the girl in the car was watching him, too, and when he reached the shrieking trooper, he pulled back his right hand, and hit him on the point of chin with every ounce of drive, of protest, of disgust and sorrow and outrage that was in his being. The blow went 'Smack!' and cut off the top of a shriek of laughter as though the man had been garrotted. He fell backwards on to the pavement, his arms and legs spread-eagled, and lay still.

Hiram saw the three storm-troopers making for him, their faces, eyes and mouths distended, black uniformed guards converging from another direction, and went to the ground rolling, and kicking out at legs and ankles as the first wave broke over him. He struck out and fought, seeking to trip and break up the white-hot, angry men, and bring them to earth. He felt blows and kicks, his hand was trampled on. There was a roaring in his ears and his chest was burning from his exertions.

He was saved for a moment by the numbers of men trying to get at him to tear him apart, their blind savagery and the confusion helping him. He had hoped to be able to get his hands on some kind of a weapon, but found nothing, and rolled out from under a tangle of shouting, flailing men, struggling to his feet looking for an avenue of escape. But he was spotted immediately, and there were angry cries and a sullen roar from the gathering crowd. Something struck him on the head and dizzied him so that he could no longer think clearly, but he knew that in the next few moments he would most surely be beaten to death. And then there was a new noise in his ears, a roaring larger and louder than that of the inflamed crowd, the grinding and exploding of a tremendously powerful motor, as like an antediluvian monster emerging out of an ancestral dream; its siren horn screaming, he saw the nickelled snout and fiercely glaring eyes of the headlamps of the lavender roadster boring through the crowd, cutting a lane by knocking bodies right and left. At the wheel, and leaning out of the side was the girl of the white face and the burning hair, and she was crying in the voice of a Brunhilde: '*Achtung.... Achtung.... Platz machen.... Achtung!*' She rammed a black uniformed guardsman in the stomach with a mudguard, and crushed the foot of a Brownshirt who tried to stop her. The blazing eyes were coming nearer and nearer to Hiram as she battered her way through the screaming mob.... She was coming to kill him, to run him down.... Hiram stood there swaying, hypnotized by the blinding rays of the headlights, and waited for the juggernaut to smash him down and trample him dead, but the lights as they pounced upon him swerved suddenly aside, and he felt a strong hand at his coat collar, jerking him toward the car. His foot found the running-board, his good hand groped for the side. He heard her yell: '*Juche!*' a strange, sobbing, eerie cry, and then: '*Festhalten!* | Hold on tight, you stupid, glorious fool!' and then with a great, leaping surge, every cylinder racketing like artillery salvos, the big car crashed away, turned, spun sharply, skidding – he would have fallen off, but a firm, strong arm went around his waist and held him jammed to the side – and was zooming down the street, picking up speed, whipped a corner in a hair-pin turn, another and another, and then shot away down a long, broad, tree-lined avenue. Hiram spat out a mouthful of blood. The cold wind was clearing his head. The girl shouted to him: 'Can you climb in now?'

Hiram wasn't sure, but he said: 'I ... I think so.... I'll try....'

Then he felt himself picked up bodily by her right arm and thrown across in back of her. He helped by crawling, and tumbled finally into the empty seat beside her, where for the moment his senses left him, and he went out into the peace of blackness. The last thing he remembered was the touch of her fur against his face as he slumped over against her shoulder.

He came to after a little, his head throbbing and singing from the crack he had received. They were just driving out of a park and on to an avenue that seemed to border it which he suspected was the Tiergarten Strasse. The girl turned the car in before a huge iron gate which rolled open silently and automatically before she had brought the car to a halt and which closed behind them in the same manner after she had driven through. She drove on beneath the portico of a large, grey stone mansion, paused before garage doors which likewise opened for her. A uniformed chauffeur was waiting as well as a butler in livery. She spoke to them sharply in German, and they leaped to the door of the car and helped Hiram out.

'Franz – bring warm water in a basin and some cotton and antiseptic. The Herr has been injured.'

The butler bowed and said: '*Jawohl. Sofort, Frau Gräfin*,' and turned to go, but she spoke again. 'Both of you pay attention. If there are any inquiries, I have not been out of the house tonight, nor has the car. If the inquirers should be persistent, refer them to Dr Grunze.'

'*Zu Befehl, Frau Gräfin!*'

Two things Hiram had understood – that the strong tall girl who had saved him was a *Gräfin*, roughly, the equivalent of a duchess, and that he had heard mentioned the name of Dr Grunze, the mysterious little hunchback who was the Minister of foreign propaganda, a man very few people had ever seen, and whom no one knew. He felt better now, and suspected that he was not as badly hurt as he had thought. The chauffeur was supporting him, but he signalled that he wanted to try it alone, and managed very well. His right hand was cut, he had been trampled and beaten, but his hat had saved him from a scalp wound.

A long passage-way led under the house from the garage. It ended in a little private elevator. The *Gräfin* entered first and when Hiram followed under his own steam, she signalled for the chauffeur to leave them. She pushed a button and the lift took them to the second floor, and let them out into a *salon* of such sumptuous magnificence and taste as Hiram Holliday had never seen before. It was old-fashioned, and yet instinctively he knew that every piece in it was sound, every beautifully illuminated painting and statue a work of art. There was a log fire burning in the fireplace. The room upset Hiram immediately. Because of his strange sensitivity to inanimate objects, the chairs, the couches, the hangings, the rugs beneath his feet told him things that he only half-understood, but that raised the short hairs at the back of his neck. The butler was standing at a small table on which were basin and water, some bottles and lint. The *Gräfin* dismissed him. Then she came over to Hiram. All of the hellish green fires were out of her eyes, and there was tenderness and concern on a face that to Hiram had at first seemed wholly cruel. Her coat had fallen open and revealed her beautiful body beneath the white nightgown, but she was unconscious of it. She took Hiram's hand in hers, and said: 'It is torn. Come, I will bathe it for you.'

Hiram drew back trembling. She exhaled perfume from every part of her, like a night flower. He knew already how this night must end, and still he retreated instinctively because he was not yet in command.

He said: 'Look – I'm really not badly hurt. I am deeply grateful for what you have done for me. If it hadn't been for you I would probably be dead by now. Would you just permit me to go and wash, and then I will leave.' He cursed himself for the stupid, stilted speech. She was there to be taken. He could press his face against her breasts if he but moved. . . .

She let go his hand and stepped back. The twin lamps in the white face began to glow again. For a second he thought that he caught an expression that was utterly simple and pure, and almost child-like in its disappointment. Then she said coolly, and with hardly a trace of accent: 'You are hardly polite, my friend. You have not even taken the trouble to tell me your name.'

Hiram rose to the challenge. 'It is Hiram Holliday. And yours?'

'I am Irmgarde von Helm. Why are you so anxious to go?' She was now standing at full height, and staring at him directly. The green eyes challenged the light blue ones behind their steel-rimmed spectacles. Hiram's face was smeared and his sand-coloured hair ruffled, and there was still a thin line of blood that seeped from the corner of his mouth and down one side of his chin. His clothes were disarranged and he looked no figure of a hero, but the eyes behind their windows, and the curl of the mouth in the round, bland, undistinguished face cried out to her: 'Be careful – I am a man,' and beneath the stoutish figure the tall *Gräfin* saw a gallant and gleaming knight and could hardly bear her yearning for his strength.

Hiram answered her. He said: 'For two reasons. I have work to do. . . .'

'And the other. . . .'

'Because I do not like you.' But Hiram's inward voice cried to him: *Coward . . . because if I stay I must get my fingers to your throat, or my mouth to yours.*

The Gräfin Irmgarde drew in a sharp breath, but before she could speak Hiram, impelled by the pictures of what he had seen that suddenly flooded his mind again, said: 'Why were you there? What were you doing there? What was there for you?'

Lies scattered themselves through Irmgarde's mind, but she could catch none of them. This strange, plain-looking man drew the truth from her before she knew she was speaking it. 'For a thrill.'

Hiram made a little sound in his throat. He was safe now. She was bad. She was evil. She had gone for pleasure to see men held helpless and beaten, and property and the collected beauty of centuries destroyed. Hiram could not keep his feelings from his face.

Irmgarde suddenly took Hiram by both shoulders: 'No . . . no,' she cried – 'don't judge. Perhaps I went to torture myself with hatred for those things which we do. Do you think that I was there because it was good what they did?'

124

'I saw you. . . . I saw your face . . .' said Hiram bitterly. 'I could have killed you . . . because everything in it was . . . evil . . .'

Irmgarde made no protest. She said simply: 'And you are good and clean and brave. I feel it. . . . I saw it. When you struck your blow it was as though in my head was the music of a great, clear, beautiful chord. And when I reach for something that is good, that is clean and honest . . .' she suddenly opened the hands that were holding his shoulders so that they were again empty of him – 'then it is no longer there. It is never there. Am I so bad . . . so bad . . .'

Suddenly she blazed at him in an explosion of temper: 'You . . . you . . . you, standing there. . . . Do you know who I am? I am Grunze's woman. He owns me, the hunchback doctor who hates the world for its beauty and who in the name of Nazi will take and destroy the beauty in every other country, as just now was destroyed the piano of Mozart. You . . . you . . . you chivalrous fool. Your country, too! The plans are made, the discord already sown . . . his agents are at work night and day. Are they all like you, over there, the men, willing to die for the *beau geste*? To strike a blow for beauty and the weak, even though they die for it? We strike at beauty and the weak, and strike and strike and strike again for the feeling of power. We must have power. Because of the power it gave me I belong to Grunze, but I have not my soul any more. Germany has not its soul any more. . . . Hiram . . . Hiram . . . let me only touch you once. Let me . . . let me . . .'

But it was Hiram who took her, dirty and bloody, and aching as he was, for in his mind he had already taken her when she told him that she belonged to Dr Grunze, and their love-making was a battle, a fierce, uncompromising struggle of souls and bodies, each fighting to take from the other and devour what they wanted, he, flame and flood and danger and the fierce brutal vitality of her, she wrestling to drain into her body all the strength and decency and pure unashamed valour and knightliness that she had seen in him, coming to him parched, as though he were a crystal fountain. Her wild, hungry contact with Hiram was almost religious in its ecstasy and longing. His blood upon her was a bath that might once more wash her clean. Hiram's passion was all male and triumphant. He took because he could not help himself, and because in taking he knew he dared the gods as well as man. . . .

It was seven in the morning when he left her. There was a passage from the house that went through another and led to an exit in an innocent little alley opening on to the Rauchstrasse so that he avoided the imposing Tiergartenstrasse entrance which might have been watched. He felt that he was half-mad from the things he had seen and the things that had happened to him, but he had his story to tell, and that drove him on. By cab he went to the Friedrichstrasse and watched the destruction and looting of the Arcade shops, and saw the children delving into the ruins for toys, their faces candy-smeared from previous thefts. He toured the textile centres in the Kronen Strasse and saw the work go on at the Tauntzien-strasse, Leipzigerstrasse and Alexanderplatz, and on the Friedrichstrasse, on the other side of Unter den Linden, he watched young boys wreck and loot and destroy.

And then he went back to his hotel and wrote his story. He had not the faintest idea of how he would get it out of Berlin, but write it he must, and his words were scorched with the fires of the burning temples, his sentences cut and splintered by the shattered glass that littered the pavements of Berlin, and bathed in the blood of beaten men. He wrote with the sounds and odours of the wild morning still in his ears and nostrils, and with all of the passion that he had found in Irmgarde and taken from her.

When he had finished he was exhausted in body and spirit, but he would not yet permit himself to sleep. An idea was gnawing at him. He had not signed the story. One copy he placed in an envelope and sent over to Biederman by messenger to the *Sentinel* office in the Dorotheenstrasse. The other he put into his pocket. He went not to a post office, but walked on foot to the Lehrter Bahnhof, and there, at the busy Government telegraph office in the branch post office, gave in his story addressed to Wallace Reck, the Hotel Ambassador, Prague. Reck was the Prague correspondent of the *Sentinel*. He paid for the telegram, gave a false name and address and walked out of the station. He then returned to the Adlon and went to bed.

Biederman received the story, read it, turned pale and began to tremble. He shut himself in his inner office, placed it in the small coal grate fireplace and set fire to it. He did not stop trembling until it was reduced to ashes and he had trampled and scattered them with his feet.

But the man in the Lehrter Bahnhof telegraph office sent the story to Prague. Later, he was sent to concentration camp for having done so. His only excuse was that he had been busy, and confused, and the telegram had not been addressed to America, or England, or France, in which case he would have, of course, notified the authorities. For Reck, Prague correspondent of the *Sentinel*, had immediately re-cabled the story to New York.

Hiram slept for eleven hours. When he awoke it was one o'clock in the morning. He was awakened by the ringing of the telephone bell at his bedside. It was Irmgarde. She said: 'Hiram ... Hiram. ... Please. ... I must see you. Will you come to me again. ... Through the Rauch Strasse. I'll wait. ... Hiram ...'

'Yes,' said Hiram Holliday, 'I'll come ...'

How Hiram Holliday Was Not but Was in Berlin

He went to her, he tried to tell himself, for many reasons, and chiefly, he clung to the idea that he was a newspaperman. There had been the hint that she had dropped off the far-reaching designs against his own country, and he wanted to know more about the activities of the new Germany in the United States.

She told him, too, because the mere presence of Hiram filled her with such love and recklessness that it banished all caution. From her he learned many curious details of the plan gradually to acquire an armed body in America so that Germany would have a million storm-troopers in the United States, which were to be placed at the service of any political demagogue pledged to overthrow the democracy and establish a Dictatorship of the Huey Long type. He gained an insight into the fantastic, far-flung Nazi propaganda organization which in its brutal and efficient activity made the Communist world revolution look like a nursery affair by comparison.

Once he had asked her in amazement: 'But the money, Irmgarde – where does the money for all this come from ?'

'Blackmail,' she had replied. 'Theft and blackmail. We steal from Jew and Gentile alike, and what they have hidden we make them disgorge. We are not yet through bleeding Austria, and when that is dry we will take Czechoslovakia. Baron Rothschild will pay us twenty million marks for his freedom. The fortune of the Fürstenhof family held in banks in England and France is estimated at ten million pounds. It will be returned to us because in Vienna we hold their boy for ransom . . .'

Hiram had felt as though he had been plunged into icy water. The scene in the battle-wrecked room in the Podebradova in Prague had swept through his mind again and he had been filled with revulsion at the cold-blooded, brutal philosophy that Irmgarde represented.

And yet he continued to go to her because the truth was that she, and she alone, drew him. He could not keep away from her. It was curiosity and danger that had appealed to him at first, but now it was the woman. It was his first encounter with a brilliant, cultured, sophisticated, morally decayed European aristocrat. And it was not a decay that came inwardly from her as a human being, but rather an outward canker, an abrasion from the life she led, her contact with a brittle, cynical European society that had in itself become degenerate. She had played the game as it had seemed most profitable and exciting to her, but underneath she had strong yearnings for such simplicities as truth, beauty and fearlessness. Inured to intrigue, artifice, the self-seeking cunning, the cowardice and conspiracy of those in power with whom she had contact, Hiram Holliday had made her his slave by his simple, brave gesture of striking a blow in protest against all of these things, and striking it at a time and place that courted almost certain destruction. Its very foolhardiness enhanced the purity and glory of the gesture. There was not a man she knew, or had ever known, not a man living in Germany who would have dared to do the same.

The next four days were whirlwinds of emotion and activity for Hiram. He worked hard during the daytime only to kill the hours that separated him from Irmgarde. There was always a tinge of caution in his own recklessness, but he trusted her to do her part, and did not know that there was none whatsoever in hers, that she had lost all caution and judgement and thought only of having him with her.

It was one o'clock, the morning of November 16, that Hiram entered the tiny private lift and went directly to the third floor of the house where Irmgarde awaited him. He found her depressed and moody. Her passion was in abeyance. She seemed to be in need of tenderness and the comfort of quiet companionship. They talked for an hour, when Irmgarde shivered suddenly, and said: 'It is cold here. Let us go downstairs, Hiram. I want to sit there by the fire with you.'

They went down the little winding staircase to the large *salon* where the fire was always burning. And the reason they did not see the man who was sitting there was because he was so small that his head did not rise above the back of the brocaded wing-chair that was turned to the fire. They were thus almost to the fire-place when Irmgarde suddenly twitched convulsively and said: '*Ach Herr Gott!*' and the man rose from the chair, or rather slid to his feet, bowed courteously, and said – 'Goot efening. . . .'

Irmgarde's hand in his had gone to ice, and her twitch had sent a little chill down Hiram's spine, but there was nothing in the man that caused him particular alarm. He was a hunchback, and so Hiram knew that it was Dr Grunze. But his appearance was not menacing. His head was large with bushy black hair, his chin was smooth-shaven and deft. His eye-glasses were attached to a black ribbon. In the buttonhole of his frock coat was a tiny swastika button. But for the hump on his back that deformed him, Hiram decided that he looked like a family doctor.

There was a terrible silence and Hiram pressed Irmgarde's hand hard to try to restore her courage. Without looking at her he knew that she was very close to fainting. The man bowed again and smiled, and he had wonderful white teeth, and said: 'Do you not introduce me, Irmgarde?'

There was no sound but Irmgarde's breathing. Hiram knew that he must break this silence, restore at least an appearance of normality. He dropped the *Gräfin's* hand and bowed. 'Permit me,' he said. 'My name is Hiram Holliday . . .' and then something, a sense of irony, impelled him to add: 'I am a correspondent for the *New York Sentinel*.' Irmgarde sucked in her breath again.

Dr Grunze smiled, bowed again, and extended his hand. 'It iss a pleasure,' he said, and then added with a shrug, and a look of mischief on his face that was almost boyish: 'A pleasure which I haff denied myself up to now. I haff never met a reporter from a newspaper. I am glad that the first iss an American. It iss a great country. We will do much wis it.'

Irmgarde said in a strained voice: 'Heinrich. You frightened me so.'

Dr Grunze patted her arm genially, and said: '*Aber . . . aber*. I did not mean to. I zink perhaps I was a little asleep.' He turned to Hiram and said casually: 'You see, zat iss ze rewards of kindness. The *Gräfin* permits me to come here and rest when I am tired from ze arduous duties of State. You are indeed fortunate, my frent, to have found this never-drying fountain of youth and graciousness.'

He spoke with great care and precision as one does who is unfamiliar with a language. Hiram could detect no trace of irony or mockery in either speech or manner. So this was the mysterious and dangerous Dr Grunze. Like all such hedged-around beings, Hiram thought, when once they were reached they became ordinary and simple human beings.

'Can we not all zit?' said the Doctor and sank back into the wing-chair. The *Gräfin* sat on a nearby chaise-longue in front of the fire. She was wearing a simple Nile-green *négligée*. Hiram, who sat in a chair opposite her, thought that never in his life had he seen a face so tragic and so frightened. There was not one drop of blood in it beyond the green eyes and the paint on her mouth. They sat in silence for a moment. Then the Doctor leaned forward, his eyes twinkling cheerfully. He tapped Hiram on the knee and said: 'My frent, I can read your soughts. You are wishing that you may interview me.'

For the first time Hiram grinned. 'Yes,' he said, 'I was. May I?'

The Doctor lit a flat cigarette with a gold tip and puffed the smoke ruminatively for a moment before he said: 'I giff to you the permission.'

Hiram forgot about Irmgarde and her desperate, warning face. He forgot about everything because for the moment he was blinded by the lines of black type: 'FIRST AND EX-CLUSIVE INTERVIEW WITH DR HEINRICH GRUNZE, by Hiram Holliday . . .' that swam before his eyes.

He leaned forward and said: 'Dr Grunze, will you tell me. What are Germany's feelings with regard to the United States? What is the reason for such obvious organizations as the German-American Bund which beneath the American flag, and protected by the laws of a democracy, propagandize against that country? What do you hope to accomplish?'

The little hunchback began to chuckle. 'Ha-ha-ha, my frent. Your question iss as naïve as your people. Germany was captured by us from much smaller beginnings than what we do in your country now. The philosophy of National Socialism must be prepared for. We are preparing you. When WE are ready for you, YOU will be ready for US.' He laughed again, heartily, and then suddenly grew serious, leaned forward and touched Hiram on the knee, a black incubus with a hump on his back.

'My frent, we will take your country, not with guns, and bomps and aeroplanes, but with an idea.' He rapped his large bulging skull-front with his forefinger. 'It iss here. We will tell zat idea to so many peoples in your country, over and over again, that they will believe it. And zat idea is zat zey were not made to rule but to be ruled over, and zat zey will be happier zat way. We will succeed because you have not ze strengs to put us in prison, or in concentration camp, or shoot us. But when we are zere in command, we will shoot, and put in prison who does not zink as we do. We haff made ze greatest discovery in ze history of man. We make all ze peoples zink in the same way. *Gehorsamkeit* – obedience. Only once before in history has it been tried, and zat was by ze Church, and it fails because zey have left to man his soul. We take his soul, too. It does not fail. Ze worse thing what has happened to zis world iss idealism – morals you say. We haf no morals. Yours we use against you to destroy you. . . .'

Irmgarde was sitting bolt upright on the couch, silent, her only motion a slight weaving of her body. She looked like a Laurencin painting, ragged colours on a white face. And Hiram listened completely bemused and spellbound with the depth and significance of his world scoop, as the little black Doctor, emphasizing his points with his long, white fingers and nods of his head, laid bare the fantastic scope of the plot against the United States. It was the Communist-planned world revolution all over again, but on a basis of philosophy and psychology so Germanic, from the red lips of the Doctor, that Hiram was appalled. Every detail of the seduction was bared. Ten years was the time allotted. 'It cannot be stopped,' concluded the pleasant little Doctor, 'otherwise, of course, I would not haff give you the interview.' He looked at his watch. '*Ach, die Zeit, die Zeit* . . .' he said. 'Perhaps that is why I am never seen, because I am too fond to talk. Irmgarde, a thousand pardons if I haff disturbed you. It iss ze privilege you haff given me. So. Gootbye, my dear. Gootbye, Mr Holliday. . . .'

During his last words he had risen, donned a Chesterfield and a black Homburg hat and picked up a gold-knobbed umbrella and pushed the button for the lift. When it arrived, he bowed to them both, donned his hat, entered the lift and sank from sight, and nothing remained to Hiram but the memory of the picture of his descending smile.

Irmgarde was shaking him by the shoulders, weeping, sobbing, crying: 'Hiram! Hiram! *Um Gottes Willen! Mein Lieber.* Do you understand? Do you understand what has happened? I have killed you! Killed you. Oh, *Gott!* What shall we do? You must not leave here tonight. You must telephone to the American Embassy in the morning to send for you. You must not be an instant alone. But still, he will find a way. Hiram . . . Hiram, what have I done?'

Her panic, curiously, struck no response in Hiram. Of all the places he had been, here somehow in the stronghold of Nazidom he felt the most secure. Closeness to them and watching them at work during the pogrom had bred contempt. He said: 'Irmgarde! Nonsense. Pull yourself together. I'm an American citizen. No one is going to do anything to me. Grunze wouldn't have told me those things if he hadn't wanted to – for his own reasons. I'm going home. I want to think.' In his mind he was already writing his story. But it was addressed not to 'Beauheld, Managing Editor, *New York Sentinel*,' but 'To the President of the United States.'

'Fool,' screamed Irmgarde, and suddenly began to beat at his chest with her fists. 'Didn't you understand? He was *reading you your death sentence.* Hiram! You cannot go. It was I who am to blame. I was not careful because I wanted to see you so. I did not make sure that he was not in Berlin.'

It was her melodramatics that made him turn so cold and stubborn. Had she explained quietly and earnestly, made him see . . .

Hiram said: 'Irmgarde, stop it! If there is any danger I'll be safer in the hotel than I will here. I am neither a spy nor a German. They'll think twice before they touch an American in Berlin. Grunze said what he did because like all Germans he cannot help boasting.'

Trembling and sobbing, she watched him go. She secured

from him a promise that he would communicate immediately with the American Embassy in the morning, that he would telephone her. . . .

Hiram let himself out through the Rauch Strasse exit. It was half-past three in the morning. The street was deserted. There was no cab in sight, but he knew that he could always find one cruising up or down the Tiergarten Strasse, so he turned to the left towards the Hitzig Strasse which would connect with it.

They must have been concealed all about the shadowed entrance of a grey stone house that he passed, because Hiram heard no footsteps, and then suddenly they were upon him, pulling him down from behind, at his throat, his legs, his arms, gagging him, tearing at his clothes. He was rolling on the ground, blinded by a cloth held over his eyes, struggling and gasping. . . . One thought raced through his mind: 'Would the fools murder an American in the street . . . ?' He set himself for the supreme desperate struggle for his life, and then suddenly he was free, gasping, breathless and dizzy, half-choked, but unharmed. He heard footsteps retreating, but by the time he had cleared his head and swung himself around to look, he caught sight of no more than a shadowy figure or two disappearing around the corner behind him.

'Oh, nuts!' he said to himself, and picked himself up sheepishly. 'Hiram Holliday, the great adventurer. Cleaned out by footpads. There's ONE that won't go into the memoirs. . . .'

Every pocket had been ransacked in the swift tussle, and turned inside out. He did not have a pfennig left. Even his handkerchiefs had been taken. His wallet was gone, and from his inside pocket, his passport and credentials.

'Oh, oh,' said Hiram to himself. 'But were they footpads ?' For a moment he considered walking to the home of one of the minor American Consuls he had met and rousing him. It was not good to be without papers in a foreign city. It gave him a terribly naked feeling. Then he thought of the ridiculous figure he would make disturbing the Consul, and discarded the idea.

Nor was there any use finding a policeman. He was not eager to be questioned as to what he was doing there at that hour. He arranged his clothes and set off at a brisk pace for the Hotel Adlon. He would telephone to the Embassy the first thing in the morning and report his loss. He reached the hotel without further incident and asked for his key at the desk. The clerk said: 'Good morning, Mr Holliday,' and handed him the key with the number '32' on the large metal disc attached to it. 'I understand you are leaving for Paris today. Do you wish to leave a call?'

'Who?' said Hiram. 'Me? Not that I know of. You've probably got me mixed up with someone else.' The clerk looked puzzled and shrugged. Hiram went up to his room. It was far around the corridor from the lift. He unlocked the outer door, hung the 'Don't Disturb' sign on it, closed it, opened the inner door, snapped on the light and froze there. There was something wrong about the room. And then he saw what it was. His bags were gone. There was other baggage distributed about the place. He examined his key. It was Number 32. He stepped out and looked at the number over the door. It corresponded. He went back into the room, leaving the door open, and inspected the battered brown handbag with the worn leather straps that replaced his own grip.

'Now what the hell goes on here?' he said aloud. . . .

The door slammed. Men poured out from the bathroom. There were green-uniformed police, black-uniformed S.S. men, and men in plain clothes. All of them carried pistols in their hands. They surrounded him. One of the men in plain clothes said: 'Hermann Weide, Communist, you are under arrest for high treason. Surrender yourself!'

Hiram looked from one to the other and grinned. They looked so earnest and savage. He said: 'You birds are daffy. My name isn't Hermann Weide, and I'm not a Communist. My name is Hiram Holliday, and I am an American citizen. . . .' His hand had half-stolen to his breast pocket before he remembered that his papers were gone. A terrible, warning flash of insight struck through him. . . .

135

'*Schweige! Kommunistischer Verbrecher,*' shouted the man who had first spoken, and then gave some sort of a signal. Hiram's cry and thrust came too late. His voice was choked off by a strip of adhesive tape over his mouth from behind. The police and S.S. men were all over him, punching and kicking, but they stopped when he was on the floor, his hands and legs manacled, and suddenly burst open the baggage, ransacking it. The Gestapo plain-clothes leader discovered a passport. It was a German one made out to a Hermann Weide. He opened it to the photograph and held it to Hiram's face for comparison. Hiram, his mind fighting for sanity and escape, saw that it was HIS picture. From another bag that seemed to have a false bottom they unearthed pamphlets and tracts, and a series of plans of what seemed to be a radio hook-up. The men handed them about to one another and spoke rapidly in German. The plain-clothes agent gave another signal. The door opened, and two S.S. men came in with a pink-faced, elderly woman between them. They brought her over to where Hiram was sitting on the floor and held her there facing him. '*Na?*' said the Gestapo man, savagely.

The woman began to beat her palms together and moan: 'Oh! ... oh! ... *Oh, Gott, oh, Gott! Ja, das ist mein Neffe, Hermann Weide. ... Oh, Gott ...* !' Then she said to Hiram in bad English: '*Ach*, Hermann, Hermann. Vy do you alvays bring trouble to us? Vy don't you in America stay und not come here und make trouble?'

The S.S. guards took her out. Hiram heard her lamentations fading down the hall-way. Another man entered, and when he was in the room, Hiram was yanked to his feet and held there for a moment. The newcomer was Hiram's build and size, and suddenly Hiram saw that he resembled him a great deal. He gazed at him silently for two or three minutes and then turned and walked out. More S.S. men came in. They helped hold Hiram while the others stripped him of every shred of his clothing and then dressed him in a new set. And then they did a very curious thing. Out of a small bag they produced some rolls of wide bandages and proceeded to bandage his head completely down to his neck, over spectacles and all, leaving only his nose free for breathing. Then he felt some moisture seep through the bandaging and his feet were kicked out from under him.

Trussed like a mummy, the person of Hermann Weide, the dangerous Communist, who had been severely injured in the struggle to arrest him, as attested by the blood-stained emergency bandages that covered his head and face, was carried out of the rear entrance of the Hotel Adlon, dumped into a military car, and driven to Moabit prison, where he was placed in a deep cell to await trial for high treason. And at nine o'clock the same morning a Mr Hiram Holliday departed on the nine-thirty plane for Paris.

How Hiram Holliday Was No Longer Anywhere

For the thousandth time Hiram Holliday walked the narrow stone cell and racked his tired brain for a thought, a glimmer, a hope of escape. It was the night of November 22. On the morning of November 23, less than twelve hours away, Hermann Weide, Communist, German citizen convicted of high treason, was to be executed. And HE was Hermann Weide. His identity as Hiram Holliday had been taken from him. What had become of it he did not know for certain, but he half-suspected the truth. There was not the slightest chance of regaining it. Once he had tried to remove the bandages from his head, and men had come and beaten him with sections of rubber hose. Since then the wrappings had remained in place. It was obvious what they were for, Dr Grunze was taking no chances that anyone might recognize him. They would still be on his head when it rolled on to the ground of the prison yard in the morning.

He did not cry out or beat his hands against the steel door. Sometimes he was so soul-sick that he could not even walk. One name beat through his head – Grunze . . . Grunze. . . . The charming, expansive little hunchback. How long had he known ? Probably from the very first. The servants in the house

137

were all his spies. Every detail of the plot had been worked out for days. A candid camera could have secured his picture for the false passport any time, any place, at a restaurant, in a bar. . . . The woman had been paid to identify him as her nephew. He had walked into it. He had disregarded Irmgarde's terror. Not even the robbery that had deprived him of his papers had warned him. He should have walked the streets that morning until the embassies opened, and gone there immediately. But the tremendous brain that had engineered the conspiracy had known that he would not, had correctly gauged him for what he was, reckless, heedless.

And he knew why he was to die. Even the game of international politics is played with some caution and regard to the rights of nations and the protection of their nationals, particularly a country as powerful as the United States. Had they merely discovered that he had written the pogrom story that appeared in the *Sentinel*, he would have been escorted over the border. But he had been caught tampering with the woman belonging to one of the keenest and most malicious brains in all Central Europe. And he had believed that he could get away with it.

His thoughts turned again to Irmgarde. Somehow he had clung to her as a last hope, but now even that had faded. She might know that a Hermann Weide, a Communist, had been condemned to death, but it would mean nothing to her. And Grunze was not the man to neglect anything. If she knew of his terrible plight, the Doctor would have seen to it that she could not use her knowledge. He wondered whether she had called the American Embassy the morning of his arrest, or the hotel. There were many gaps in Hiram's knowledge of the snare into which he had walked. But he felt them. He had not understood the testimony at the trial. But from the number of times the word 'Paris' had been mentioned, he had an idea of how impregnable and immovable were the jaws of the trap. And he had remembered suddenly that the clerk had questioned him about his intention to leave for Paris in the morning. Grunze had overlooked nothing. There was no loophole. In the morning they would come for him, lead him out, kill him and bury him. The death notice of Hermann Weide would be splashed on Berlin's bulletin boards. And what had become of Hiram Holliday, no one would ever know.

He wondered how he would die? He knew that another was scheduled to die with him, a Fritz Gorner, convicted of selling military secrets to a foreign Power. Gorner was to be executed first. He would watch him die. Already he felt the pressure upon his arms as they pushed him forward to the block. A crack on the back of the legs to bend his knees, a push from the rear to grind his face into the block. . . . He would feel the swift, powerful movement of the executioner, even if he did not see him swing his axe, hear him suck in his breath from the effort of raising it and then. . . . Hiram's hands went to his throat again for the hundredth time, and then as it had, hour after hour, his mind swung around like a cyclorama on hinges, groping, reaching, probing, grasping, searching for a hope, an idea. And inevitably the cyclorama swung back again to the bitter contemplation of his blindness and his folly, his misjudgement of the polite and pleasant Doctor, his blind, headlong plunge into disaster with Irmgarde, and his vainglorious belief that he would be able to deliver to his country as well as to his paper, the details of the Machiavellian designs upon the United States as told him by Grunze – Grunze, who already knew that he was telling them to a dead man. The cyclorama swung again. And again, and again.

There were footsteps down the stone corridor outside, but Hiram paid no attention. They stopped at his door. Keys rattled. The door swung open. It was the turnkey and a deputy governor of the prison. Behind them was another figure hidden in the shadows of the poorly lighted dungeon block.

The deputy governor said: '*Hermann Weide! Durch Spezialverordnung des Minister Doktor Grunze werden Sie von der Gräfin Irmgarde von Helm besucht. Halbe Stunde Sprechzeit gestattet.*'

Hiram did not understand him. All he knew was that the cell door clanged shut, the footsteps retreated. And the Gräfin

Irmgarde was in his arms, sobbing, and pressing him, and whispering. . . . She was dressed in a long black velvet cloak with a Capuchin hood, and around her throat and face were wound yards and yards of the white tulle she affected. She continued to sob until the footsteps had died away completely. Then she sprang back and dropped her hood, and Hiram saw that she was not crying at all. Her face had life and colour, there was an excited cunning on her mouth, and her eyes were gleaming and sparkling with excitement. And she began to speak at once in a low voice, rapidly, cutting off his questions to save time. . . .

'Grunze told me,' she began. 'Tonight. He could not resist to boast. I know everything. They told me at the embassy and the hotel that you had left for Paris. At first I thought you were safe. And then Grunze told me what had been done. Quiet. Listen to me, Hiram. Every second counts. You do not exist any more. Your papers were taken by a man who went to Paris with them under your name. He went to a Paris hotel, the St Régis, and registered in your name. He even sent several cables to your office. Then he simply returned to Germany under his own passport. So you have disappeared from a Paris hotel. Your papers were found in your room there. They are now in the hands of your representative there. Only Grunze could think of something so clever. But he had to boast because it would hurt me. He couldn't wait. And so we defeat him. I made him give an order that I could see you alone to say good-bye to you . . . wait . . . don't interrupt . . . that I could do because . . . because of what I can withhold from him. . . . Now! You must do exactly as I say instantly. We will change clothes. I had the highest possible pass to come here, Grunze's own. You will not be disturbed when you leave, if . . .'

'My God, no!' said Hiram Holliday, flatly and definitely. 'And leave you here. . . .'

For the first time since he had known her, Hiram heard Irmgarde laugh. Her face was one dancing mischief. She said: '*Mein Liebes.* . . . Now it is you who are making the great melodrama. Don't you know who I am? I am the Gräfin

140

Irmgarde von Helm, who is under the protection of Minister Doctor Heinrich Grunze. They can do nothing to me. Yes, they will call Doctor Grunze. And then I will laugh at *him*.'

The first ray of hope took Hiram's heart on the upswing. 'Irmgarde. . . . Are you telling me the truth?'

In her enthusiasm and sincerity and excitement she lapsed for a moment into German: '*Ja, ja, ja, Lieber, dummer Mann.* . . . You must understand. Grunze has been TOO clever. No one but he actually knows that Hermann Weide is Hiram Holliday. All the others, the men who made the arrest, the woman who recognized you as her nephew, the man who went to Paris, all, all, were obeying orders blindly in the German way. When Hermann Weide is gone, and I am found here, it will be Grunze who will have to hush it up so that there is no scandal. When you are Hiram Holliday again, you are safe. . . .'

Hiram was half convinced. What the *Gräfin* had said was true. The very air-tight nature of the frame-up could defeat it – if he were free, if he were Hiram Holliday again. But between the condemned Hermann Weide in the cell in Moabit prison, and his old self there was such a vast unbridgeable chasm. He said: 'Irmgarde. . . . It sounds impossible . . . how. . . .'

She knew she had won. She laughed at him again, and Hiram saw the daring, brilliant woman, thrilled to the core by her adventure, and he remembered why she had driven that night to the pogrom, the night that seemed so many years ago. 'For a thrill,' she had said.

Now she said: 'First we change clothes. *Marsch!* Immediately! Then I tell you. Quick!'

Her *tempo*, her excitement caught Hiram up. If this then was to be the last adventure, at least it was still adventure, and better to go out with the obliterating beat of bullets. . . .

They stripped and changed. They had to chance that Grunze's name and order were really powerful enough to leave them their half-hour unobserved. But Irmgarde knew the German capacity for obeying an order implicitly. She helped Hiram into her clothing. She had even thought of wearing flat-heeled sports shoes of a larger size. He got his feet into them. The hood covered his head, and she wound the white tulle around and around his throat.

'Bandage me carefully, carefully, my Hiram . . .' she said. 'Make no mistake.'

Hiram wound the bandage around her head as it had been around his, carefully covering every speck of the flame-coloured hair that she wore caught up tightly in a net. She had thought of everything. He bandaged his spectacles on to her swathed face, leaving the eyes free as his had been. She said: 'Have no fear of the colour of my eyes. They will not notice it tonight. And in the morning, the red-haired *Gräfin* will be awaiting them, green eyes and all.'

They completed the exchange in seven minutes. Then Hiram Holliday was the *Gräfin* and stood there, cloaked and hooded, and Irmgarde, suited and bandaged, was Hiram Holliday, and sat bent over on the steel cot, and said to him in her low voice: 'Listen carefully. Mark everything I say in your memory. Do not interrupt me for I must finish before they come. Gather together your nerves like steel. And do not disobey me in the slightest for everything has been thought of, everything has been planned. Obey to the letter.

'Listen now. When they come, stand as you are. In your right hand hold this paper I give to you, hold it so at all times it can be seen. With your left hand keep my handkerchief to your mouth, and you are sobbing, sobbing, always sobbing. You are broken and sobbing, as I would be were I leaving you. I will be standing in the corner, my back to the door, my head upon my arm. I, too, am despairing. Follow the man who will lead you, always sobbing, sobbing. Look not to the right or the left. Go behind him, the paper showing. You will pass through the office of the Governor. Do not stop, do not speak. Walk as a woman walks who has lost her lover. He will then precede you to the door and lead you to the outside. Your car and chauffeur is waiting there, the car and chauffeur of the Gräfin von Helm. Say nothing. Get in. He has his instructions. He will drive you home. When you arrive there he will say: '*Hat die Frau Gräfin noch befehle?'* Remember the sound of that. You will still be sobbing. Shake your head for 'no,' and enter quickly the house with the key that you will take from your – my purse. Go up in the lift to our . . . my room on the third floor. Leave there that paper which is Grunze's highest pass, which permits him or his representative to go anywhere.'

She paused for a moment to let her instructions sink in. Then she said again: 'Good. It will be eight o'clock when you leave here, quarter-past eight when you are home. In my room you will find clothes that will fit you, a suitcase with linen and necessaries. In the clothes will be money. Dress. Place my clothes neatly as I am accustomed. Disturb the bed. Wet my tooth-brush. Spill mouth-wash in the bathroom. Use the soap. Wait until nine o'clock. Leave, not by the lift, but by the staircase. Do not pause. Do not hesitate. Go on down. Do not under any circumstances go into the *salon* or any other room. Let yourself out by the door you know, carrying the suitcase. Walk quickly away. Do not take a taxicab until you have walked for five minutes. Then drive to the Friedrich Strasse Bahnhof and go in. It will be a quarter-past nine.'

She stopped again. Hiram's heart was beating so that he could hear it. She went on: 'Go into a telephone-box. Telephone to your people in Paris. Be clever. Be cautious. Do not mention your name. Make them understand that they must send you your papers by the night aeroplane so that you will have them in the morning. The express from Paris arrives at twenty minutes to ten. Go to the gate, and when the people come out, mingle with them as though you had just arrived. Go out, enter a taxi and drive to the Hotel Adlon. Register there as Hiram Holliday. Make some remark calling attention to your trip to Paris and your return to Berlin. You are very tired and anxious to go to your room. If he asks for your passport tell him you will send it down in the morning. Go to your room. Telephone to all the friends you know, and say that you have returned to Berlin from Paris. Be natural. Be normal. Make appointments. . . . From then on, if you do as I say, you are safe.'

Far down the corridor the footsteps began. . . . 'And above all, my dearly beloved man. Never call me. Never seek to see me again. Never speak of me. Never give sign that ever you knew of me. Now, summon your great and dear courage.' She paused again, then crossed herself quickly and said: *'Gott sei mit uns. . . .'* The footsteps were louder. . . .

Hiram Holliday began to concentrate. There was no turning back now. He thought of what little Lisette, the circus queen in Paris, had once taught him of the foundation of classical pantomime. It was to believe with every ounce of strength, spiritual and physical, that you WERE what you were pretending to be. He believed. He was. His body began to take on the form and pose that had been Irmgarde's, his head to hang at the tragic angle of a weeping woman. He sobbed as he had heard her sob the night she had begged him not to leave her house.

The turnkey came with two soldiers. He tapped the unhappy *Gräfin* politely upon the shoulder. They had no more than a perfunctory glance for the prisoner who stood with his face to the wall, his head resting on an arm. The iron door grated into place. The long, slow march through the prison to the outer air began, the three men in the lead, the broken woman following. In his cell, the prisoner sank to his knees and bent his head over his folded hands, and remained there while the sounds of the departing footsteps, and the half-hushed, torn sobbing of the departing one had been stilled by distance, and for long, long afterwards, so long that it was safe to turn the prayer from supplication to thankfulness and praise.

How Hiram Holliday Was in Berlin but the Woman with Red Hair Was Not

Hiram Holliday walked into the Bahnhof Friedrichstrasse at sixteen minutes past nine by the station clock. He was dressed in a dark suit, wore a raincoat of the type he had always had, carried a leather suitcase on which were labels from London and Paris hotels. He went into a red telephone-box and put in a call for Clegg, the Chief of the *Sentinel* Bureau in Paris. His line of action was half-planned. He hoped that Clegg would recognize his voice when he came to the wire and understand what he wanted, but he was not certain that he would. He had not had much to do with him in Paris.

The call went through. He heard the French operator, and then heard Clegg say: 'Hello. Yes, this is Clegg, Paris Bureau. Who is it?'

Hiram spoke strongly and robustly: 'Hello, Clegg. Say, I'm back in Berlin again. Will you fellows send me that stuff of mine that I left in Paris?'

It didn't work. Clegg said testily: 'Who is this speaking? I don't know what you are talking about. Who is this?'

And then Hiram had an inspiration. He said: 'Hayseed, on vacation!'

There was a long silence from the other end, and then Clegg said: 'Oh, oh! I get it. Wait a minute. How do I know?'

'Try me,' said Hiram and waited. There was another pause and then Clegg asked:

'What's a "20 Head"?'

Hiram grinned in appreciation and answered immediately: 'Two Column two-line 18 pt Cheltenham Bold Lower Case banked head, 23 units to the line.' One did not spend fourteen years on a copy-desk for nothing. It was clever of Clegg to have remembered it; as clever as his translation of 'Hayseed, on Vacation,' to 'Hiram Holliday.'

'Okay. You back at the Adlon? I'll get it off on the midnight plane. You'll have it in the morning. You been having some bad weather over there?'

Hiram understood him. He replied: 'Thanks. It's fine here now. Cleared up a lot. Adlon is right. Much obliged,' and rang off.

Then he called a taxi and told the chauffeur to drive to the Adlon. He felt better, but his nerves were still terribly shaken. His escape from the prison had been bad enough, but the task of changing his clothes in Irmgarde's room and getting out of the house had seemed even worse, because for some reason he could not fathom he was in a sweating fear from the time he entered the house as the Gräfin von Helm, and quit it as Hiram Holliday. On the way out he had come close to entering the wonderful, graceful, old-fashioned *salon* for a last look. His hand had been on the door when he recalled her warning, 'do not pause, go on down, do not go into the *salon* or any other room,' and he went on. She had taken a terrible risk for him. He owed her implicit obedience. The feeling of fear left him once he was outside the house.

He walked into the Hotel Adlon and went up to the desk. The clerk automatically shoved a registration card at him in a little leather holder, and then looked up and said: 'Ah, Herr Holliday. Back wis us so soon again. I did not know you first wisout your glasses. You enchoy your little trip to Paris? Let me see, what room you haff before. Sirty-two. You like that one again?'

'Yes, thank you,' said Hiram steadily, 'that will be fine. Broke my glasses on the train. Damned nuisance.'

The clerk made a clucking noise and said: 'You let me haff your passport, please. . . .' Hiram was about to speak when he said: '*Ach*, it is not necessary. I haff all se information from last time. You can let me haff it tomorrow if I should need it. We are glad to see you back. . . .'

Hiram went upstairs. Not even Room 32 could shake him any more. He carried out Irmgarde's last instruction and called up two of the correspondents from the American Press services he had met, announced his return from Paris, and made tentative luncheon engagements. Then suddenly all his strength seemed to melt from him. He reached the bed and fell on it, worn out, exhausted, and in a minute fell asleep. He was awakened by the telephone ringing. He was still in his clothes and badly befuddled. The clerk said: 'Mr Holliday? We have a *Rohrpost*, a special delivery letter for you downstairs. Shall we send it up?'

The letter was from Clegg in Paris. It contained his passport, credentials, Registered Marks, traveller's cheques and letter of credit and a brief, unsigned note. It had not been opened at the border. The note read: 'Here you are. Next time don't be so careless and leave stuff like this around in hotel rooms. Messaged Beauheld after our talk. He says thank you and please go to Vienna at once and look after our interests there. Particularly interested in synopsis of "Man in the Iron Mask", for early publication. Regards.'

The cryptic reference stumped Hiram only for a moment until the sleep cleared from his head and then he grinned suddenly, and his admiration for Clegg grew. The Man in the Iron Mask was the most famous prisoner of France. Who was the most famous prisoner of Vienna but von Schuschnigg. To get a story on him. . . . The assignment excited him, and he swung his legs from the bed and sat up. Then he looked at his watch and saw that it was nine o'clock in the morning and all the terrible memories came tumbling down upon him. Nine o'clock. The execution of Hermann Weide had been scheduled for eight, and he, Hiram Holliday, was still alive and safe. They had by this time discovered Irmgarde. Perhaps Dr Grunze was already at the prison. He tried to picture the scene, and grinned a little. The Doctor was in a bad spot, and was going to be very angry. Hiram called the porter and asked about planes to Vienna and booked on the one o'clock ship from Tempelhofer Feld. Then he called the American Embassy and asked for the under-secretary he knew there.

He said to him: 'This is Hiram Holliday speaking. I am back from Paris. I am very nervous, probably for reasons that are wholly imaginary. But I am going to take the liberty of calling you every hour. If I do not, will you be so kind as to make immediate inquiries as to my whereabouts. At one o'clock I am flying to Vienna, and I will call you once more when I arrive there. I know it is nonsense, but it will make me feel better. Thank you.'

Then he went out and bought some more clothes and linen, and secured another pair of spectacles at an oculist's. It was not difficult because he was only far-sighted, and it was easily corrected. At twelve o'clock he was at the magnificent Tempelhofer Feld, the Berlin Airport, from where he telephoned the

Embassy again, and stood for some good-natured chaffing from the under-secretary.

He went to the *guichet* and checked his ticket and struck up an acquaintance with the Lufthansa man, a personable young chap who spoke excellent English. It appeared that he had been to New York and had even done some flying out at Roosevelt Field. Hiram had taken flying instruction there. The Lufthansa man knew the hangar out of which Hiram had flown. They struck the quick, easy footing of brother amateur pilots.

Hiram wandered about the waiting-room. His spirits were returning. He had been a fool, and very near death, but he was alive and beginning slowly to realize the fact again, and to return to the appreciation of the joy of living. He was still too close to past events to know fully by what a hair line his existence had hung. Enough that he was out of it, with his head still attached to his shoulders. He thought of Irmgarde with tremendous gratitude and affection. There had been no slip-up. It had worked out exactly as she had said it would. And part of the bargain was that he was never to see or try to speak to her again. It closed the book. But there was one thing that was not closed, and thought brought little chills of excitement to him again. He still had the fantastic story that he had had from the mouth of Dr Heinrich Grunze. Somehow, he would manage to get it out of Vienna. That, too, he owed to Irmgarde. He suddenly saw in his mind her tall figure with the white face surmounted by the flaming hair, and remembered the laughter around her mouth when she visualized the Nazi officials finding her in the cell.

He studied the huge bulletin board that stood just inside the entrance to the Airport Main Hall and facing the exits to the planes, so as to greet the incoming travellers. It was covered with travel-posters and schedules. He breathed deeply again – Sweden, Norway.... Come to Picturesque Dalmatia.... Visit Rome.... The Tyrol Calls To You.... The world was there for him to see. Yes, he, Hiram Holliday, was still there to see it....

It was a quarter to one. He went and drank a glass of beer, and bought a couple of Tauchnitz edition paper-books to read on the plane. There were boys going through the waiting-room calling: '*Bay-Zett Am Mittag, Bay-Zett Am Mittag. . . .*' They were selling the famous Berlin afternoon paper, *B.Z. Am Mittag*. Hiram saw large black headlines, but ignored them since he could not understand German, much less the newspaper type-face.

At ten minutes to one he went back to the *guichet* to say good-bye to his friend the Lufthansa man. The German suddenly held up the *B.Z.* in front of Hiram's eyes and said: 'Have you seen this?'

Hiram could read and understand the headline. It said: 'DR GRUNZE TOT!' Dr Grunze dead! Dead! What did it mean? When? How? Irmgarde had counted upon his protection. . . . Irmgarde! Grunze!

The iron voice of the loudspeaker system bellowed: '*Passagiere nach Wien! Bitte einsteigen! Passagiere nach Wien bitte. Ausgang rechts!*'

'That is your ship,' said the Lufthansa man, and extended his hand. 'You go out to the right there. Happy landing. . . .'

Hiram hardly saw him because of the choking doubts and fears that clamped and bit into his heart. He said in a voice that he heard apparently from a distance, pinched and strained:

'This Dr Grunze. Tell me . . . what else does it say? Where . . . How did he . . .'

The Lufthansa man did not seem to notice anything strange in the query. He said: 'The paper says he was found dead in his bed this morning at eight o'clock from heart failure . . .'

Grunze dead! Eight o'clock in the morning! Irmgarde!

'You know . . .' the Lufthansa man said, beckoning to Hiram to come closer, and dropping his voice confidentially, 'there is a rumour already all over Berlin. Of course the paper must print what is given. You understand. I heard it an hour ago. The rumour is that he died in some other way, and that he was not in his home. But of course one cannot tell. There are always rumours. Your plane is waiting. Good luck . . .'

'*Passagiere nach Wien!*' Hiram's porter, a boy in a sailor-suit and cap, was drifting towards the exit gate with his bag . . .

Grunze dead! Rumour! Not in his own home! Some other way! Hiram was suddenly standing alone, far out on a point in stellar space, and the world, whirling, spinning, roaring, was rushing down upon him to crush him. . . .

What did it mean? What had happened? WHY HAD IRMGARDE FORBIDDEN HIM TO ENTER THE SALON? *What had been in there that he must not see?* And now he pictured the room again, the couches and tables, the soft rugs and paintings and the precious knick-knacks scattered about, the ever-burning log-fire. And he saw again the deep wing-chair, with the little black hunchbacked Doctor sitting in it, with his huge head, red lips and deft chin. But now he was leaning back. His arms were at his side. And something was sticking up out of his chest, something curved and bright . . .

Irmgarde! Irmgarde!

Had she? And then a shocking certainty gripped him so hard that he felt it clutch him physically at the nape of his neck. *The man who had laid the snare that had enmeshed Hiram Holliday and nearly brought him to his death would never, while still alive, have given up his 'laissez-passer' from the All Highest to Irmgarde or permitted her to see him.*

There was no choice now. He must go to her at once. As fast as they could take him there. To Moabit, to Moabit, to Moabit prison. Ring the bell, crash his fists against the gates! *Hola! Hola!* Let me in! Let me in! I am Hermann Weide the condemned Communist. . . . The Gräfin Irmgarde von Helm must go free!

Go free! And yet if she had murdered Grunze . . . He turned his back upon the plane for Vienna and moved heavily towards the doors that led from the waiting-room.

He was walking towards the great bulletin board. There were two workmen standing in front of it with bucket, brush and poster. They unfurled it, blood red. Whick! It was smacked up against the board! Sweck! The wet paste-brush smacked across it, and battened it there, gleaming and dripping, the droplets trickling from it in little streams like thin bleeding. . . .

Hiram saw the words, the terrible, burning words:

'FRITZ GORNER
HERMANN WEIDE
EXECUTED TO-DAY NOVEMBER 23 FOR
HIGH TREASON.'

Hermann Weide! Hermann Weide! But he, Hiram Holliday, was Hermann Weide. And he was alive and staring at his own death notice. His own? The poster was blood red, redder than Irmgarde's hair. Irmgarde! Weide! And then the world that had been rushing upon him split open with a crack of thunder and engulfed him, and he knew. Irmgarde had never removed the bandages. That was why he was safe. In crackling flashes he saw and understood. Irmgarde had killed Grunze, forged the order for the prison visit, and from the dead man had taken the powerful pass that had got her through to him. She had lied and acted. With a dead man on her soul she had laughed and acted and made him believe that she was safe. She had meant to die, but to die with one last, desperate reaching for the light and the sun. To die destroying a thing of evil, and giving life to him whom she loved.

When they came in the chilly, grey, November morning to execute sentence upon Hermann Weide, the figure in his clothes had arisen calmly and marched between the guards into the cold, bleak courtyard, where waited the man with the frock-coat and white gloves and silk hat. He saw the grotesquely bandaged head with the steel-bowed spectacles, laid upon the block. Hiram flung his hands before his face and cried aloud:

'Irmgarde! Irmgarde!'

He felt a twitch at his sleeve. It was the sailor-boy with his bag. He said: *'Mein Herr! Das Schiff ist bereit. Gehen sie, oder gehen sie nicht?'*

Hiram stared at him. The boy switched to English: 'Se aeroplan. Iss retty. Come you?' He dragged a little at Hiram's arm. Hiram permitted himself to be led. He did not know that he was walking. The boy led him through the portal and out to the waiting ship. The gate shut behind him with a rolling, sonorous clang that echoed through and through the waiting-room.

FLIGHT FROM VIENNA

*How Hiram Holliday Listened to Folk-Song
in Vienna, and a Princess Obeyed Orders*

IT was the Baron who suggested that Sunday afternoon late
in March, Hiram Holliday's last day in Vienna, that in the line
of a farewell party they go to Franzl's in Grinzing to hear Mitzi
sing *Gassenhauer*, old Viennese folk-songs, later go on to the
Cobenzl Terrace, overlooking all Vienna, for dinner, and
perhaps wind up the evening with one of their absurd whirls
through the 'Wurstl Prater,' the famous old amusement park.
Hiram didn't care. He was leaving Vienna for Rome the next
morning and was gloomy and depressed with a sense of failure,
and yet in a way glad to be going.

They drove out to Grinzing through Döbling and Heiligen-
stadt in Hiram's rented car with Hiram at the wheel, silent, and
Baron Willi von Salvator at his side chattering gaily. The
Baron felt the depression of his strange American friend and
was trying to cheer him. Hiram needed cheering. In Vienna
he had learned that the life of a European correspondent can
sometimes be as drab and routine as – well, perhaps as sitting
fourteen years at a newspaper copy-desk.

Newspapers have their own ways of doing things, and Hiram
knew that he had been sent to the dull post in Vienna for
seasoning and experience, in spite of the series of fantastic and
sensational stories he had turned in to the *New York Sentinel*
almost from the time he had left his post at the copy-desk there
to go to Europe for his first vacation in fourteen years.

He had not wasted his time entirely. He had employed
tutors nights and had worked furiously, and now had a fair
knowledge of French and German. He had acquired the routine
of reading and translating the local press for stories, the daily
visits to the various ministries and consulates, and in a cautious

way had learned how to establish a pay-roll of informants and tipsters, but above all, he had realized that to be of use to a newspaper in a fixed post in a dictatorship such as Nazi Germany, a man must be marked 'dull, unenterprising, amenable,' in the files of the Propaganda Ministry, and definitely 'harmless,' in the dossier of the Gestapo, the secret police.

Hiram steered the car through the slanting, cobbled streets of Grinzing, on the outskirts of Vienna, where were the famous wine restaurants that in the late summer and fall placed green boughs before their doors to announce the *Heuriger*, or new wine. The plight of Vienna and the Austrians, under the Nazi terror had eaten deep into his soul and gave him constant hurt. He had never known the old gay Vienna, but in his stay in the great, grey city, he had learned to feel it pulsing beneath his feet. It was his first experience living in a conquered country, and he was witness to the age-old European custom of the victor guzzling the spoils, and the daily contact with it was harrowing, the persecutions, the disappearances, the constant spying. . . .

After he had been there two months he had been offered a change. It had come in the shape of a curt cable from Beauheld, his managing editor in New York: 'You are doing your job. I like a good soldier. Do you want to try something else?'

Hiram had been sorely tempted to snatch at the relief from the heavy, depressing atmosphere of the tortured city where he had been further oppressed by a sense of personal failure. He had not managed to see the imprisoned Chancellor Schuschnigg, for which his paper readily forgave him since Beauheld was too intelligent to demand miracles. But he had also failed in the three months to find the slightest trace of, or clue to, the whereabouts of the kidnapped Duke Peter von Fürstenhof – and for this he could not forgive himself. His own words spoken that night in gloom-ridden Prague to Princess Heidi were an obligation upon him, words said at the time in the full meaning of Domnei, the ancient chivalry, but which now, as he thought upon them, had the ring of vainglory.

He had cabled Beauheld: 'Thanks, I'll stick,' because the obligation was still unfulfilled. And the task was no nearer completion now that he had his definite orders to quit Vienna and report to Rome for duty. Well, Hiram had told himself, romanticism was one thing, but one learned things from bitter lessons. One of them was not to be a fool. Life was run on a basis of getting on with one's work.

Baron Willi said: '*Rechts hier!* To the right. We go to Franzl's. If Mitzi does not take that ugly look from your face then you have been in Vienna four months for nothing.'

Hiram relaxed into a grin, slowed the car, and swung it to the right up a narrow cobbled street with tiny old one- and two-storey houses with arched doorways and peaked roofs on either side. He would be sorry to leave the Baron. The friendship had in many ways lightened the task of his stay in Vienna. Hiram was by nature a warm hero-worshipper, and his heroes were the stalwart adventurers of the world, the men who could ride and shoot and fly and fight, men who by their courage and physical equipment could live in any age, take care of themselves, and win.

Wilhelm Franz Baron von Salvator was such a man, a former Austrian Army officer, wealthy, an aristocrat, member of the famed Spanish Riding School. He had already at the age of thirty-two, seven years younger than Hiram, fought four duels, three with swords, one with pistols. He was brilliantly handsome, tall, black-haired, blue-eyed with crisp military moustache, accomplished, light-hearted, fearless. It was hard to know what had drawn him to Hiram unless it was Hiram's frank admiration for him in which he liked to bask, or perhaps it was because he felt or guessed a kinship with the plain, quiet American of the steel-rimmed spectacles, tousled sandy hair and roundish face, who in no manner whatsoever was the figure of either hero or adventurer. They had met when it developed that they lived in the same building in the Strohgasse, where Hiram had taken two furnished rooms on the top floor. Chance acquaintance had grown into a genuine friendship.

Franzl's was one of the largest and most famous of the Grinzing restaurants with an arched courtyard into which Hiram drove his car and parked it next to a large black limousine, in which a chauffeur was waiting.

'I was here two weeks ago,' said the Baron, as they climbed out of the car. He screwed his monocle into his left eye, said: '*Die Mitzi! Herrlich!*' He blew a kiss into the grey afternoon sky.

'Thanks for nothing,' said Hiram. 'You kept her for yourself for two weeks. Now that I'm going, I can look. . . .'

The entrance from the courtyard led via a passage to the tiny foyer off the street. Laughter, noise, music, clatter burst upon them, and the smell of wine and beer and cigar smoke. The large room was jammed with people sitting at the rough-hewn tables, as were the two wings that led off from it, one on the right, the other on the left. In the centre in front of the two kitchen doors was a small, square raised platform on which sat the *Schrammel Orchester*, a red-faced band of musicians, in peasant costume, consisting of trumpet, violin, accordion and zither. They were playing a lusty waltz and it seemed to Hiram as though everyone in the room, seated, was swaying slightly to the rhythm. There was no place vacant, but when the proprietor saw Salvator he squeezed a tiny table in close to the door and provided two chairs. The Baron ordered a Gumpolds-kirchner '32 and asked about Mitzi. The waiter said: '*Ja, ja, ja. kommt scho*'.'

The low-beamed room was rocking with gaiety, and Hiram found himself unconsciously thumping the beat of the peasant waltz with the bottom of his heavy wineglass. The waitresses were solid, red-faced, healthily sweating, wearing peasant dresses, with straw-coloured hair coiled in thick knots. Here and there at the tables there was a Brownshirt, or a German Army officer in the grey-blue uniform, and a black-shirted, black-uniformed S.S. man or two. The hot, steamy gaiety of the place was infectious, and Hiram grinned cheerfully at a pretty girl three tables away who had slyly lifted her glass to him.

'Aha,' said Salvator, 'that is better. But is she smiling at you or at me?' They were talking in German.

And suddenly for no apparent cause the band stopped playing and a dead silence smothered every sound in the room. No one moved. Not a glass or a dish rattled. All eyes were turned towards the door. There were two men in plain clothes standing framed in it. Policeman was written all over them. They began to move slowly into the room, threading their way through the closely-packed tables, their eyes shifting rapidly. Suddenly a little man at one side of the restaurant gave a half-strangled cry, rose and tried to run towards the kitchen.

'Halt!' the two men called harshly. The fugitive's flight led him past a table where a sour-faced, bullet-headed Brownshirt sat. The Brownshirt stuck out his hand and seized the fleeing man's coat-tails, saying: '*Na na, Bursche,* not so fast. A couple of people want to see you here.'

The two plain-clothes men fastened upon their victim. Each took an arm. They led him towards the door. The little man's face was grey, and although his mouth was saying something, no sounds came forth. Hiram felt sick to his stomach, and his clenched fists were white at the knuckles. 'My God,' he muttered to Salvator, in English, 'why can't they leave these people alone? All they want is to laugh a little and drink a little. . . .'

When the three were abreast of their table, the Baron cleared his throat and spat. It struck full on the lapel of the plain-clothes man nearest them. The whole crowded room seemed to take part in a long, indrawn gasp. The policeman's face turned a dirty red. He glared at Salvator and his free hand went to his pocket. The Baron sat calmly gazing up at him, his monocle screwed into his eye with a look of absolute cold insolence upon his face.

'My respects,' he said raspingly, 'and apologies for my poor aim.' For a moment the policeman stood glaring, uncertain whether insult had been directed at him or the victim. There was nothing in the chilling stare of the Baron to enlighten him.

Then the three passed out through the door. The band burst into a *Ländler*, dishes rattled, voices picked up, the room was again a-crash with noise. 'By God,' said Hiram, banging the table with his fist, 'that took courage.'

'Nonsense,' said Salvator, lighting a flat, gold-tipped Regie, 'it took – spit. *Na, na! Wo ist die Mitzi?*'

But the lift that Hiram had felt upon coming in to the *Lokal* had vanished. Somehow, the incident, a common enough one to him during his stay there, seemed to crystallize all of those months. Failure . . . failure. This was a country of failure. Gay, light-hearted weaklings. Their new masters, the men of evil, struck. They flinched under the lash, and then ordered a *Frischen Schoppen Wein*, like the Baron, who after his incredibly gallant and insolent gesture which might have cost him his freedom, not to mention his head, merely said: 'Where is Mitzi?'

Hiram was working his fist into his fingers, for now he felt he wanted to go and kill the Brownshirt who had held back the poor frightened little man, when he felt Salvator's hand on his arm. The Austrian spoke to him in English as though he had read his thoughts.

'Come, come, Hiram. . . . Do not be too hard on us. Remember the thing that is called Time. You think you are seeing something that is new and terrible in this Nazism? We are lost? We give in? No, no, my friend. It is not new. It is not Nazism. It is Germany. We have belonged to Germany once before. And before that, Germany has belonged to us, a State of the Habsburg Empire. Then we were strong. Now the German State is strong and we are weak, so we bow before it *und Witze machen über Hitler*, make jokes. The Austrian can always make jokes. And the rest Time does. There is nothing new in Central Europe, nothing that has not happened before. . . .'

Hiram was looking at Salvator curiously. He had never known this side of his friend. The Baron expanded and continued: 'Those pigs?' With his head he indicated the Brownshirts. . . . 'They are always. But when the Monarchy returns to Austria they go back to their stys where they belong. You think because we have had Socialism here, or a republic, that it is over with kings? My friend, it is never over with kings. You cannot wipe out the habits of two thousand years in twenty. The French killed a king, proclaimed a republic and acquired an emperor. It will be so again. We Austrians are monarchists by habit. Monarchy is not dead with us because of events. Power changes, but not human nature. The seat of power in Central Europe, the barrier against the East, and the tides of the yellow races, is not Germany, but Austria. History has proven that. It will be so again. . . .'

'You mean Otto, or one of his brothers . . .' suggested Hiram.

'*Ach*,' said Salvator, and dismissed Otto and his clan with a flip of his cigarette. 'Time, Hiram, Time. History strides not in days or months, but in quarter- or half-centuries. The Ottos will be gone when the wheel turns again.' He dropped his voice suddenly and shifted closer. 'There is in Austria now, today, a boy – you are leaving tomorrow. I can tell you this. He is of the Hapsburg blood, but the clean and good strain. He is in the hands of the Nazis. When the Nazis took Austria, his aunt, the Princess Fürstenhof of Styria, escaped with him and the Fürstenhof fortune. The Germans stole him from her and brought him back and are holding him for the return of the money. When the money is paid they will probably kill him. But before that can happen, he will be rescued. There is already an organization here in Austria. Perhaps I, Willi Salvator, will be the one who will find him and bring him to safety. And thirty years from now, maybe forty, that boy will sit upon the throne of a Middle-European Empire. Think in large terms, my friend.' He paused, gave his moustache a twist, and waited to see the effect upon his friend. It was disappointing.

'Hmmmmmm,' said Hiram, and lit an American cigarette with a hand whose steadiness surprised even him. Here it was again, and he had to face it. Holliday, the great adventurer! Sardonically he bowed to the Fate that had dealt him this last slap in the face before his departure. It was the Salvators who were gaited for such play, not the Hollidays. He drew what comfort he could from the knowledge that his friend would go on where he had failed, and probably succeed.

A sudden loud burst of hand-clapping brought him back, and a yell from the Baron who had raised his glass and was toasting: 'Mitzi . . . Mitzi. . . . Die Schoene, Mitzi. . . .'

And Hiram turned to look at the girl who had stepped up on to the stage and was preparing to sing. She had glossy, chestnut-coloured hair parted in the centre and worn in two braids, the braids coiled into little buns, one around each ear. She was dressed in a Dirndl costume, with a neat embroidered apron over a red dress. She was standing with her hands beneath the apron, swaying a little to the rhythm of the vamp the orchestra was playing. Her face was red and shining, and there was a dimple in her cheek. Even from the distance at which they sat Hiram could see that her eyes were blue and dancing. She was smiling softly and gazing all around the room, taking in every table. When she suddenly looked him straight in the face Hiram's heart crashed against his ribs again and again until her glance passed on and she began to sing in the quaint Viennese dialect:

> 'Weist du Mutterl was i tramt hob,
> I hob im Himmel eini g'sehen,
> Do warn so viele schoene Engerl,
> Zu dennen mag i gerne gehen. . . .'

Hiram put his head between his hands for a moment and held it, and then looked up again at the girl, and in doing so stared on beyond her into the wing on the right where his gaze held at one of the tables and the group of people sitting there. And then for the first time his hand shook violently, so much so that he spilled his wine and had to put his glass down. Salvator saw nothing because he was enchanted with Mitzi. He kept saying over and over: 'Entzückend . . . entzückendes Kind . . .' and then to Hiram: 'Isn't she an enchanting child?'

It brought Hiram back with a start from the mad, unreasonable places where he had been. 'What? Eh? Yes, she's good. Very good.'

'*Ach*,' said Salvator half-angrily. 'Very good. You are not flesh and blood, you Americans. It's that damned ice-water you drink all the time. I show you a Viennese enchantress who looks like an angel and sings about angels and you say very good. Is there nothing that can get you out of your mood?'

'Yes,' said Hiram Holliday suddenly and flatly, 'there is. Look, Willi, those people in the other room at the right, the third table on the wall from the archway, the fat man. Do you know them?'

The Baron half-rose from his chair to see better, and stared through his monocle. There was a fat man at the table with a woman, tall, elderly, angular, and a child, the latter with his back to them. But it was the man who caught and held his eye, because he was enormous, a mountain of obesity with a round, shining dome of a head, naked of hair. Ripples and rings of fat rose out of his huge collar, he looked like the rubber man of a famous old-time French tyre advertisement. He had a huge stone crock of beer in front of him which he rested on his swelling chest when he drank. The woman was drinking wine. The rough, tousled hair of the child just showed above the back of his chair.

Salvator sat down laughing. '*Ach*,' he said, 'the fat one and his family? A typical Viennese high-liver. Put it in your book of types. Stuffed with beer and *foie gras*. The fatter he gets, the thinner his wife grows. *Aus Ekel*. Out of disgust. I never saw them before.'

Hiram grunted and said nothing. He was watching Mitzi again. She was singing another song, this time a broad *Gassenhauer* – in a rough voice, her hands on her swinging hips. She had turned so as to face the right wing:

'*I hob zwei habi Rappa ...*'

She checked suddenly as though the second line would not come, or she had forgotten it. Hiram saw that she was staring

161

at the fat man who had not even turned his head to look at her. Then she caught the second line:

'Keine besser'n finds du nicht . . . '

No one but Hiram noticed anything, Hiram whose breath was suddenly coming fast and hard from the turmoil of the emotions that boiled within him. The girl finished her song, made a curtsy and left the stage. The applause was long and loud, and insistent, but she did not come back. The orchestra struck up another piece. In the wings, the fat man and his family were making motions towards paying their bill, gathering up belongings. Salvator turned to say something to Hiram, and stopped with his mouth open. The placid roundness had gone out of the American's face somehow, his hair was up on end and the light blue eyes behind the steel-rimmed spectacles were shining with what to the Baron looked like madness. He seemed even to have grown in stature and his stoutish figure to have taken on a hardness. He was on his feet and had dropped a ten-mark note on the table. Then he had Willi by the arm. 'Come on,' he said, and even the voice was different. 'At once.' The Baron had been a soldier long enough to know a command. He followed Hiram out of the door and down the long passage-way to the courtyard exit, expostulating:

'Hiram! Are you crazy? What is the matter?'

They were at the door. 'There's no time,' said Hiram. 'Do. Do what I tell you. I'm relying on you. Go and get in the car. Take the driver's seat and start the engine. Put it in gear but hold the clutch out. You may be joined by someone in the back seat. Say nothing. Appear to occupy yourself. Keep your hat well pulled down over your face. Sit and wait until I give you the word. Then go like all hell for Vienna.'

A figure suddenly appeared in the adjoining doorway, leading apparently to the kitchen, a woman in a green *loden* cape with the hood over her head. Hiram did not hesitate an instant. He went to her and said: 'Mitzi! There is no time to talk now. Do as I say and there is a chance. Go to that blue car next to the big one. Follow that man. Get in back and sit quietly. . . .'

162

She went immediately without a word.

Salvator had half-turned around and seen the girl. 'Yessus Maria, it's Mitzi. And I said that you were all ice-water. Hui! That is the fastest work I have ever seen, my friend.'

'God damn it, go on,' Hiram yelped savagely.

Baffled, and shaking his head, Salvator got into the car, started the engine and waited with his foot pressing the clutch pedal down. He heard the girl climb into the rear seat. Hiram went back a little into the passageway until he heard heavy footsteps. 'It's got to be,' he said to himself. 'God, let it be. It must be his car. . . .'

Figures came down the passage. Hiram turned his back and walked slowly across the courtyard towards his car, calling out to Salvator in German: 'What do you think, shall we drive out to Cobenzl?'

The Baron took his cue. 'We could. It's still early.'

Hiram put one foot on the step of his car, opening the rear door as he did so, and then bent over and began to worry his shoe-laces. His back was to the big black limousine next to them. He heard the engine start, and bending his head still more he could see the elephant of a fat man with his angular companion holding the child by the hand coming across the courtyard. He heard the door of the limousine open on the other side and knew that the woman had helped the boy up first and had followed him, the chauffeur assisting. Hiram waited until the heavy puffing and grunting told him that the man was attempting to edge his enormous girth into the car and then struck.

He made a series of motions and they were so fast that there was almost no time between the sounds. He whirled, ripped open the door of the big black car, snatched the boy from the seat, holding him close, slammed the door shut, dumped the child on to the floor of his own car, slammed that door, tore open the front door, threw himself in yelling: 'Now, Willi! Move! Duck, everyone!'

And they were turning the corner of the courtyard into the street before the first scream from the woman, the bull-like roar of the man and a sharp explosion, reached their ears. The bullet went 'Wang-YEEEE-eeeeeeee' off the body of the car, and they were down the street, turning a corner, doubling another, cutting in and out of the Sunday traffic, Hiram looking back, and the Baron grinning like a fiend and handling the car as though it were a racer on a track. The big black limousine was not in sight as they headed towards Vienna again after back-tracking through the narrow streets of Neu Gersthof.

'*Ganz brilliant gemacht,*' said Baron Willi. Through the mirror he could see that the girl had the boy in her arms and was sobbing. 'Would it be too much to inquire of you whom we have kidnapped just in case a policeman should ask me?'

Hiram laughed triumphantly. 'You're a hell of an Austrian, Willi,' he said. 'Keep on going. You've got Princess Adelheit von Fürstenhof and her nephew, Duke Peter, the next Emperor of Central Europe, in the back of the car. And that fat guy was Dr Anton Virslany, the most dangerous Nazi agent in Europe.'

'Yessus Maria!' said the Baron Willi again, and took a corner on two wheels, and then slowed the car down to a sedate pace. He looked at Hiram as though he were some strange animal. 'And what do we do now?'

Hiram's heart was surging with elation. He hadn't failed. . . . 'To the Wurstl Prater. Protective colouration. It's the last place they'll look for us. . . .'

How Hiram Holliday Puzzled a Small Duke and Patronized a Shooting-Gallery

The Duke Peter was enchanted. His beloved Aunt Heidi had been returned to him and he was in the Wurstl Prater. His Uncle Virslany, the fat man who had taken him from Prague, had never gone to the Wurstl Prater with him. He had behaved with Uncle Virslany, because the uncle had promised him that soon he would see Heidi again, and so he had waited instead of trying to run away. And it had all come true, just as it had been promised, except, the colour of Heidi's hair was different. And Uncle Hiram was there, too, and a new, strange, nice man with fine moustaches. And here they were in the Prater, the gay, wonderful Prater where a band was making fine music, and people in Sunday dress were walking and children were screaming and playing on all sides, and there was a Punch and Judy show, and they went on all the exciting rides, and jaunts, ponies and scenic railways and boats, through the dark tunnels where every so often they came upon little miniature scenes out of fairy-tales, and the wonderful trip on the Giant Wheel that took them so high that all Vienna lay at their feet.

Uncle Hiram and Uncle Willi – that was the name of the new man – did strange things sometimes, but they were always exciting things. And Uncle Hiram could talk German now. That was wonderful because now he could speak with him. The nine-year-old Duke had been puzzled when Uncle Hiram had insisted upon leaving their beautiful blue car, so much prettier than Uncle Virslany's black one, in a side street, and had called a taxi-cab, but the taxi-cab had taken them straight to the Prater, and that was all that had mattered. And Aunt Heidi seemed to know who Uncle Willi was, and like him. How good it was to be back again with people he really loved.

Once, during the boat ride through the black tunnel, the Duke Peter had asked: 'Aunt Heidi, why is the colour of your hair different? It was so pretty when it was golden,' and Aunt Heidi had placed her soft hand over his mouth, and whispered: 'Shhh, Peter, my sweet. Do not talk. Understand there is much danger. Just enjoy yourself with us. I had to change my hair to be with you sooner, to help to find you. It will be golden again, I promise you, only do not speak, whatever you see, whatever happens.'

The Duke was puzzled that Heidi should have had to change the colour of her hair to find him, because Uncle Virslany had been promising him that Heidi was coming all the time, but consoled himself with the idea that perhaps they were all playing the game again, like the time in London when some strange men had tried to steal him and Uncle Hiram had made

165

him pretend that he was a little English boy going to the country. Grown-up people always did strange things and talked in strange, un-understandable ways, not sensibly like young people. For instance what had the new Uncle Willi meant when he had said: 'It will be almost impossible to get out. They will forge an iron ring around Austria,' and Uncle Hiram had replied: 'Hm. . . . Well, perhaps if we can't break it we can bend it a little.'

And again in the boat tunnel, just as they had come to the delectable scene of Snow White and the Seven Dwarfs, he had heard his Aunt Heidi say: 'This strange play of Fate, Hiram. Always, when all hope is gone, it is you who appears. When I did not hear for so long, I had to do something. They were pressing me to ransom him. When I was a little girl in Styria the peasants taught me the old folk-songs. I thought if I changed the colour of my hair and worked in Grinzing, that sooner or later I would see Virslany and through that find Peter. But if it hadn't been for you . . .'

'For Willi,' Uncle Hiram had said. 'If it hadn't been his idea to go to hear Mitzi sing, and his handling of the car. . . .'

No, these snatches of conversation were nothing for a small boy, though he was sharp enough to gather from what he heard later that his Uncle Virslany was not a good man, that he had stolen him, and that he had never meant him to see his beloved Heidi again.

But that which happened at the shooting-gallery! Ah, that was something! *Jucheee!* Hurrah for Uncle Hiram! Hurrah for new Uncle Willi. It had started when they walked down the Hauptallee of the Prater after the most wonderful Merry-go-Round ride, in which Uncle Willi had pretended he was a cavalry officer on his horse and rode like a king, and Heidi and Uncle Hiram and he, Peter, had had a race, and they all laughed as though they were mad and said that Peter had won and was the best rider of them all.

On the Hauptallee, on both sides of which there were the most wonderful booths, Uncle Hiram kept looking back all the time, and all around, as though he were searching for someone

166

he expected to meet, and once he took Uncle Willi by the arm suddenly and then they both looked back, and quite strangely they all seemed to be walking a little faster, which Peter did not like because he was getting tired. But then Uncle Hiram had said: 'I think we will all just go to a shooting-gallery and see who is the best shot.' Hurrah, what fun! How Peter loved shooting-galleries. And were they really going to let him shoot? Now he was glad to hurry, too, and when Hiram turned around again and he looked back also, all he could see was three men walking together a little way behind them.

The shooting-gallery was wonderful, with iron clowns that had targets in their middles, and when you hit the bull's-eye they beat on drums and clashed cymbals, and there were clay-pipes and clay-birds to shoot at, and rabbits that were attached to a wheel that went around, and an egg that was miraculously balanced on an upshooting stream of water, and he was given a gun and allowed to shoot real bullets while Uncle Hiram and Uncle Willi had a brave contest with little shot-guns with two barrels, blazing at cardboard ducks that were pulled up to the ceiling on a string, and when they hit them with the little tiny shot, no bigger than poppy seeds, the ducks would flutter to the ground. And while the two men were shooting, they were talking things that Peter could make neither head nor tail of, such as when Uncle Hiram said:

'We're in for it, Willi.'

And Uncle Willi replied: 'Yes. You are right. Was that why we came here?'

'Yes. It is rough, but it cannot be helped. Who has not eyes cannot see. For God's sake, don't miss.'

At that moment Peter's gun was empty and while the man was reloading it he had turned to see what Heidi was doing, and she was looking very pale and frightened and was reaching for his hand. Perhaps, thought Peter, it was because of those three men who were now coming over to them, each with a hand in his pocket. Something in their faces frightened even Peter, and when one of them said: 'Yes, that is they!' and they came nearer, he crowded to Heidi, but Uncles Hiram and Willi just turned quietly around with their silly little guns in their big hands, and the little guns suddenly went 'peng – pang – peng – pang,' like fire-crackers going off, and then there was the most tremendous excitement, with people screaming and crowds running and trampling, and the three men were yelling and spinning around, half-doubled up, tearing at their eyes with their hands, and there was even some blood, Peter saw it on their faces, and Willi and Hiram at first seemed to be helping the three men until the crowd grew bigger, and then all of a sudden they were out of the pushing and yelling and turmoil, in the middle of things, and came back and took him and Heidi by the hand, and they all slipped behind the shooting-gallery booth and went through some bushes and across a lawn, where they all got into one of the tiny cars of a miniature train pulled by a little locomotive no bigger than a St Bernard dog, but perfect in every detail, that was just starting out for a trip around the Prater, and the locomotive went 'Hooo hoooo, ding, ding, ding, ding,' and off it went chuffing just like a real train, and when it got to the other end of the Prater, they got out at one of the exits and all went into a taxi-cab. Hui! What fun and excitement there was for a boy when Uncle Hiram was around. . . .

How Hiram Holliday Met the Ancestors of the Princess Heidi

On Sunday night, Vienna goes to bed early. By half-past ten the streets were almost deserted. It was cold and there was a chilling drizzle falling out of a fog that hung down over the house-tops and spun a halo around the street lights. Two men, a girl, and a small boy came from the more brightly lighted Kärntner Strasse, the Broadway of Vienna, through the short Schwangasse and crossed hurriedly to the west side of the darkened Neumarkt, skirting the lovely Donner Fountain. As they went a military car with four officers riding in it came crashing out of the Schwangasse and caught them in its head-lights for an instant.

'Steady ... steady ...' said Hiram. He could feel Heidi's arm trembling under his hand. They were wet, cold and hungry. They had not eaten, and dared not go into any restaurant or store. They had heard the radio on the street cry out that their arrest was wanted – two men, a girl and a boy. They had had to abandon cabs. There had been another narrow escape when they brazened the Kärntner Strasse. Hiram's luck on taking to crowded, frequented places was running out. It was Heidi who had saved them, by breaking suddenly into nasal, high-pitched French scolding Peter shrilly, and when the startled boy burst into tears, and replied in French: *'Mais, je n'ais rien fait ...'* they were passed by as tourists.

In the light of the car-lamps, the Baron suddenly gave a little tipsy skip, faced sideways, teetering precariously on the kerb and raised his arm in the Nazi salute. There was a burst of contemptuous laughter, and the iron car rolled on past.

'It's here,' said Heidi. They were in front of the plain, austere white facade of the baroque Kapuziner Kirche. Heidi counted two doors from the closed entrance of the church. There was an iron portal there under an arch.

'Are you sure?' said Hiram Holliday. For the first time, his voice was strained and anxious.

'Oh, yes ... yes .. I must be,' breathed Heidi.

Hiram rapped sharply on the iron door with the edge of a coin held in his fist so that the knock rang unmistakably. He counted many seconds before there was an answer. It came in a deep, sonorous voice, and it sounded muffled and hollow as though caverns lay behind the iron barrier. 'Who is there?'

Hiram Holliday spoke rapidly, as loudly as he dared. 'In God's name let us in. It is the Duke Peter of Styria, and the Princess Fürstenhof.'

There was a moment of pause, and then the voice boomed like a muffled bell from behind the door: 'We do not know you.'

'Verdammt!' snapped the Baron. 'Open the door, I tell you. I am Willi Franz von Salvator. The Duke and the Princess are in great danger. ...'

Again the voice tolled the words that sounded like the ringing of the doomsday bell: 'We – do – not – know – you.'

Cars were passing. Any moment, one of them might stop, men would pile out reaching for them. . . . Hiram was white and shaking with rage and helpless exasperation.

'Wait. . . . Oh, wait,' Heidi whispered. . . . 'I remember now. From when I was a little girl. The ritual of the Hapsburg dead when they seek entrance here for their eternal rest. Wait. . . .'

She rapped on the iron door with her knuckles. Hiram thought that this time they would no longer answer, it took so long. But again the question came: 'Who is there?'

And Heidi answered: 'Four humble Christian souls who are weary and seek rest and sanctuary. . . .'

A bolt shot with a sharp 'Spang!' Slowly the great iron door swung open. A huge, brown-robed monk stood framed in a passage-way. His full beard came almost to his waist and his eyes glittered in the light of a taper he held aloft. For a moment he contemplated them. Then he spoke, but this time gently.

'Leave behind all earthly titles, ye who enter here. Come in. You are welcome, my children.'

They poured into the passage-way and heard the monk close and bolt the door behind them and, too, they heard a car pass with a siren wailing, but the sound of its rising cry was dampened now, as though it came from another world.

There was a long flight of stone steps, downward, at the end of the passage. The monk lighted them down, marching ahead with the smoking taper. There was another corridor at the bottom of the steps and then another shorter flight. It led them into a plain, white marble vault, the walls faced with Carrara. Candles burned in wall-brackets. Four bronze sarcophagi stood in the vault. Hiram could see that other vaults opened out from the one they were in. It was a place of sombre grandeur.

'Where are we?' he asked.

The monk smiled. He had wonderful white teeth. 'You are in

the Kapuziner Gruft, the burial place of the House of Hapsburg.'

And then Hiram knew why Heidi had come there. After the narrow escape on the Kärntner Strasse he had said savagely: 'Civilization! Damn! If this were in the Middle Ages, we could at least find sanctuary,' and Heidi had said suddenly: 'Yes ... yes. ... Sanctuary. I think I know where. Come with me.'

And so she had brought the little Duke Peter home to the shelter of his ancestors.

The Baron was outlining their story rapidly to the monk whose name was Brother Leopold and who listened gravely until Salvator had finished. Then he said: 'Those things have not touched us yet. We live with the dead. You may remain here for the night. You will be safe. Come, let us go above, where you shall eat and dry your clothes. In the morning we will determine what is to be done.'

Hiram suddenly noticed that Heidi and the boy were no longer with them.

'Peter. ... The Princess! Where are they?' he said.

Brother Leopold glanced in the direction of the large vault behind them. He said: 'They went in there.'

Hiram looked. Only a single candle burned in the chamber. He went over to Brother Leopold and indicated the taper in his hand. 'May I?' he said. Then, holding the light high over his head, he turned and descended the step into the grotto. He had advanced no more than a few yards when he stopped. For he saw there a sight that he was never to forget as long as he lived.

The vault was domed, and in the waxing and waning yellow light of the fluttering paper, Hiram saw that the ceiling was painted with a Biblical scene. In the centre, slightly raised on a stone dais, stood a great bronze double sarcophagus. On the cover were two figures in bronze, half-reclining, crowned and sceptred, their hands folded, the fingers pointing to heaven, and Hiram knew that they were the effigies of Maria Theresa, Austria's greatest queen, and her husband, Francis of Lorraine.

And the light of his flickering taper showed Hiram, too, that at the foot of the great Royal bronze coffin there knelt the Princess Heidi and the Duke Peter.

They were kneeling there, silent, in the ancient classic attitude of prayer, palms together like the figures of the tomb, their heads bowed over them, and the flame of the burning wax showed the yellow, ruffled hair of the boy and the chestnut, dark-dyed coils of Heidi's braids. The hood of her cape was thrown slightly back and its folds draped her like the bronze folds of the Royal robes on the cover of the great sarcophagus. Heidi's lips were moving silently. And with a cold, thrilling chill, as though an icy wind had blown through the grotto, Hiram Holliday suddenly realized that the living blood of the mouldered great in their metal tomb coursed through the veins of the two children who knelt at their feet to make their prayer.

He stood there, plain Hiram Holliday, holding his taper aloft and gazing down upon them. Who was he, and who were they? Duke and Princess Royal, seed and fruit of the ancient house of Hapsburg, a boy and a lovely girl, and about them the dust of the men and the women, and their children, too, who had ruled in Europe for six hundred years. And Hiram Holliday, ex-chair-holder of the copy-desk of the *New York Sentinel*, foreign correspondent and would be king-maker.

Six hundred years and the bones in every leaden or bronzed coffin in the great burial grotto stood between this girl and himself. He thought suddenly of the line attributed to Maximilian the First, the greatest of Hapsburg princes who ruled all Central Europe: 'Austria does not make war. She marries.' For nearly three hundred years these Hapsburgs had ruled Germany as well as Austria. Salvator had been right. The wheel had turned. It would turn again. What right had fifty years to say that the day of Royalty and pomp was done, fifty against so many thousands? . . . Who could say that this boy would not some day wear the Hapsburg crown . . . if . . . Ah, if!

King-maker . . . king-maker. . . . Would there be any then to say that years ago an American, named Hiram Holliday, had

172

saved King Peter from the Germans and brought him safely out of the country? What was the fate of the king-makers? Ingratitude, oblivion. . . . Who remembered them?

There was no sound in the vault, but Hiram imagined his own breathing was the rustle of the dead. Here they lay, and because of these pinches of dust and whitened bones enough blood had been spilled to fill the Danube from Vienna to the Black Sea.

Who remembered the king-makers? And then Hiram knew that he did not care. One could not sit upon a throne unless one were born to it. One could aspire to a princess, and never achieve her. But one could, sometimes if one were called and blessed, for one brief moment move the King and Queen upon the chessboard of history.

History! The word seemed to ring through Hiram's mind like a deep, thrilling bell. Was this history, this little bit of dirt in carved boxes, all that remained of a great house? Or was it in the flesh and blood of the two who knelt and prayed? Or was it he, Hiram Holliday, himself for a moment? Would the curved dome of the painted ceiling close in and crush him for the rashness of his thought?

Perhaps, thought Hiram, because he was where he was and saw what he saw, he had lost Heidi for ever. The lightness and gaiety was out of the adventure of the fair-haired Princess and the lost Duke. These who were entombed here had been served and loved, and those who had served and loved them had vanished even as they. Hiram Holliday could, if he chose, love and serve too, and make his faint mark upon the blank page of things to come, and vanish too.

The boy and the girl finished their prayers and arose. Heidi took Peter by the hand and led him away. The child was sleepy and his eyes were barely open, but on Heidi's face there was the expression of one who looks into great and deep distances. She had to pass close by Hiram, but she never saw him as she went, or knew that he was there, as she climbed the step and passed into the other room where Brother Leopold and Salvator were waiting.

For another moment Hiram remained looking at the bronze effigies. He raised his hand in a queer sort of half-gestured salute to them. Then he extinguished the taper and followed after Heidi.

How Hiram Holliday and the Princess Were Cornered on the Roof of the World

During the night the Baron Salvator slipped out of the monastery. It was safe for him to do so because his connexion with the fugitives was not even known. And the next day Hiram Holliday was introduced to something he had long suspected, but never would have seen under any other circumstances – the underground railway out of Austria for aristocratic suspects and political refugees.

At nine o'clock in the morning a small, closed delivery-van drove into the monastery. On its sides was painted the legend: '*Bäckerei Lanzer, – Mödling.*' It discharged sundry loaves of bread and packages of rolls and also the Baron Salvator who said: 'It isn't *de luxe*, but it will get us where we must be by tonight. Tickets, please. . . .'

They received the blessing of Brother Leopold and climbed in. The stolid-looking driver came around and closed and locked the rear doors of the van. Light filtered through from a small window back of the front seat. They felt that they were moving. The Baron spread out a map of Austria on the floor and they knelt around it. For the first time Hiram was glad that matters were out of his hands. From now on they were in Salvator's keeping. The Baron indicated a wavering, winding route that wandered down through Styria, crossed Salzburg and the Tyrol and ended at the Swiss border. 'Once we are into the Tyrol,' he said, 'we are practically safe. The Tyroleans do not love the Germans. We are spending the first night at the château of my cousin near Krumbach.'

Hiram studied the map, and with a finger traced the Italian border. He said suddenly: 'Heidi. What has become of your . . . of Count Mario?'

The girl looked startled for a moment. 'I . . . I do not know. He was recalled to Italy without notice shortly after I left Prague for Paris.'

The sudden surge of joy and hope that went through Hiram belied his experience of the night before. He quelled it fiercely. The picture of Heidi kneeling came back to him. Aloud he said: 'Damn! In bad? I mean, out of favour?'

Again Heidi hesitated before she replied: 'I . . . I do not know. I have not heard from him.'

Salvator raised an eyebrow and looked at Hiram, who explained briefly, 'The Count Mario d'Aquila is the fiancé of Princess Fürstenhof. . . .'

'So?' said the Baron Salvator and fell to studying the map again. But Hiram had seen his face. Salvator, too? And yet, why not? A Salvator could marry a Fürstenhof. Blood. . . . He hated the word. Blood and perdition! The men through whose veins these so-called noble streams had flowed had taken what they wanted and held it by their strength. Wasn't it acts and deeds that ennobled? He fell to bitter introspection. What acts, what deeds were there for him, a stoutish reporter, close to middle age? Heidi was for heroes, for men who could take her and hold her. . . .

That night a servant of the château reported that an enormous elephant of a fat man, a stranger, had taken lodgings at the hostel in the village a few miles away, and was asking questions: 'Had anyone seen or heard of a girl, a boy and two men travelling together in the neighbourhood?'

'Damn,' said Hiram. 'Virslany. . . . I'm sure of it. He knows that unless he doesn't get the boy back he'll spend the rest of his life in a concentration camp. We've got to move.'

They left at five o'clock in the morning, this time in a furniture van.

They went west and southwards, always ahead of their pursuit, but never far enough. They travelled in vans, in horse carts, once even for a long stretch on horseback, which Peter loved. But Hiram was worried. The Baron's underground route was far from perfect, and several times they had had to switch destinations, or remain in their van because of advance information grape-vined that Virslany had put in an appearance in a village for which they were bound. Hiram was sure that the secret agent was out-guessing them, for if Virslany knew exactly where they were he would strike. But he didn't KNOW. He suspected, and where he suspected, he appeared, asking his eternal questions. He never seemed to have anyone with him.

They tried going north-eastward again for two days, hoping to throw him off. He did not appear. It was almost as though he knew they were headed away from the border again. They went south to avoid Innsbruck and headed for the Brenner Pass. At Stafflach they paused at the Weisser Hirsch, where the proprietor was one of the links in the far-flung chain of the system. They were in a closed pedlar's wagon that they had procured at the last stop in the north where they had had two days of rest and comparative safety. Salvator himself was driving it. The fugitives inside the wagon were stiff and cramped. They had been under way many hours.

Salvator climbed down from the driver's seat and stretched himself, drinking in the clear, cold air. They were high in the mountains now. The Weisser Hirsch had a roof porch. Out on to it came an enormously gross and obese man swathed in bundles of clothes until he looked like a great, dark, round ball. He came to the edge of the rail and stood there looking down, his round, naked, pudding of a face wreathed in the steam of his wheezing breath. The proprietor of the inn came out, his hands stuck in the pockets, sauntering leisurely, and said: 'Nothing today, thank you. Have you those glasses with you for the Adler Hütte at St Jodok? They are anxious for them there.'

'*Ja, ja*,' said the Baron, and climbed lazily back into the driving seat. 'I am going there now.' Inside the van Hiram was in a cold sweat.

'He! – you pedlar,' called out Virslany from the porch above, 'do you have any pistol cartridges?'

Salvator tipped his cap as he swung the car around, and said: 'Sorry, Your Worship. Not permitted.' The fat man frowned and turned away. They took the road to St Jodok in line with the suggestion of the inn-keeper. They had escaped only because Virslany did not *know* Salvator. But had they? Was Virslany only playing with them? An idea was gnawing at Hiram's mind, one he could not catch, or pin down. It had been growing for many days, but he had not spoken his fears to Heidi or Salvator.

At St Jodok, at the Adler Hütte, the news was bad. Anton, the proprietor, a powerful Tyrolean, came out, smoking his long-stemmed pipe, and leaned on the front of the little van, apparently chatting affably and bargaining. But what he said was:

'The Brenner is closed. On the Swiss border they have struck. They came to the *schloss* of Graf Bentingen and took him away. It is useless to go there. You cannot stay here. I am suspected. There were two men here three days ago and they asked many questions. It is good you did not try to go through Innsbruck. Go east again, and wait. It is safer. You can go to Ginzling. Go to Franz Gussler's hut. The road is still open. Good luck!'

Eventually, Hiram and Salvator sat before a log-fire in the mountain hut of Franz Gussler at the mouth of the Floitental, outside of Ginzling. Heidi and the child had been put to bed, exhausted. It had been snowing for eight hours. The van would be useless for transportation for many days. Behind them, almost sheerly, rose the great white wall of the Grosser Löffler, rising to twelve thousand feet, barring them from Italy. Running into the wall a sharp angle from north to south was the Rosswund, another icy, ragged group of peaks of the great range of Zillerthaler Alps. From one of the windows of the hut Hiram could see the line of the funicular that carried the little cage-car six miles over land and then hauled it up six thousand feet to the great Schwarzenstein Hotel that lay snuggled on the mountain slope to the south-west of the Grosser Löffler.

The Baron had lost his gaiety which had been unfailing

during the flight. He said: 'I knew our luck was too good at the start. We should have got through if Bentingen had not been taken. Apparently, the Nazis had better information than . . .'

'Willi,' said Hiram Holliday, 'give me that map.' He unfolded it, and with a pencil traced another line on it, the route of their dangerous, tedious journey. Then he marked with an 'x' the villages where Dr Virslany had been seen or reported, and further shaded the portions leading to the borders where they had been advised it was dangerous to go.

'We've been herded,' Hiram said. 'I've felt it, but I wasn't sure. I am now. They've been stalking us like animals. Do you see it?'

The Baron nodded gloomily. 'But if they knew, why did they not take us?'

'But they never knew. They couldn't find us. And so they played it blind. Only Virslany could have conceived it. Look. The Gestapo, with the aid of the military, concentrates on the borders. Word gets around to your own people that it has been made impossible to get through. A few of them are arrested. They get the wind-up and warn us off. Closing the borders that way leaves Virslany free to conduct the search – his search. Look how the x's are grouped, and then see our line. For all his weight, Virslany is tireless. He travels constantly from village to village asking questions. He is playing a kind of blindfold chess.

'He says to himself: "Where I am, where I have been, they will not be. They will be elsewhere, either north or south of my imaginary line. I will then go to the north. If they are in the north I will drive them south. If they are not in the north then they are already in the south and I will go there next and eventually corner them." You see how he has zig-zagged? Two out of five times he hit us even though he did not know we were in the same village. Here and there he must have picked up scraps to guide him, leaks, tipsters. The only time he miscalculated was when we back-tracked. But he didn't mind that, because as long as we were heading back into

Austria he didn't care. The longer we stayed in Austria the sooner we would be betrayed.

'Now look here. We are coming into South Tyrol, and are running out of places to go. It is like cornering the king in chess. You see how he drives us up into this pocket. . . .'

Baron Salvator groaned. 'It is brilliant. Brilliant. We . . . I have been played with. And now here we sit like birds in a net waiting for him to come and pick us out. We cannot leave, but he can come in by sleigh. Hiram, my friend, what is there left to do? *Das süsse Mädel*. Hah! When he comes, I shall kill him.'

Hiram shook his head. 'It wouldn't do. That would be the end for us. But there is always one move left when mate is imminent.'

'Yes. . . .'

'Deeper into the trap. We will make him reach for us. We will move on to the square where the next move made by the enemy will end it. And there is not a chess-player worth the name who will not hesitate a moment before making the mate move under those circumstances.'

Salvator frowned. 'But in the end it's still mate . . .'

'In chess,' said Hiram Holliday. 'But we are human beings. Rules limit what a chessman may do. Nothing limits a human being but his own capabilities. When he is driven into a corner . . .'

'There is no place left to go. You have said it yourself. He has driven us as far as we can go, the van is useless.'

Hiram looked out of the window at the thin black thread of the funicular against the white of the mountain barrier. 'We will go up to the Schwarzenstein,' he said.

Salvator stared at him. 'What the devil have you in your mind, Hiram?'

'Nothing – yet.'

Dr Anton Virslany came to the end of his quest with a sigh of relief. It had not been love of his work or country, but fear that had made him carry his enormous bulk on the blind chase for the three who had taken the Duke Peter from him, the Princess Fürstenhof, the American corespondent, Hiram Holliday, and the unknown. He stood in the depot of the funicular railroad and interrogated the conductor. With him were two police officers and four soldiers. The conductor was frightened. Yes, he remembered taking up a dark-haired girl and a young boy, and a man with a round face and steel-rimmed eye-glasses. Yes, there was another man with them. When was it? Hmmmm. Three ... no, four days ago, because on the trip back the line had been out of order for two hours. Had they come down? No, they had not. He was certain he would have remembered. The young lady was extraordinarily good-looking.

The obese Doctor rubbed his hands. Good. They would go up. But it was five o'clock in the afternoon and the last trip had been made. Ah, the Herr Doktor had a special authorization? Please enter. The machinery began to hum. The hanging car moved up towards the Schwarzenstein.

It arrived there at six. Then Dr Virslany commanded it to wait and posted two soldiers at the gate. With the others he went directly to Herr Matthias, the proprietor of the huge resort known as the Schwarzenstein Hotel.

'The four who arrived here last Monday, Herr Matthias, two men, a girl, and a young boy about nine years ...'

'Ah, you mean perhaps the Princess Fürstenhof, Duke Peter, and the American gentleman, Mr Holliday. ...'

Dr Virslany's eyes started from his head. They had used their own names? He was shaken, but he recovered. 'Yes ... yes. Where are they?'

'Hmmm,' said Herr Matthias, and permitted himself a long draw at his Tyroler pipe. 'They were off ski-ing this afternoon. Toni and Seppl are with them. They ordered a special supper to celebrate the expected arrival of a friend. They should be back by now. It is almost dark.'

'I will wait,' said Dr Virslany. 'You are to notify me at once when they return.'

He posted the two policemen at the ski-house. The other

two soldiers he took with him on to the glass-enclosed terrace where he sat down. While he waited, he watched with enjoyment the group of ski roysterers studying the half-moon that was rising out of the mountains to the east, through the huge Zeiss six-inch telescope that was a feature of Herr Matthias' magnificently equipped establishment. Any moment now the quarry would be in his hands, and he shook a little with anticipatory laughter. He had not laughed for many days. It was good that he had them. For if he had failed, he would most certainly have blown his brains out with the little pistol he carried in his pocket and for which he had finally found bullets. For the enormous Doctor knew too much about concentration camps and their conduct. . . .

How Hiram Holliday Led the Princess Down From the Roof and Made His Apologies

The six stood on the high, sharp, Alpine ridge, curiously grouped in pairs. The two guides were in the lead. The girl and the slim youngster were side by side. And the two other men were a little off from the group.

'You are still determined to go, Hiram?'

'Yes.'

'Even though it is impossible. No one has ever done it. The Lattler ridge to the Gross Moselle is at places no more than three feet wide. And six thousand feet deep.'

'It has been done. Once. I found it out. Seppl and Hannes Schneider did it, three years ago. Seppl remembers the way. The leader is the important thing in a descent. The others simply follow.'

'If they are experts.'

'Heidi and Peter are both experts. Peter has been on skis since he was four.'

'And yourself?'

'I . . . I have skied. I will do the best I can. You will not come with us?'

The half-moon on the snow made it very light. The ridge on

which they stood was almost razor-backed. On one side, deep in the shadows, lay Austria. On the other Italy.

The Baron sighed. He was taller than Hiram, but somehow at that moment he looked smaller. 'No, Hiram, my friend,' he said finally. 'I will return where I belong, and perhaps try to profit from the lesson I have had from you. And besides, you see, Heidi *hat mir den Korb gegeben*. She has refused me.' He shrugged his shoulders and laughed a little, and then suddenly clapped Hiram on the shoulder. 'Go on, Hiram Holliday. You will succeed, not I. I am the weakness that is Austria. You know now. The Heidis are not for me. They are for you, my American friend, who have the strength and the courage and the energy to win them and hold them. For a moment I thought I could play the king-maker. I remember I boasted to you in the restaurant at Grinzing.' He shrugged again. '*Auf Wiedersehen*. I shall go on down into the valley. There is enough light. I know it like a book. I have done it often. Good luck.'

He poled over to Heidi and said: '*Auf Wiedersehen*, Mitzi.'

'Good-bye, Willi,' Heidi leaned over and kissed him. 'Willi . . . Willi . . . my good friend. I am sorry.'

'I understand, Mitzi. Good luck. Hiram will take care of you.'

'Hiram will take care of me,' echoed Heidi.

'And we'll all meet at Maxim's in Paris a year from now. Ski *Heil !*'

'Ski *Heil !*' howled the guides.

'Ski *Heil*, Uncle Willi,' cried Peter.

There was a scuffing of ski edges on hard snow, a flirt of ice crystals, and the Baron was gone. They saw his figure diminishing, a tiny black spot on the whiteness.

'Ready,' said Seppl. They adjusted their rucksacks containing food, brandy, kindling, matches, first-aid kits, clothing. The guides carried lengths of rope at their waists and resin torches which they did not yet light. Hiram looked at his wrist watch. It was nine o'clock. The climb had taken three hours.

Heidi asked: 'Hiram, can this be done ?'

He answered harshly, almost savagely. 'It can be done. We will do it.' Then he said: 'Heidi, if anything should happen to me . . .'

Heidi looked him straight in the eyes. 'Hiram, if anything should happen to me . . .'

Maria Theresa in her bronze sarcophagus was so many miles away.

'*Hui!*' called Seppl. 'Ski *Heil!* In order as decided, ten metres apart.' He turned to the right, shoved once with his poles and was off. Heidi followed him. Peter was next, standing straight upright like a young sapling. Hiram pushed off behind Peter. Toni brought up the rear.

The slope at the start was surprisingly easy, broad and gentle, like a roof, the roof of the world, Hiram thought, as he bent his knees and leaned forward. He was wondering, without a good deal of concern, whether he would survive. Perhaps it was better this way at night. Heidi and Peter would not see the dangers they skirted. But he, Hiram, knew them. He had heard them from the guide. He had gone over them a thousand times in his mind.

The descent had been originally planned for the daytime. Hiram had thought of it long before they had arrived at the Schwarzenstein Hotel. Virslany had herded them into the terrible barrier of the Gross Löffler and Moselle because he knew that it was impossible to cross it. Impossible? Then he, Hiram Holliday, must *make* it possible. In the old days in New York when he did his eight-hour trick on the copy-desk, day in and day out; he had in his spare time acquired some lessons in skiing under rather curious circumstances. At the Schwarzenstein he had queried and talked to every guide and teacher. And he had finally won over Seppl, who had agreed to take them.

It was just past five that evening that they had all been on the hotel terrace. Young Peter had been amusing himself looking through the big telescope. Suddenly he had cried out: '*Ach* . . . look, Tante Heidi. Uncle Virslany is coming up. I can see him. . . .'

Hiram had jumped to the powerful instrument. He heard the

183

funicular machinery whirring as he did so. In the clear air he could plainly see the form of Virslany in the cage, although he figured it would take him still forty-five minutes to get there. It had cost Hiram fifteen of those precious minutes to persuade Seppl and his partner Toni to make the descent with them at night. Their rucksacks were all packed for the morning and the skis and outfits they had acquired days before. Ten minutes before the cage had clanged into its berth at the Schwarzenstein, the party had turned the corner of the hotel and on a back slope had begun the 3500-foot climb to the ridge beyond which lay Italy. They had left Herr Matthias a story to tell Virslany.

Hiram noticed that the icy wind was biting more sharply against his face. Their speed had increased, and suddenly they were in shadow as towering crags they had passed cut off the light of the moon. A yellow light flared ahead, and one behind, as the guides fired their torches. Peter turned his head and flung back over his shoulder: 'Seppl says to keep your head down now and follow the ski-tracks.'

Ah, that was it. He had imagined it that way. Look neither right nor left, but down at those white lines and follow them, follow them, follow them.

Seppl was checking his speed now with graceful Christianas. Hiram had to stem hard to keep his place in line, and the stemming began to tire his legs, already weary from the long, hard climb. He fell and slid on his back. Toni was on him like a flash helping him up, and they had to speed to catch the others. The slope was narrowing now, and needles of rock thrust upward from the snow, and the angle of descent had increased. Hiram's legs were aching from the constant stemming, and his hip hurt him where he had fallen. They crossed a narrow ridge beneath some outcroppings of rock, and Hiram felt himself wavering. He was breathing hard. When the ridge broadened to a slight up-slope and they stopped to rest, Hiram fell again, trying to stop, but picked himself up gasping, his lenses clouded with snow.

'It will be harder now. Are you all right?' inquired Seppl. Hiram panted. 'Yes. . . . Yes. I am all right. Go on. . . .' Heidi was looking at him with a curious expression on her face.

They came to an ice-crusted declivity so steep that it appeared almost perpendicular to Hiram. The others zigzagged it slowly. Hiram simply fell, sliding and slipping, turning on his back, his body banging against rock. He never saw the awful chasm just to the left of where he was tumbling. When he regained his feet, he thought he had lost all feeling in his left wrist.

They skied down a narrow gorge with high walls on both sides which enabled Hiram to recover a little, and then suddenly they shot out of it into bright moonlight that shed itself over the white-capped ocean of tossing peaks. They skirted a ridge and then the way went hogbacked again, a long, narrow stretch that twisted and turned with blackness on both sides. Hiram heard Toni behind him grunt: 'Lattler Rücken! Steady nerves, boy. Look only straight ahead.'

Heidi and Peter did not know what lay on either side of the terrible track they followed, but Hiram did – sheer drops of five thousand feet. The speed increased. The ridge, the only passable link connecting Austria and Italy at that point, had to be taken at gravity. The last strength and control went out of Hiram's legs. He could no longer stop. He did not know how he got around the curves. He felt that now he was lost and that the easiest thing would be to give way, to slide off, to right or left and have it over. But the awful terror of the fall into blackness to spin down to the final obliterating crash, kept him going. His chest was burning and his ears roaring. It was no use. There was nothing left. He felt himself sinking into the bottomless darkness, but fell instead on hard snow. The terrible ridge was over. Toni was pouring some brandy down his throat. He recovered. 'Can you go on?' Heidi asked, her voice trembling.

'Yes, yes. I can go on. It can be done. . . .'

He could never afterwards break down the rest of the descent into any parts. He had entered a nightmare world of grinding rock, pouncing shadows, ice and snow, trees into which he caromed. He had lost his spectacles somewhere, his hands were ripped and one of them, the left, was useless. Sometimes the world of black and white rushed past him with fearful speed, and he thought that he had left the ground and was flying. And then again he was falling, falling, tumble after tumble battering him, and he could not tell whether each contact with the ground was new agony or just the continuation of the last.

He was no more than half-conscious when the last slope finally flattened out and on one side stood a dark, shapeless mass. Both Heidi and Seppl caught him and kept him from pitching into the side of the hut. A light gleamed from an upper window and then a door opened and a stalwart man in a Tyrolean jacket came out and said in German: '*Herr-je*, where do *you* come from?'

'From Schwarzenstein,' said Seppl.

'*Yessus Maria!* Over the Lattler Rücken! Impossible! Mother, come down here. Some people need help. And the little man did it, too? Yessus.'

Hiram fell to the ground and beat his head with his fists. 'God, oh God,' he groaned, 'I've failed. We're still in Austria!'

'*Na, na*,' said the man. 'We're Tyroleans on this side, but you are in Italy.' It was the last thing that Hiram heard.

Hours later he came to. He was in a bunk. Heidi was at his side, pressing a cloth to a bruise on the side of his head. He found he could speak.

'Did we make it?'

'Yes, Hiram . . .'

'No one hurt?'

'You have been hurt a little, Hiram,' and then: 'Hiram. Tell me something. Where did you ever ski before . . . before tonight. . . .'

Something silly began to quake in Hiram Holliday, some deep-set laughter. There it was again, his great moment of drama! Hiram the king-maker? Hiram the clown! It would be good for him to tell. He managed to turn his head a little.

'The name of the place probably won't mean a thing to you,

Princess. It was at Saks Fifth Avenue in New York on an indoor alp made of Epsom Salts. I got a diploma after ten lessons. There's your hero. Oh, for God's sake, Heidi, laugh. Laugh as I'm laughing at me, the eternal fool. . . .' He wrestled bitterly to retain consciousness, and then lost to a blinding hysteria. The others came and stared wondering at this wild, battered man laughing, laughing unknowingly, while at his side, holding his head to her heart, the Princess Heidi between sobs called his name: 'Hiram,' time after time, and buried her lips and face in his hair, and called him brave and glorious, and beloved, until the wild laughter that clouded his mind died away, and he grew calm and fell to sleep still in her arms.

DUELLO IN ROME

How Hiram Holliday Listened to the Voice of Rome
and Acquired an Ancient Sword

IT had been in mid-September of 1938 that passengers on the gigantic liner, S.S. *Britannique*, Europe bound, were asking one another a question, half in jest, half in genuine curiosity, with regard to one of their fellow-passengers. The question was: 'Who is this Hiram Holliday?'

This curiosity had been engendered by the fact that although a man by that name had distinguished himself most dramatically in certain shipboard competitions and had sent the ship's fencing instructor to the doctor to have three stitches taken in his arm, no one could ever remember having seen or noted him.

But seven months later, April of 1939, to be exact, the same question was being asked, and by no means in jest, in London, Paris, Berlin, Prague, and one other capital city of Europe.

In London, in an inner office of the British Intelligence, an elderly moustached officer called over to a youngster at a nearby desk: 'I say, Reggie, did we ever find out who did for those Nazi chaps in Green Park, the night of the crisis?'

The young man consulted a file and said: 'American, by the name of Hiram Holliday.'

The officer looked blank and said: 'Who the devil is Hiram Holliday?'

In Paris, an underling of the famous Deuzième Bureau, the secret service, was ushered into the presence of his chief, bursting with pride and information. He said: '*Mon Chef!* I have established it finally after months of work. But never have I given up, never relented. The great clown, Grognolle, who convulsed us so at the Cirque Antoine at the time of the Vinovarieff plot. It was the missing American, Hiram Holliday. I have the proof.'

The chief smiled and said: '*Ah oui! C'est bon, mon vieux.* And now if you could apply this same talent and energy to telling us exactly who is this Monsieur Holliday . . .'

But most serious of all were the repercussions in Berlin, where the Gestapo nursed a well-filled dossier labelled, 'Hiram Holliday, American Newspaper Correspondent and Secret Agent.' The last, though it was not true, would have flattered Hiram enormously.

It contained an account of his share in frustrating their plans to seize and hold for ransom the person of Duke Peter, nephew of the Princess Adelheit (Heidi) von Fürstenhof of Styria, in London, Prague, and Vienna. And it held the notation: 'Very likely concerned in some manner with the death of Auslands Propaganda Minister Dr Heinrich Grunze, and the disappearance of Gräfin Irmgarde von Helm', and concluded: 'At present in Rome as Foreign Correspondent for the *New York Sentinel.* Under surveillance. It is necessary that an action be taken with regard to this agent.'

And the simple man who had left his mark upon the capitals of Europe stood one afternoon, late in April, on the worn flagstone of the Via Sacra in the Foro Romano, the ancient Roman Forum, and looked up into the light blue Italian sky, through which roared seven giant Caproni bombers, wing to wing, their hooded snouts thrust forward, the sun ringing their whirling propellers. Beneath his feet lay the dust of those who had created and lost the Roman Empire. And in between was Italy.

This combination was as profoundly disturbing to Hiram Holliday as it was at the moment to all Europe, again in the throes of a nerve-racking war crisis. Italy had seized Albania. Greece trembled. The English kept watch at Corfu. Men massed in the Dodecanese. The great booms had been swung into place blocking Gibraltar, the French and British fleets massed in the Mediterranean and three-quarters of Europe was under arms. The powder train was laid again, and this time Italy was holding the match. One more move, and . . .

Hiram smiled grimly as the deadly scythe of the warplanes

drew across the sky. There seemed to be in his ears not the thunder and grumble of the powerful motors, but mocking laughter that rose from the tufa and all the ancient rubble at his feet. Hiram was listening to ghosts again.

He was in Rome, he knew, as a reporter of the current European scene, and reporters are not supposed to concern themselves with the half-heard voices of the past, but rather are expected to deal with the present and the tangible, the signs and portents that indicate the moving of the minds of the rulers, the dictators and their satellites. But Hiram could never at any time in Rome succeed in disassociating himself from the shouts, the groans and warning cries of history that swirled up around him, rising, seemingly from every crack in the pavement. At times it was almost as though the ground was heaving beneath his feet from the pent-up laughter of those who lay beneath.

Past glory! Past glory! It was Mussolini himself who had caused to be affixed to an ancient wall along the broad, compelling Via Impero that led from the Colosseum to the Piazza Venezia, that series of maps in coloured marble that traced the rise of the ancient Roman Empire from the pin-point of the Rome of Romulus and Remus to the vast domain that took in three-quarters of Western Europe and stretched eastward into Mesopotamia. Hiram used to pause whenever he passed them, musing. He could remember no great, dead Empire of the past that had ever sprung resurgent, Phoenix-like from its own ashes.

The fascination that ancient Rome poured over Hiram was the subject of some laughter in the Rome Bureau of the *Sentinel*, in the Via Colonna. Fred Proggi, the Bureau Chief, was a trifle nettled. Hiram Holliday was always on the Palatine, in the Forum, in museums, or reading in the American Academy. A crisis, thought the Bureau Chief, was no time in which to pursue studies of ancient history.

But then, Holliday was definitely strange; he did things in his own way, and orders from New York were to leave him alone. If he chose to write and mail back home what Proggi considered dull articles on the military organization of the

Empire contrasted to the modern Italy, or comparisons of Mussolini with Julius Caesar, or Gaius Octavian, and if he chose to waste hours puttering in antique and curio shops in the Via Babuino and spend all his money there, why that was undoubtedly his business. Still, Proggi would have appreciated help. The paper wanted to know just one thing – war or peace? He would have been very much surprised if he had known that in his own way Hiram Holliday was hitting very close to the truth.

No one knew what was going on in Hiram Holliday's mind or the curious things that were happening to him in Rome. There was, for instance, the little incident of his most precious treasure which hung in his rooms in the fine old Hotel Russie. Shortly after his arrival in Rome, when his blood was racing wildly with the excitement of the wonderful city, he had wandered into the curio shop of Salvello Salvelli on the Via Babuino. He loved to inspect and finger the old, old objects, coins and vases, ancient rings and bracelets and statuettes, for the poignant, vivid emotions they shot through him. Among his many curious qualities not to be expected in an ex-copy-reader, Hiram Holliday had a fourth-dimensional sensitiveness, to inanimate objects. Old things sent him vivid, inescapable messages.

Signor Salvelli himself waited upon him. He had grown to like this quiet, shy man. On the curio-crowded wall, back of the counter, two swords hung side by side. They were short, no more than twenty inches in length. The hilts were of bronze with no cross-piece, knobbed and thinner in the middle with welts for gripping. The blades were of iron, broad two-edged, tapering to a sharp point. They were green with the mould patina of the centuries.

Hiram pointed to them. 'What are those?'

'Ah, ha!' said Signor Salvelli. 'Well may you ask. That is the *gladius*. The famous sword of the Roman Legionary. One is an original from the excavations at Ostia. The other is a reproduction. It is magnificently made. It is nearly impossible to tell the difference. If I did not know . . .'

'I can tell the difference,' said Hiram Holliday. 'Give them to me.'

Smiling, Salvelli took them down and laid them upon the counter. 'I will make you a little wager, my friend. . . .'

'Don't,' said Hiram curtly, 'you'd lose your money,' and took first one and then the other in his hand and balanced it for a moment. Then he handed one of them to Salvelli and said: 'This . . . this is the original . . .' and the proprietor wondered for a moment why the American's voice shook.

'*E vero!* But yes! Brilliant! You are the expert then, *un Professore?*'

'N-no,' said Hiram. 'I want it. What is the price?'

He had been shaken by the sensation of utter, brutal strength, truculence and power that had flooded him, a swaggering fearlessness, a picture of a man with a bursting gorge who cared for nothing that walked on two legs, a vitality and indomitable will. Every nerve in his body told him that the weapon had belonged to a fighter such as there are few left on earth today.

'Hah! My friend. I am afraid. . . . It is a piece of the museum. . . . I could not under seven thousand lira. The reproduction I can give you for six hundred lira. So well made, one who is not like yourself could not tell the difference . . .'

'No. . . . No . . .' cried Holliday. He had the weapon in his hand again and it transformed him somehow. Behind the steel-rimmed spectacles his strange-coloured blue eyes were burning weirdly, he seemed inches taller. He raised the sword aloft and in a strange voice cried out: '*Marcus . . . Marcus Severix, ave!*'

Something very much like a chill ran through Signor Salvelli.

'I must have it. Never mind the price. I will pay you each week,' said Hiram. 'I must have it.'

'In that case, my friend,' Signor Salvelli heard himself saying: 'I give it to you. As a present. It is yours.'

Not until Hiram was out of the shop did Salvelli realize what he had done. He hung the reproduction back upon the wall and shrugged his shoulders. He was a healthy man. Strange things happened when one dealt in the possessions of the ancients. Many little pagan gods dwelt in his shop. Perhaps they had looked down approvingly upon what he had done and would bring him luck. . . .

The bombers had passed and were a distant humming, and the spell was broken. Hiram wandered on past the slab of black stone covered with a sheet of metal to protect it, and known as Caesar's Rostrum. He came from behind it. In front there stood a tall slim girl with deep violet eyes, and dark chestnut hair. A young boy, eight or nine years old, was beside her. The girl spoke to him in German. 'See, my Peter,' she was saying, 'from that stone Marcus Antonius faced the cowards who had murdered Caesar and over his dead body spoke his funeral oration.'

Hiram raised his hat. 'Heidi! And Duke Peter,' he said. 'How fine to find you again.'

The boy flew into his arms with a yell of delight. 'Onkle Hiram . . . Onkle Hiram! Where have you been?'

But the Princess Adelheit von Fürstenhof of Styria said quietly: 'It is good to see you again, Hiram.' She did not hold out her hand. She thought that he had changed since that first fantastic night in London so many months ago when they had met. He was leaner-looking and harder, with much of the roundness gone from his face, and there were lines in it that had not been there before.

He looked at her gravely, conscious of the coldness in her.

He said: 'Are you well – and safe here?' He glanced at Peter.

'Yes,' said Heidi, and there was no colour in her voice. 'The Italians have been kind. Or perhaps Peter and I are a bargaining point for them with Germany. We are going away soon – to where it will be safer. . . .'

There they were, talking like casual strangers, the girl he had led over the impassable Lattler Rücken that bridged the Gross Löffler from Austria into Italy, on the wild, night ski-run.

'And Count d'Aquila,' inquired Hiram politely, 'that brave man who fought like a lion for us, in Prague?'

Heidi lifted her head. 'Mario?' she said. 'He is in Rome. He is at the "Russie." He loves and admires you very much, Hiram. Why don't you try to see him?'

'I will,' said Hiram. 'I am at the same hotel.' Commonplaces, commonplaces. What was the barrier between them? His last sight of her had been at the end of the terror-ridden flight from Vienna over the Alpine pass. When he had recovered consciousness in the Tyroler hut, on the Italian side, she and Peter had been gone. The people there had explained that if Heidi and the boy had remained, questions would have been asked and it would have been dangerous. And so they had sent her on, passing her from house to house and village to village.

'What happened after we made the crossing, Heidi? I remember very little.'

The girl gave a small cry. 'Hiram,' she said. 'What – what do you remember?'

'We came to the broad slope in the darkness where the house was. I know I fell. That night was a torture of everlasting falling. I thought I would crash again, but someone held me. And after that I do not remember any more, except that there were dreams, horrible ones of black abysses, rocks and ice, and a dear one, where you were Heidi, and one in particular that I have tried to dream again . . .'

The girl drew in her breath sharply. Her hands sought for Peter's. 'It . . . it is so late. Come, Peter, we must go. I . . . I am glad you are well, Hiram.'

He stood there and watched them disappear. Only the boy turned around and waved to him. 'Hiram Holliday, the kingmaker,' he said to himself. 'How do you like it?'

And then like a blinding lightning he was riven by the thought – supposing the dream had not been a dream, that she had held his head in the darkness of his delirium and called him brave and beloved, and wept over him. . . . What had he known, battered and broken at that time, where dreams had ended and truth began? He turned to run after them, but they had vanished.

He shrugged his shoulders and made his way to the exit of the Forum on the Via Impero where he hailed a horse-drawn carriage and directed the driver to the office of the *Sentinel* Bureau. He wondered whether his last article had been printed in New York. He had written a scathing comparison of the opponents picked by ancient and modern Italy for battle. There might be a message from Beauheld. He wondered how the piece would go down with Fascist Italy if it had been translated and cabled back, as was the work of most of the foreign correspondents.

The answer to his question was there when he arrived. In addition to Proggi, there were two unexpected callers awaiting him, a Lieutenant Di Cavazzo, and a Commendatore Ara-Pesca. The former he knew personally, the latter by reputation. And with very few words wasted, they made their business with him plain.

For certain men in one of the inner bureaux of the Italian Government were likewise asking not only: 'Who is Hiram Holliday?' but 'What is to be done about him?'

In the ordinary course of events, Hiram would have been asked to quit Italy within twenty-four hours. But there was in the Bureau a letter in an envelope bearing the Gestapo seal, in which Italy's axis partner sent a digest of the dossier on Holliday, and made a number of specific demands. The demands themselves did not go down so well since the Italians rather resented the implication that Gestapo business took precedence over the varied problems of the Italian secret police. But the prime consideration was that Hiram's articles had touched the Romans on their weakest spot – their pride. It had been newly dusted off and refurbished for them by Mussolini. They had become boastful of their military power in the manner of all the totalitarian nations as part of the propaganda to impress and disturb the democracies. The Italians, however, being naïve, had swallowed their own propaganda. The powerful higher-ups in the Government in addition to being wounded in their national pride, for the

Italian is a true patriot at heart, saw that Hiram was on the verge of hitting upon a further truth which if widely disseminated as counter-propaganda might wreck expansionist schemes and result in a genuine calling of the totalitarian bluff. If this were to happen they might be forced either into a disastrous and losing war which would wipe out all the gains they had made since Mussolini came to power, or, their bluff called, slip back to the status of a third-rate power. For this reason alone they were in agreement with their northern partner – that the axis powers could but benefit by the elimination of the individual by the name of Holliday. But they cast aside the crude suggestions of the Gestapo and went at the matter in a truly Italian manner.

And the means to their end were supplied by the statement of one Lieutenant Di Cavazzo, a member of the Secret Council, the only one of their number who not only had ever seen the man Hiram Holliday, but, it developed, knew him personally.

Di Cavazzo, it appeared, frequented the huge, sombre *salle d'armes* beneath the colonnades of the big Stadio P.N.F., the sports stadium of the National Fascist Party. To this *salle*, reported Di Cavazzo, himself a sabre-fencer, came this man Holliday three evenings a week for fencing instruction and practice. He was taking lessons from Captain Rozzo, the Italian Army champion, the *épée*, or duelling sword, appeared to be his weapon; and while by no means brilliant, he was a capable and competent fencer of many years' experience, to be rated in class B, perhaps, and one who made up in enthusiasm and love for the sport what he lacked in skill, practice and speed of legs, hand and eye.

'He is quiet and earnest,' reported Di Cavazzo. 'A true sportsman, and well liked. I have observed him, have fenced with him myself and judge him to be a visionary and a romanticist. As you know, one learns a man's character, his strength and weaknesses, more quickly at the end of a sword blade than in any other manner. It is unusual to find in an American the instincts of a medieval bravo. He savours a bout to the last stroke, and it is easy to see and feel that in his imagination he is playing without mask and button.'

At this point the Chief of the Council, a spare, dry man with a bald head and a monocle, interrupted and said: 'Sufficient, my dear Di Cavazzo. You are a capital fellow, and your powers of observation and analysis will take you far. You have shown us the solution to the problem. At this moment, Signor Holliday is either a dead man, or one who is so discredited that he will be of no further menace either to us, or our – ah – friends in the north. Observe how we will impale him upon the horns of a dilemma from which there is no escape between the choice of death or disgrace.'

He then made clear the details of his plan, which were exquisitely simple.

How the Forces of Evil Challenged Hiram Holliday to a Duel He Could Not Win

'Good evening to you, Mr Holliday,' said Lieutenant Di Cavazzo in the *Sentinel* Bureau. 'Permit me to make known to you Commendatore Ara-Pesca, one of the editors of *Il Popolo d'Italia.*'

Hiram acknowledged the introduction. Signor Ara-Pesca was a little man with a dark face and shrewd eyes.

'We have missed you at the fencing *salle*,' said the Lieutenant.

Hiram replied that he had been busy with some special work, but hoped to be there again in the near future. He was racking his brains for a pre-glimmer of the real purpose of the visit, so that when it came he would not be unprepared. He had long had a vague inkling that Di Cavazzo was more than a mere Army lieutenant.

'Ah,' said Di Cavazzo. 'You have been occupied no doubt with the preparation of your articles for the American Press. Articles which you were certainly aware must be exceedingly offensive to the Italian Government.'

Hiram grinned. The Lieutenant, wonderfully dapper in his black uniform, swagger cape and shining boots, seemed suddenly comic opera to him. 'Well,' he said, 'I didn't think you'd exactly like them.'

It was now the Lieutenant's turn to flash white teeth. '*Per Bacco!* Spoken as I expected. I can see that you are our man. The Government indeed has been deeply offended, and it was with difficulty that the Commendatore and myself were able to dissuade certain members from ordering your immediate expulsion from the country.'

Proggi, the Bureau Chief, a tall, white-haired man, looked baffled and disturbed. He had not thought Hiram's articles that important, if important at all.

The comic-opera notion faded from Holliday's mind. He said evenly: 'That was white of you, Lieutenant. And to what do I owe your benevolent interest in my fate?'

Di Cavazzo was not at all disturbed. 'Ah,' he said. 'To that I was coming. A matter of precedence. If the articles were offensive to the Government, as indeed they are, they were doubly so to those whom they directly impugned.'

The first alarm bell sounded in Hiram.

'You have reflected upon the honour of the Italian soldier, minimized the glories of his recent achievements, and cast reflections upon his courage.'

'That's true.'

Di Cavazzo drew a sharp breath, and Ara-Pesca turned red. The Lieutenant recovered himself and continued in his calm, even voice. 'The Army has been able to persuade the Government that it holds every prior right to demand satisfaction. Thus, Commendatore Ara-Pesca, himself a distinguished journalist like yourself, and I, are here to represent the interests of Colonel Rafael Del Tevere, of the Italian Army, who requests that you do him the honour of meeting him at such time and place and with such weapons as you or your seconds, as the challenged party, shall decide. If you will be good enough to name someone to act for you we can arrange the details.'

There was then a silence broken only by the breathing of the four men in the dingy, littered little office.

'Hell's bells, Hiram,' exploded Proggi, suddenly. 'You're being challenged to a duel.' He turned upon the Lieutenant. 'You chaps must be nuts. Americans don't fight duels. I'll have this out with the Ministry. Holliday has never had a weapon in his hand in his life. I know Del Tevere. He won the Olympic Military Pentathlon. He has killed three men in duels already.'

'On the contary,' said Di Cavazzo quietly, 'Mr Holliday is an able and experienced fencer, and, I am given to understand, a more than competent pistol shot. I myself have had the pleasure of crossing blades with him in friendly bouts in the *salle* at the Studio, where he had honoured us by his presence for the last few months. It is the hope of Colonel Del Tevere that Mr Holliday will select a weapon in which he feels himself the most at home, preferably, of course, the sword, the weapon of officers and, ah – gentlemen.'

'And what,' said Hiram Holliday, suddenly, 'if I should refuse?'

Di Cavazzo shrugged. 'Then', he said, 'it would be the unfortunate duty of the Government to insist upon your immediate expulsion from the country.' He paused for a moment, and his dark eyes glittered from his olive face: 'Not, however, for the offence given by your articles.'

'But . . .' said Hiram.

'It will then be necessary for my colleague, Commendatore Ara-Pesca, whose articles, whose every word, is quoted not only in the newspapers of the Continent, but those of your own country as well, to write that you have been expelled from Italy, not for your opinions, but for lacking the courage to back them with, ah . . . the kind of action that you decry as failing in the Italian soldier, and also to indicate that your continued presence here under those circumstances would necessarily be contaminating to all Italians.'

The beautiful simplicity of it staggered Hiram for a moment. But he said: 'And if I should agree to meet Colonel Del Tevere, and win?'

The Lieutenant showed his fine white teeth again. 'In that

case,' he declared, 'the Army will be happy to maintain your right to express your opinion – ah . . . as long as you are able to – ah – defend it so ably.'

Proggi swore suddenly. 'Damn your impudence,' he shouted. 'You're planning a murder. Say the word, Hiram, and we'll throw the pair of them out of here.'

Di Cavazzo never even turned his head. He was regarding Holliday with a slight smile on his face.

Hiram shook his head. 'Thanks, Fred. No. I . . . I want to think this out. I've got to think it out. Don't you see, if I decline . . .' He turned to the two Italians: 'Gentlemen, will you come to the Hotel Russie tomorrow morning at ten o'clock? I will give you my answer, and if it is in the affirmative, I shall have my second with me. You have explained the affair quite clearly. Thank you.'

In Berlin, Hiram Holliday had been trapped by an elaborate, heavy-handed typically German plot, and landed in a death-cell in Moabit prison. But now, pacing his old-fashioned apartment in the Hotel Russie, he realized that that had been childish compared to the simple ingenuity of the snare that was now laid for him in Rome. It was Italian to the core. Physically and psychologically, it was air-tight. He saw no choice between death and disgrace. And he had no illusions as to the truth that one or the other was imminent. It was so Roman-like to have added the torture of giving him his choice.

He had gone over the consequences of refusing to fight, a thousand times. That path led back to safety, it was true, but safety on the rim of the copy-desk of his paper, and to that he knew there could be no returning. There would be many who might applaud his stand in declining to fight a duel. But to the majority he would be the man who had been chased out of Italy, not with the honour that fell to other correspondents who had been forced to leave because they were incorruptible and uncompromising, but as a coward who had been ostensibly offered his chance to remain and had failed to accept it because of regard for his skin.

Because Hiram was a human being, the approbation of his

fellow-man was important to him. But above all, because he was Hiram Holliday, his own self-esteem was more important than anything. It was himself he had to face, waking and dreaming, in the knowledge that when the moment came for which, following his romantic bent, he had been training himself through the long, dull years on the copy-desk, when in his free hours he had learned to fight the weapons of ancient, as well as modern man, and had drilled himself in the physical accomplishments of the heroes of another day, he had failed, had deliberately turned his back upon this other world in which he had lived in his mind for so long and sought the safety of the law and the narrow life.

And the alternative was to bleed away his life because of a sliver of steel run through his heart or lung by a stranger.

For he had no illusions either as to the outcome of the duel. He was too capable a fencer for that. Colonel Del Tevere was not only an Olympic fencing champion and a master of the French *épée*, or duelling-sword, but he was also a veteran of personal combat, having fought some seven duels, three of which had terminated fatally for his opponent.

It is a curious thing about fencing that a little knowledge is more dangerous than none. A good fencer is in much more jeopardy against a wild, unorthodox novice, who, discarding form, is liable to land with a lucky point. But the more the habits of a man are grooved into the classic and orthodox lines of defence and attack, the more certain he will fall victim to the superior speed, craft, strength and skill of one who is a champion.

And because he himself was a classroom fencer, with his muscles set, Hiram knew that Del Tevere would most certainly kill him. He might play the Colonel for a time, in fact, Del Tevere would most certainly prolong the end as long as possible to avoid any possible charges of an assassination, but there could be but one finish to the fight. The farther it went, the worse it would be for Hiram. His legs would tire, his arm grow heavy, his point would waver, there would be a grunt and a lightning movement and he would be spitted. He wondered whether he would feel it as a hot, searing pain, or merely as a merciful blackness from which he would never emerge. Or whether, all strength gone from his limbs, he would sink to the ground to cough out his life from a punctured lung.

It was a warm, fragrant, stilly Roman night. Hiram went out on to his terrace overlooking the famous Russie gardens. Bits of white statuary glimmered, star-lit, through the shadows of the lacy shrubs and flowers. Was he a fool, to think of passively leaving this deep beauty for ever for an outmoded ideal? He did not believe Di Cavazzo's story of the challenge. It went deeper. The presence of the important journalist Ara-Pesca alone was an indication of that, for the man was a party mouthpiece. Hiram knew that he had mounted up an account in totalitarian Europe. In Germany he had been loved by a woman belonging to a dangerous statesman. In Vienna he had succumbed to the sweet lure of the romantic role of kingmaker. Now the bill was being presented for collection. Did they know the truth now in Berlin? Was the long Nazi hand reaching into Italy? Did not that give him the right to secure his own safety? But what safety, and what security? A discredited correspondent? The phrase, 'Chased out of Italy,' would follow him as long as he lived. Men like Hiram Holliday could not live under stigma.

He thought, too, of Heidi, the Princess Adelheit von Fürstenhof of Styria, and their curious casual meeting that day in the Roman Forum. Who did she love, this immaculate Princess of another day whom he had aided in the purest meaning of Domnei, the old, medieval woman service? Was it d'Aquila, the valiant and dapper little Italian Count who served her, too? Once, when they, Hiram and Heidi, had stood ski-shod on the summit of the Gross Löffler, that supposedly impassable barrier between Austria and Italy, and prepared to risk the descent to the Italian side, Hiram had thought that he had conquered when she had looked him in the eyes and said: 'Hiram, if anything should happen to me . . .' Had she meant what he had when he had said the same thing, that if he died in the descent, he died loving her?

And what if she had? Probably already she regretted it. What was there in life for them both? A flat, a radio, an ice-box and a car? Was that an end for people who had lived dangerously and romantically, for a woman who by her blood was a dynast? One did not go on and on having adventures until sooner or later bullet-hit or knife found its mark, but neither did one, the vows spoken, surrender to the Philistines.

Perhaps the Colonel and his needle-pointed sword were the answer to a great many things, the answer, in fine, to everything. Hiram shook off the mood and went back into his rooms. He would wrestle with his dangerous dilemma until there was no longer a grain of sand in the cup of the hour-glass.

All over Rome the bells great and small began to toll midnight. They tolled in dissonance and polyphony, in twos and threes like a roundelay, until at last midnight was done and there was silence again. A breeze, heavily scented, blew in from the blossom-laden gardens and stirred a drape against the wall and disturbed the Roman sword that hung there. It clashed and rang gently against the wall the barest whisper of old, strong iron, the merest susurration of a distant call to arms.

And Hiram leaped to it and tore it down, held it in his right hand and shook it, and again it told him all that he had felt in the dingy curio shop, and this time a hundredfold more.

Again he felt the presence of its owner, stocky, powerful, swarthy, brutally beautiful, black hair, mocking eyes and mouth, reeking of sweat and garlic, but brimming with life and strength and vitality and the conqueror's spirit. He had fought them all, the Parthian, the Macedonian, the Egyptian, the Jew and the wild woad-painted Briton, and his own brother, too, in the civil wars that had torn the old republic. With the sword and the wild, unquenchable ferment in his blood, he, the Roman Legionary, had carved out his destiny and his fortune in burning heat or bitter cold, in plenty and in starvation, because of that vital seed of conquest that was in him. He was tough and hard as his father and his father's father before him had been because in his veins the Roman bloodstream had flowed undiluted by the weaker currents of the world.

No wonder Hiram had heard the mocking laughter when the big bombers flew by. Men, not machines, warred upon men. Therein the world never changed. The Italian was a Roman no more, and not a million proclamations could make him so. The Empire dreams of Caesar, of Antony, of Augustus, had been founded upon the men who could carve them out of the flesh and bone of other men. And they were gone – gone. The seed was dead and the blood was thinned. There he was, the Italian of today, enchanting, endearing, artist, easy-going, gay and sunny, loving life and good things, brave enough in his way, but the hungry, restless, roving fighting conqueror? Never! Never again! And his leaders KNEW IT.

There was the answer, the answer that Hiram had sought in the musty libraries and museums and among the ruins, and, too, in the street and restaurants of Rome and in the Campagna where the peasants tilled the soil. All the uniforms and the panoply and the machines for war were there, but the urge, the bitter, hungry urge and the strength were not.

Strength! Strength of men! The old sword poured it into Hiram, until he cried aloud with the joy of it. Man's work! What had it to do with pause or fear or reflection, or dalliance by the wayside? One was born but once, and the struggle never ended until the grave.

'*Ave,*' cried Hiram Holliday in his lonely room. '*Ave, Marcus Severix!* And, by God, I'll prove it!'

He crashed his typewriter open and began to write the story that he had been searching for in Rome, the story that had been in his mind and soul from the first glimpse he had had of modern Rome shot through with the tall, glorious white skeletons of her past, the story that had needed the message of the sword to free it.

He poured it into his machine. Bluff! Bluff! Bluff! Italy would make no war. The harsh, virile bloodstream of conquest was thinned by twenty centuries. The Legionary who had conquered the earth was gone, and on his bones dwelt a different people.

The Rome of old would have had its teeth in England's throat to obliterate or be obliterated, to be destroyed or destroy as they had shattered Carthage. Romans never had fought as mercenaries as Italy had done in Spain. In old Rome's Pantheon hung the shields of Mithridates, of Jugurtha, of Hannibal and Cleopatra, of Cicengetorix and Boadicea, Aristobulus and Josephus. Not even a puppet king had been captured to grace a modern Roman triumph. Weak Zog had fled to Greece, Haile Selassie, the Lion of Judah, dwelt beneath his umbrella in the English countryside. The disgrace of Guadalajara in Spain had been barely wiped out against a starving, handcuffed nation.

'They never come back!' wrote Hiram. 'Where were the ancient nations? Greece, impoverished, living under the protection of England. Egypt the same. Spain a bloody wreck, Turkey a bare fraction of her former power, Persia, the Aryan fountain-head, weak and helpless. Where are those dangerous, powerful sprouting seeds of conquest? In the blood of the Germans and in the rising torrent from the Orient?

'The twenty centuries' admixture of blood in the Italian has made him culturally and artistically one of the great nations of the earth, but it has robbed him of the feckless, brutal fighting strength of his Empire ancestor, and no amount of posturing and shouting by his leaders, no easy, set-up victories over weak and helpless nations can bring it back.

'Italy will not fight England or France except as the tail to Germany's kite. Read that written on the ruins!'

He then wrote what was probably one of the most famous 'Notes to Editor' ever appended to a reporter's copy. Beauheld, Managing Editor of the *New York Sentinel*, printed it at the head of Hiram's story. It read:

'Note to Beauheld. This may be my last story to you. It's too long a thing to go into. I've been challenged to a duel here. It's all tied up with this story, and anyway, it's my affair. But, by God, I'll prove that either they or I am right. Hold this yarn until you hear. If something happens to me chuck it into the Hell Box. If I give you the word, you can splash it because it will be the truth. I say they can't take cold steel, man to man, no breaks and no edge. Give my regard to all the dopes on the copy-desk. HOLLIDAY.'

It was six o'clock in the morning when he had finished. Outside his door the gardens were dew-lit and bathed in pearl-coloured light. He sealed the story in an envelope with a note to Proggi: 'Get this through to New York somehow, if you have to fly a man to Paris with it. And don't worry about me. I know what I'm doing.'

Then he picked up his telephone and said: 'Get me the apartment of Count Mario d'Aquila. Yes, I know it is early. He won't mind being disturbed. Tell him it is Hiram Holliday asking for him.'

How Hiram Holliday Accepted the Challenge and Named His Weapon and was Visited by a Princess

At the stroke of ten, Lieutenant di Cavazzo and Signor Ara-Pesca were ushered on to the terrace of the Russie overlooking the gardens where they found Hiram Holliday and the Count Mario d'Aquila sipping vermouth. The two men rose and bowed, and Cavazzo was obviously surprised at seeing d'Aquila. The dapper little count with the slicked black hair and small teeth was smoking an elegant gold-tipped cigarette, and his smile was charming.

'Good morning, gentlemen,' said Hiram Holliday. 'Your punctuality bears out everything I have ever read about the ritual of duelling. I see that no introductions are necessary. Count d'Aquila has very kindly consented to represent me in this matter. Won't you sit down, and what may I order for you?'

Di Cavazzo suddenly spoke sharply in Italian to d'Aquila, who answered him in the same language, and there was a brief bristling passage between them before d'Aquila turned to Hiram and said: 'Pardon us, my friend. The lieutenant had the kindness to point out that it might be dangerous for me, an Italian, to represent you, an American, in an affair hinging upon Italian honour. I explained to him that selection of a second was rather a matter of personal friendship than private opinion, and besides that it was my own business. I then invited him to go to the devil. Instead of which he has decided to join us in a vermouth-cassis, a most sensible attitude.'

Hiram heard another warning bell. He was convinced now that more than a simple challenge lay behind the affair. Otherwise Di Cavazzo would have been at d'Aquila's throat.

'So then,' said Ara-Pesca, 'we may take it that you have decided to accept the challenge of Colonel del Tevere, Mr Holliday, a decision which, I may add, does you much honour.'

Hiram said dryly: 'Thank you. I am glad that you are pleased.'

'Good,' purred Di Cavazzo. 'The time and the place?'

'We leave to your most excellent discretion,' said d'Aquila. 'Except that my principal, Mr Holliday, begs that it be out-doors rather than in the *salle*. A slight touch of claustrophobia – way back in his family. . . .'

Di Cavazzo stiffened slightly. Was he being laughed at?

'Very well. And the weapons?'

'The Roman sword,' said d'Aquila quietly.

Relief appeared on the faces of the two other men. 'Hah!' said Di Cavazzo. 'Good. Your choice again does you credit. If I may suggest, there are a number of tested duelling *épées* at the *salle* which I will submit to you for your inspection and choice, and . . .'

D'Aquila interrupted him gently, as gently as though he were speaking to a child. 'My friend,' he said, 'I do not think that you understood me. I said nothing about duelling *épées*. The choice of my principal, Mr Holliday,' and here his voice suddenly lost its gentleness and became harsh and biting, 'is the *gladius*, the Roman military short sword as worn and used by the Roman Legionary under the Empire.'

In the dead silence that followed the splashing of the little fountains in the garden sounded like a waterfall.

'What?' said Di Cavazzo. 'Are you mad?'

'You heard him,' said Hiram Holliday. 'Do you accept?'

The Lieutenant was badly flustered: 'Why . . . why . . . it is fantastic. I . . . I . . . must confer with my principal . . . I . . .'

D'Aquila leaned forward suddenly and tapped Di Cavazzo on the knee. 'You must do nothing of the kind, my friend. Under the code, Mr Holliday, as the challenged party, names the weapons. You may either accept or decline. If you decline we will be happy to receive a written apology from Colonel del Tevere for wasting Mr Holliday's time, and a guarantee that there will be no further talk of expulsion from Italy under the circumstances you mentioned.'

Ara-Pesca was purple. 'But this is unheard of. You dare to make a joke of a serious affair. Kindly remember, Count d'Aquila, even though you have abandoned your own, that you are dealing with men of honour.'

D'Aquila flushed. 'Your first statement, Commendatore, I will be glad to debate with you at any time under your own choice of arguments. As for the latter, it is exactly what we have kept in mind. Mr Holliday is anxious to spare Colonel del Tevere the embarrassment of having to defend himself against a charge of political assassination such as the American Embassy would undoubtedly bring. My principal is no match for the Colonel either with swords or pistols. He therefore has selected a weapon, no less deadly, with which both he as well as Del Tevere are unfamiliar, at the same time graciously yielding that by birth and heritance from the glorious past, Del Tevere should feel the more at home with it. It is in short a weapon admirably suited for the settlement of his argument since it places a minimum of weight upon skill and practice, and a maximum upon ah – strength and courage.'

'You toy with impossible conditions,' rasped Ara-Pesca. 'Where are such weapons to be procured?'

'My Principal has acquired a very fine specimen which he will be glad to lend you as a model. There are duplicates of it in the Museo delle Terme, in the Museo Romano, the Museo Mussolini and in the hands of Salvello Salvelli, the collector.'

Di Cavazzo was in a rage. 'You are earnest? You insist then in making a farce of this affair.'

'Farce, hell!' exploded Hiram Holliday and arose towering from his chair, and it was d'Aquila who noticed at that moment he looked more Roman and rugged, with his sandy hair, drawn face and queerly coloured blue eyes, than any of them. 'Do you want to fight, or don't you? Will you fight if you haven't got an edge? You were willing enough to have Del Tevere slaughter me with his own duelling sword. He hoped I'd pick the weapon of a gentleman, eh? Well, I've chosen the weapon of a fighter. It's your own. You conquered the world with it once. You're boasting that you'll do it again. Well, you've still got to lick a white man. Let's see him fight with this weapon man to man, until one of us is dead or quits.'

He threw the Roman sword that he had held concealed on to the iron-topped table where it fell with a shattering clang.

'Do you take it or leave it?'

They stared spellbound for a moment at the squat, business-like thing with its broad, flat, two-edged pointed iron blade.

'We ... we accept provisionally,' said Di Cavazzo. 'You will hear from us.' He and Ara-Pesca bowed like automatons, turned and withdrew.

'Now what the hell does that mean?' said Hiram Holliday.

'It means,' said the little Conte d'Aquila, smiling crookedly, 'that they have, as you Americans say, the lost goat.'

D'Aquila called Hiram at noon. He said: 'Del Tevere has accepted. I am given to understand he was furious that Di Cavazzo hesitated. He is a sportsman. He wishes to ask if you will agree to the use of the Roman shield in the combat.'

Holliday laughed. 'Tell him helmet, cuirass, greaves and the S.P.Q.R. standard, if he wants.' He said: 'When?'

'Tomorrow morning at six. A short distance out on the Via Appia, there is a suitable place in a cypress grove.'

'The sooner the better.'

'You are still determined to go through with this?'

'Yes, Mario, I am. Can I get a square deal?'

There was a pause. Then Hiram heard Mario say: 'Hiram,

I, too, am an Italian. I swear with my life that it will be a fair and honest combat. I will see you at the hotel tonight.'

'Thanks, Mario. I'll be there after nine o'clock.'

He remained away from the office, though he would have liked to know whether they had succeeded in getting his story through. He spent most of the day in the library of the American Academy, reading. He did not feel nervous and he wondered why. He dined alone in the Ulpia restaurant built into the ruins of the Trajan Forum and returned to the Russie shortly before nine o'clock. There was no message from d'Aquila. He found his rooms lonely and stuffy and closing in on him. He wanted the freedom of the sky overhead. He realized that reaction was setting in. He left word for Mario at the desk and went out into the lovely sombre gardens filled with the scents of jasmine and orange blossom. There he sat on a marble bench, and like a thirsty child, drank in every beauty, the patch of starlit sky caught through the tree-tops, the twists of the flat-topped Lebanon cedars, and the gloomy martial rise of the cypresses, the gentle sound of the fountain and the murmur of the city without, the curved stem of a sleeping flower, its bent head closed for the night, for he was wondering whether he would ever see these things again.

He was startled when his name was called, and called again. He arose. A figure was coming down the winding path. He knew it at once. He said: 'Yes, Heidi . . . I am here.'

The Princess Fürstenhof came and sat beside him. She was dressed simply in white. Her face was quite pale and in the light that filtered through from above she looked unearthly and inhumanly lovely. At last she said, her voice low and earnest: 'Hiram, my dear, dear friend. Why are you doing this? Why? Mario told me. Why? Is it worth it? Have you reflected? To die. For what? Because men are proud, romantic fools?'

Something had Hiram at the throat, something brutal and savage, and when he spoke it was in a voice that Heidi had never heard from him before.

'Heidi! What right had you to come here?'

Presently she answered. 'The right of our friendship and

the things we have been through together. Is not that enough? And because there are not many like you on this earth, because I will not see you wasted, Hiram. Is it your pride driving you to this? Can you face me and tell my why?'

'Yes,' said Holliday, 'I can. Because I must. I know why now. Because I hate these Fascists and their brutality and their anti-human philosophy. I have lived in Europe seven months now, and I have seen what they have done to human beings, in Berlin, in Vienna, in Prague and here, fear in every soul, every decency of human liberty abolished. I have been in their trial rooms and prisons, Heidi, I've talked to the frightened men and women whose families have disappeared, and seen the men who have been beaten and broken until they were better dead. And this is the rule they want to stretch to the ends of the earth, to my own country. By God, Heidi, I can strike one blow against it. This is my protest, the protest that is groaning in me to be released. To stand just once with a naked sword, and strike, and strike and strike, and get it out of me, this rage that I feel. And then maybe I can be at peace again. . . .'

He was standing now in the glimmering darkness with his arm upraised as though his weapon were already in his fist. And as suddenly he checked himself with a groan, and sank back on to the bench. 'Oh, my God, Heidi, will I never quit posturing and posing?' He paused for a moment and then said: 'No, Heidi, no. This isn't a pose. No, not this time. I feel it. I'm hungry for it, to strike one blow against this thing that is false, vicious and tyrannical. They've put forth their champion, and they're going to let me meet him. Don't you understand that, Heidi? Even if we are only symbols. You must see it, Heidi. And if . . . if you are the kind of person I have carried in my heart and my mind for so long, you won't try to stop me. You wouldn't. You'd . . .'

'Send you out to die, Hiram? No. But stand in your way? No, not that either. I have learned to know you, Hiram. In you there is all the beauty that man has attained and can put forward against the eternal forces of darkness, all the strength, the love, the gentleness and chivalry of the good.

There are so few of you left, Hiram, and like you, just like you, there are none. Nothing could stop you, nothing I feel or could say or do, because you are a man. And men must listen to those things that are within them, and follow them, and not pause, or stop for . . .' she paused, and then with her head dropped, whispered so that he hardly heard the words, 'for anything.'

Hiram took first her hand and kissed the fingers, and then he took her head between his own two hands and kissed her lips. He said: 'Princess,' and it was the first time that he had not called her Heidi, 'Princess, help me. I do not trust in moments. I'm not ready yet. First I must do. Strange things have happened to me in Rome. It is as though I have at last isolated the emotion of ambition and tapped the reservoir of strength to drive it. I feel I must rip and tear through this world, Heidi, and by the force and urge of my mind and body, carve out a piece of it that will be mine because I have won it. I have been asleep for twenty years. I must go alone, Heidi, until I have done these things that I must do, used what I have now, tearing at me inside, the thing that gives me no rest.'

He went on, speaking as though all was plain between them. 'I mistrust words, Heidi, and night enchantment. Life is lived in daylight, and things undone leave one bitter. We both have still much to do. And if I am a fool to start now to do what should have been done long ago, I won't admit it. I won't believe it. The power is there, Heidi. I've found it. I understand it. It lives up here right in my throat. . . .'

He said: 'When I have used it, Heidi, when I have made a life that can be lived . . .' he stopped because there were no words, but his arms were lifted again, and his hands seemed to be groping for the patch of night sky seen through the trees, and its freight of distant stars.

Heidi finished the sentence for him: ' . . . high on the mountain-tops. . . . When you are ready, my dear. . . . When you are ready, Hiram . . .'

She said no more, but took his face this time and kissed him. They arose and stood for a moment held together tightly, less by the pressure of their arms about one another than by the power of their deep understanding of one another. Then she turned, and without looking back went down the winding path and out of his sight.

Hiram went up to his room where he found d'Aquila waiting for him. The sleek little Count looked at him curiously.

'Well?' he said.

'Hello,' said Hiram Holliday. 'All set. I have left a call for four-thirty in the morning, but we'd better double check on it.'

D'Aquila nodded. 'By all means. It is necessary to be punctual in affairs of this kind.' He stopped and was quiet for a moment. Hiram said nothing. The Count finally broke the silence:

'Ah . . . I hope you are not offended with me, my friend.'

'Eh?' said Hiram, 'offended?'

The Count was examining his smoking-case and taking a long time to select a cigarette. He said: 'I . . . ah . . . took the liberty, unpardonable, I am afraid, of – ah – informing the Princess Fürstenhof of the . . . the affair of tomorrow morning. I beg of you to forgive me, Hiram.'

Hiram suddenly felt a very great love for this dapper little man, because again he was being permitted a glimpse behind the glossy hair, the absurd dab of moustache, the dress of a dandy, to the man that lay beneath. And because he loved him, it made him inarticulate and powerless to move. He would have liked to put his arms about him in friendship.

But d'Aquila had Italian intuition. He said: 'I thank you for your silence.' He lit his cigarette and sent the blue smoke towards the ceiling. Then he looked over the top of Hiram's head to a copy of Raphael's Madonna that hung on the wall and spoke again.

'Strange,' he said, 'I feel as though it were I, instead of you, who goes to duel tomorrow. I might almost wish that it were so. This is a curious time in which we live, trapped, as it were, between the old order and the new.' He seemed now to be talking not to Hiram, but to himself, or to the picture. 'When I was a young boy, a marriage was arranged for me as was still done in Europe. The Princess and I were associated much as children. We grew up together. It was always understood that we were to be married. That is the way great houses are strengthened. And if love should come – *Bene*, then they say the marriage is doubly blessed, eh?'

He chewed upon his lip for a moment. 'And when the great houses are no more? When they are shattered by the new order and seized by the usurpers, and there are left only the men and women who inhabited them and escaped from the fall? *E vero!* Then there remains but man and woman, and it is the woman who chooses. And freed from her duty she chooses where her heart lies. *Basta!* . . . I believe, my friend, when this is over, that I must see whether Ara-Pesca is not inclined to continue our little discussion of this morning with me at some suitable spot.'

Now Hiram understood what d'Aquila had told him, and he followed his bent and went over to him and put both arms about him for a moment, and then held him off by the shoulders, and looked down at him and said: 'I . . . I wish I were a man like you, Mario.'

The little Count grinned, all his white teeth showing. Then he gripped Hiram by the hand. 'Until the morning, eh?'

That night Hiram Holliday slept next to the sword of Marcus Severix, one-time Legionary of Augustus Caesar and the Empire.

How Hiram Holliday Duelled with the Forces of Evil and Learned that there are still Honourable Men

Five miles out of Rome from the Porta St Sebastiano, along the Appian Way, and a short distance past the Tomb of Seneca are the ruins of an old tower known as Fort Appia Antica. Behind it and to the left there is a thick grove of Roman pine and cypress. In the centre of this grove the trees mysteriously stop growing about a circle some thirty yards in diameter where there is an open space with a slight rise at one end.

Archaeologists know that it was a ceremonial grove, and that beneath it probably lies an altar, but it has not yet been excavated. The ground is even and well turfed. A cone of light cuts down through the opening of the tree, illuminating it like an amphitheatre.

And it was here at six o'clock of a morning late in April, a group of men gathered for the strangest duel fought in modern times. The two parties arrived simultaneously, and entered the grove from opposite sides, where they bowed to one another and began the arrangements for the combat.

With Hiram came Count d'Aquila, and a friend of his, Rafael Campanare, to act as the other second. Colonel del Tevere's party was larger. In addition to Lieutenant di Cavazzo and Commendatore Ara-Pesca, it included two doctors, Rezzi and Tagliafone, and the dignified, white-haired old General, the Conte di Brabazon, who had been agreed upon by both d'Aquila and Del Tevere to act as referee.

Holliday had his first look at his opponent. Colonel del Tevere was a fine-looking man of about Hiram's height, but slightly younger. He had a strong nose, dark hair and shining black eyes. When he stripped to the waist even as Hiram was engaged in doing, he showed a barrel chest and finely muscled arms.

Hiram found himself amazed at the speed with which matters went. There was no unnecessary talk or delay. D'Aquila and Di Cavazzo busied themselves inspecting the weapons. The two doctors had removed their coats and, opening their bags, laid out instruments, sutures, dressings, a minature first aid station. Hiram, bared to the waist, bent over to tighten his shoelaces. He was wearing rubber-soled oxfords. He noted in a most detached manner that his legs were trembling slightly. He wondered if they would go on doing that during the fight. D'Aquila carried Hiram's sword, and a small round shield, the *clipeus* of the Roman Legionary. It was of tough, hard, iron-like leather with a bronze facing. On the inside were affixed two straps, one through which the left forearm was slipped, and another near the edge for a hand grasp.

General di Brabazon called out in English: 'Ready, gentlemen?'

Hiram ran his left arm into the shield and had a momentary thrill of appreciation. It was light and well-balanced. The two parties moved towards the centre of the enclosure where Del Tevere halted, and he and his adherents gave the Fascist salute which D'Aquila and Campanare returned. Hiram bowed briefly.

Del Tevere spoke. He said: 'Before we begin, I wish to tender my apologies to Signor Holliday for any – ah – delay shown by my seconds during the negotiations. I wish to state that his choice of weapons does him and me the greatest honour. I am proud to wield the arms of our illustrious ancestors in their irresistible march to the glory of the Roman Empire.'

All the seconds and the two doctors cried: 'Bravo, bravo!' Hiram found that his legs were no longer trembling and that he was saying to himself: 'That is a very pretty speech, my friend, but I wonder how you are going to like the business end of it when you get it. . . .'

'Gentlemen! Your attention, if you please,' said General di Brabazon. 'I am given to understand that it is desired by both parties from their dispositions and their choice of weapons that this be a combat to a finish. You are to use your weapons as you choose. At the signal which will be a blast from my whistle you are to fight and continue fighting until one or the other is disabled or yields, at which time I will again blow my whistle when no further blows are to be struck. During this time there is to be no interference whatsoever. The entire terrain upon which we stand is at your disposal. But whosoever retreats beyond the limit of the surrounding trees shall be deemed to have yielded himself and acknowledged defeat. Seconds retire. Gentlemen, may I beg that as brave men you salute one another.'

They stood facing one another, ten feet apart. Hiram had removed his spectacles. His mouth was closed, the lips hard-set, and his light eyes were shining with excitement. The two men rendered one another the traditional fencer's salute. Hiram was standing braced, knees bent, his left foot slightly forward, the shield raised and held slanting to cover throat and chest. He saw Del Tevere fall into a pose, and with an angry mutter quickly change it. He had stood at first with his right arm and side turned to Hiram, before he turned left side forward. But Hiram had noted it, and in noting it, very probably saved his life. For he said to himself: 'Be careful, Hiram! The man is a fencer. He'll fight the weapon as much like a fencer as he can.'

In the thin, early sunlit morning air, the whistle piped, and before it had ceased, Del Tevere flashed forward over the intervening ground in a crashing *balestra*, the dark blade of the short sword hissing overhead in a direct attack at Hiram's head. It was that first warning glimpse that Hiram had had that dictated his own reply. He jumped backwards and held his shield steady, and the hard leather took the shock of the Colonel's lunge. It had been a sabre attack, beginning with a feint for the head. Had Hiram raised his shield to protect against the cut, he would have taken the blade driven full power through his chest.

For a fraction of a second, Del Tevere's point was stuck in the leather. Hiram jabbed straight for the eyes. Del Tevere got his shield up in time, and with a grunt, freed his point and jerked backwards crying: 'Hah!'

Hiram followed him, edging forward like a boxer, right foot behind left foot, and blessed the time he had put into boxing lessons. He could follow his left foot forward. Del Tevere, the champion fencer, knew only one way to advance comfortably, his right leg ahead, knee bent. In distance, he made a sharp, short lunge for the Colonel's exposed right side. Del Tevere parried well in time in *sixte*, carrying Hiram's blade outward. But the riposte never came, because Hiram's weapon slid along the top of his, there was no hilt or guard to stop it, and the razor edge cut the back of Del Tevere's hand from the knuckle to the wrist. It was only a surface cut, but the Colonel jumped back out of range, and Hiram heard d'Aquila cry: '*Per Dio!* First blood!'

Hiram was thinking furiously: 'Hah! fencer . . . fencer . . . you can't help being a fencer, Del Tevere, and if you fight that sword like a fencer you'll be killed. Forget everything you ever knew about fencing, Hiram. Don't make a single move like a fencer. You've got to put two thousands years between you. Go back . . . back to the man who used this weapon once. Fight the way he fought. This was made for close quarters, man to man. Get in. Get in. . . .'

He pressed forward. He was beginning to feel that he understood his shield and sword. Del Tevere thrust at his shoulder. Hiram was a fraction slow protecting and felt the point rip the flesh on the outside of his shoulder. But the lunge brought Del Tevere close, and Hiram ripped up his shield and the bronze-bound edge caught the Colonel under the chin, gashing it, and staggering him so that he tottered backwards and fell. Hiram stepped back and waited for him to get up. General di Brabazon called out sharply: 'It is not necessary to wait. If one or the other falls the other may close in and force him to yield. . . .'

Hiram moved forward, again coaching himself: 'Use your shield, Hiram, . . . feed him iron . . . fight him . . . fight him.' With a crashing shock, they locked. Del Tevere had learned something and struck with his shield, but Hiram whipped his head out of the way and clinched, and twisted away in time as the Colonel brought his knee up. Del Tevere's chin was dripping blood and his eyes were glaring wildly. Hiram felt a sharp pain in his right leg and knew that he had been cut. With a fierce effort he threw his opponent off. But he was tiring, his chest was beginning to burn and he thought he felt a numbness in his leg. He paused for a moment to get his breath, and in that pause Del Tevere charged like a wounded bull, a hundred and eighty pounds of man-driven bone and muscle behind steel and bronze.

Hiram was never able to tell why or how he knew the Roman trick of the old Legionaries, whether somewhere he had read it, or whether it came to him from the ancient weapon that he grasped, but it was in him like a clear light. He met the head-on, devastating charge by dropping to one knee, his shield raised over his head, and as he felt the body shock ripped upwards viciously with his short sword and felt it go home. The force of the charge spun Del Tevere half-way around, and when he recovered his balance his left arm bearing the shield hung useless, the blood pouring from the wound that had severed the shoulder ligament.

'*Ave !*' cried Hiram wildly: '*Ave Marcus Severix*. . . . For liberty and decency!'

He edged forward again. Del Tevere backed away from the blaze of the oncoming figure with its craggy head and fighting eyes, and the naked steel point. . . .

'Back . . . back . . . back . . .' cried Hiram, 'or I'll kill you. . . .'

From the woods towards which they were edging something cracked spitefully, and a small bit of turf flew up close to Hiram's feet, but he neither heard nor saw.

'Back!' he cried again. He was dragging his right leg behind him now as Del Tevere gave way step by step: 'Quit or take it. . . .'

He was suddenly conscious of running feet and yelling, and thought he heard d'Aquila's voice. Again came the vicious crack from the woods.

'Back you . . .' The last word was trapped in Hiram's throat by the terrible searing blow that took him in the chest and he fell to his knees, wide-eyed and puzzled. Del Tevere had not hit him. Of course not. Why, there was Del Tevere lying on the ground, collapsed from loss of blood. And then he knew, and swaying on his knees, began to laugh aloud, an awful, rising, choking laugh: 'Hah! The edge! I knew it. You won't fight without the edge. You can't whip a fighting man. It took a bullet to do it. Hah-ahg. Go on and finish it, but I'm right . . . I'm right . . . you haven't got it . . . you'll never have it again. . . .'

He was still on his knees, facing into the woods from which his death was spitting at him when d'Aquila reached him crying: '*Corpo di Dio !* No! No! Assassins! Murderers! God of Gods, you are no Italians.' He flung himself in front of Hiram as the rifle cracked again. The Count said: 'Ahhhhhh,' very quietly, and slipped to the ground in front of Hiram, who stared at him and saw him die.

But now there were rippling shots from behind him. The General, Di Cavazzo and Ara-Pesca were running forward, and they all had pistols in their hands, and Hiram saw the little burst of sparks fly from their muzzles and the sharp cracking seemed to split his ear drums. They went on by him, screaming with rage, their pistols flaming. They crashed into the woods.

Hiram began to sway a little now. He reached over and patted d'Aquila on the shoulder a little. 'You weren't one of them, friend,' he said. 'Again we don't think far enough. Who will tell when my ashes are delivered whether I died of sword or bullet?'

They were coming back out of the woods dragging something behind them. Hiram watched, a consuming curiosity fighting off his slipping consciousness. It was the white-haired General di Brabazon who fell to his knees at Hiram's side and cried with tears in his eyes: 'Look! Look! Oh, God give you life to know and understand. Look! He is not an Italian. He is a Nazi. See, we have killed him. His gun is German. The cowardly assassin sent to murder a brave man. He is not of us. I swear it. Look, there at your feet is an Italian who has died for you and for Italian honour. Rather I were dead myself than that you did not believe. . . . Di Cavazzo – show him the papers found on that dog we killed. . . . Sir! Brave man! Do you see. . . .'

'I . . . I . . . am – very – glad – ' said Hiram Holliday slowly because he was beginning to drift out of all pain – 'to – know – that . . . that – there – are – still – honourable men.'

Then quietly he fell forward over the body of the friend who had died for him and honour, as the two surgeons rushed to his side.

It was two months before Hiram Holliday was far enough along in his convalescence to undertake the trip home in response to the summons from New York. The doctors had given him up on those first days, and marvelled that he refused to die. Sometimes the spark was so faint that they turned from him to report that it was extinct. And then some tremendous force within him would bring it back to glow again and they would come out to report – 'He still lives . . .' He was unconscious for nine days and never knew who watched ceaselessly at his bedside.

And then on a bright warm day in June he sailed from Naples on the huge *Rex*. He was drawn fine, and very pale and he still used his cane to walk.

He came up on deck and sat in a chair to say farewell to Europe. The white-plumed cone of Vesuvius slipped by on the left. The bow of the ship turned towards the north and began to glide past the blue, villa-dotted coast-line.

Hiram sighed and murmured: '*Finis*. But at least homeward bound. . . .' He took out his cigarette-case and lit one, and stared for a moment at the inscription inside the smooth, white-gold surface. It read: 'To Hiram Holliday, the bravest of the brave – di Brabazon, Del Tevere, Ara-Pesca, Di Cavazzo, Rome, April, 1939.'

He shut the case with a snap. Two figures came walking up the deck. Hiram stared, unbelieving, at the girl in the white dress and smart close-fitting white hat over hair that was again the colour of clear, strained honey, and the young boy at her side.

They paused at the side of his chair.

'Heidi . . .' cried Hiram. . . . 'Heidi and Peter . . .'

She looked down at the pale, drawn man and smiled a little. 'Yes,' she said, 'we, too, are going home, a new home, to rest where there is freedom and honour and peace, where people are . . . are like you.'

She reached for his outstretched hand and held it tightly. 'And thank God that you lived, Hiram – for. so many, many reasons, and thank Him now again that you can and will go on . . . on to those high places where you must go.'

MORE ABOUT PENGUINS, PELICANS
AND PUFFINS

For further information about books available from Penguins please write to Dept EP, Penguin Books Ltd, Harmondsworth, Middlesex UB7 0DA.

In the U.S.A.: For a complete list of books available from Penguins in the United States write to Dept DG, Penguin Books, 299 Murray Hill Parkway, East Rutherford, New Jersey 07073.

In Canada: For a complete list of books available from Penguins in Canada write to Penguin Books Canada Ltd, 2801 John Street, Markham, Ontario L3R 1B4.

In Australia: For a complete list of books available from Penguins in Australia write to the Marketing Department, Penguin Books Australia Ltd, P.O. Box 257, Ringwood, Victoria 3134.

In New Zealand: For a complete list of books available from Penguins in New Zealand write to the Marketing Department, Penguin Books (N.Z.) Ltd, Private Bag, Takapuna, Auckland 9.

In India: For a complete list of books available from Penguins in India write to Penguin Overseas Ltd, 706 Eros Apartments, 56 Nehru Place, New Delhi 110019.

PAUL GALLICO

LUDMILA/THE LONELY

Two short novels: a charming pastoral legend of old Liechten-
stein is balanced by an account of the war-torn love affairs of an
American airman stationed in the Midlands during the forties.
The two subjects could scarcely be more dissimilar. But
both bear the unmistakable stamp of Paul Gallico's unique gift
for telling a story, and for celebrating life – even in the midst of
the most ordinary, even sordid, reality.

Also published

CONFESSIONS OF A STORY-TELLER

FLOWERS FOR MRS HARRIS

JENNIE

LOVE OF SEVEN DOLLS

MRS HARRIS GOES TO NEW YORK

THE SNOW GOOSE AND THE SMALL MIRACLE

THOMASINA

TRIAL BY TERROR